Christmastime 1945

··

A Love Story

LINDA MAHKOVEC

Other books by Linda Mahkovec

The Dreams of Youth

Seven Tales of Love

The Garden House

The Christmastime Series

Christmastime 1939: Prequel to the

Christmastime Series

Christmastime 1940: A Love Story

Christmastime 1941: A Love Story

Christmastime 1942: A Love Story

Christmastime 1943: A Love Story

Christmastime 1944: A Love Story

Christmastime 1945: A Love Story
by Linda Mahkovec
...
Copyright © 2019

ISBN: 978-1-64704-018-5

Distributed by Bublish, Inc.

Cover Design by Laura Duffy
©JohnAnderson/iStock

To my family, with love

Chapter 1

꩜

The snow fell softly over Manhattan as Lillian
Drooms hurried home. She was still smiling from
her meeting with Mrs. Huntington and the art
director of children's books. Her drawings had
been well received and Mrs. Huntington hinted
that Lillian had a good chance at being selected to
illustrate a children's adventure series – she would
love nothing more! She lifted her face to the sky
and inhaled deeply. Happiness and Christmas were
in the air. Wanting to catch even more of the holiday spirit, Lillian decided to walk up Fifth Avenue
and cross through Central Park on her way home.

The crowds thickened as she neared and then
turned onto the avenue. All around her, the sense
of excitement was palpable – in the carolers and
newspaper boys, the honking and braking of traffic, the calls from the vendors: "Hot chestnuts!
Pretzels here!" Workers rushed from jobs, couples
walked arm-in-arm, shoppers ducked in and out of
stores – their arms laden with packages and shop-

ping bags – and groups of servicemen explored Manhattan while they awaited their final train or bus ride home.

Lillian took a moment to look around her at the bustling city, so alive! And this was just one avenue. She knew that the harbor and piers, and Grand Central and Penn Station all bustled with returning soldiers. The roads into and around New York City were crowded as never before – the city was bursting at its seams. At long last, the war was over! And this first Christmas after the war was sure to be a memorable one.

Bumped and jostled by the throng of people, Lillian tucked herself into a doorway to take in the post-war Christmas euphoria. The very air tingled with promise and future, and she smiled out at the swirl of commotion. She observed the faces passing by, all united by a sense of cheerfulness and gratitude. A soldier and a young woman strolled by, briefly stopping to embrace and kiss. A family, with the father in uniform, stopped to buy bags of roasted peanuts at a street cart festooned with red and green bows. An older couple laughed as they nearly collided with a ho-ho-hoing Santa Claus bell ringer. Across the street, a group of WACs – such smart, confident women – chatted with a group of GIs. Further down the block, a cluster of sailors pointed and gawked at the skyscrapers of Rockefeller Center.

Lillian stepped back out into the stream of people but continued to look all about her. The signs of Christmas were everywhere – wreaths, red ribbons, and garlands of shimmery tinsel appeared in nearly all the windows and doors. After the gray of war, everything vibrated in color. Was it her imagination? Was it her own happiness coloring the world? No, indeed, the dresses in the department store windows boasted brighter shades, young women sported bolder makeup, brighter lipstick that suited their flashing smiles. And the lights! Strings of colored bulbs shone everywhere – outlining windows and doorways and awnings. It was the first time Christmas lights were used freely since before the war and no one was holding back.

The war was over, Christmas was in the air, and Charles would be home soon! Out of habit, Lillian checked her thoughts, not trusting to such perfect happiness. She would muster the calm and pragmatism that had gotten her through the war years. Charles was not home yet – in fact, she hadn't heard from him for several weeks. It could be January or February or later before his arrival. But he *would* be home – and he would never have to leave her again.

The smile she tried to suppress burst into bloom again at the thought that Charles would soon see his daughter. They were a family of five! It was hard to keep such happiness tamped down.

Lillian stopped at a street vendor on the corner to buy a bag of roasted chestnuts for Tommy and Gabriel. At the newsstand next to the cart, she glanced at the front page of a newspaper featuring *Operation Santa Claus*, the joint-military effort to bring as many servicemen home before Christmas. And that included Charles!

She paid for the chestnuts and hoped they would stay warm until she got home. She filled her eyes one more time with the bustle of Fifth Avenue and then made her way into the quieter atmosphere of Central Park.

Despite the snow, the park was crowded with mothers and their children, lovers strolling and posing for photographs, nannies pushing baby carriages. When Lillian crossed the arched stone bridge, she paused for a moment to look back at the Plaza Hotel. Her eyes found the windows of the room where she and Charles had stayed last year, and a surge of pleasure shot through her. She continued walking. How could she stand the wait?

By keeping busy, she decided. Working on her drawings. Getting ready for Christmas – shopping, baking, decorating the apartment. And she would focus on the children. They were looking forward to the ten days they would have off for Christmas this year. Lillian stopped to watch a group of boys and girls making a snowman, and a few others pulling a sled – all enjoying a little after-school fun before dinnertime. The thought of dinner caused her to pick up her pace – Tommy and Gabriel would be hungry. She soon exited the park and walked towards her home.

She sometimes worried that Tommy and Gabriel were too much on their own now. The birth of Charlotte had taken so much of her time and attention. And though the boys seemed to be happy, there was something different about Gabriel that she couldn't quite put her finger on. She would have to ask him about it.

Her happiness increased as she turned onto her street, knowing that her children were waiting for her. She had been gone for less than three hours, yet already she missed them. She glanced up to the third floor of her brownstone and smiled – in the window hung the paper snowflakes the boys had made when they were little.

She hurried up the stairs and when she opened the door to the apartment, her heart swelled – there sat her children. The living room lamps cast a golden glow upon Tommy, Gabriel, and Charlotte, the Christmas tree sparkled with lights and ornaments, and music from the radio softly played.

"Look, Mom, she's laughing." Gabriel's smile grew wider as three-month-old Charlotte smiled and kicked her arms and legs. "She looks like those jumping jack toys that you pull the string and the legs and arms kick out."

"We gave her a bottle a little while ago," said Tommy, smiling at his baby sister. "But she doesn't seem tired. She only slept for about ten minutes since you left."

Lillian took off her hat and gloves and wriggled out of her coat. "Hello, my darling!" She lifted Charlotte, causing the little arms and legs to move faster in excitement. She walked around the living room with her. "How is it you're still awake? I wish I could rock you. You'd be asleep in no time."

Tommy darted a glance to Gabriel, who gave him a knowing smile.

Lillian turned to the boys. "There are chestnuts for you in the bag."

Tommy jumped up and set the bag on the coffee table. "Still warm." He and Gabriel reached for a few chestnuts and began to peel the split shells. "Did you have a rocker for me and Gabriel?"

"I did, but I gave it away to Vera in Brooklyn – remember her?" Lillian nuzzled Charlotte and kissed her fingers. "I didn't in a million years think I would ever need it again to rock a baby to sleep."

Lillian ruffled Tommy's hair. "Did Mr. Mancetti mind you switching days?"

Tommy shook his head. "As long as I can work a few days a week to restock the shelves, he doesn't care which days they are."

"And you're sure it's not getting in the way of your school work?"

"Not at all," he said, holding up his math book.

Gabriel saw an opening and decided to bring up the subject again. "I wish I could get a job."

"Gabriel, you're only eleven. Perhaps in a few years. Besides, when would you have the time? You're extra busy with your new school projects. You have Boy Scouts one night a week, and you help me with Artists for Victory at the hospital on Tuesdays."

"Tommy does all that too, and works three days a week. And he still has lots of time."

"I only work a few hours on my shifts, Gabe. And one of those days is Saturday." Tommy gave Gabriel a look that said to lay off the subject. He had been working at Mancetti's for almost a year now and loved it. He had been adamant that it wouldn't interfere with his homework and studied even harder to prove it.

Gabriel ignored Tommy and persisted. "Still, it's feasible. I could find a job – "

Lillian cocked her head at Gabriel's choice of word. "Feasible? Hmm. We'll see in another year or so. Besides, I need you more now that I have Charlotte."

Gabriel's mouth twisted in disappointment.

"How'd your meeting go?" asked Tommy.

"Swell. I'll tell you all about it. I'll just change first." Lillian took Charlotte to the bedroom and changed into a housedress.

As soon as they heard the bedroom door close, Tommy turned to Gabriel. "Stop talking about getting a job. You have to wait your turn. And you don't have any time – you're always at the library after school. What project takes that much work? It's more likely you and Billy are goofing off."

Gabriel ignored his remark. "Did you hear what she said?" He leaned forward and spoke in a whisper. "I told you a rocking chair is the perfect Christmas present."

Tommy nodded. "I guess so. But the ones we looked at were all too expensive. And we didn't like them."

"I think I found something. Mr. G at The Red String Curio Store has been on the lookout for one. I stopped by there today – he has three! One of them is just the kind Mom would like."

"No junk, Gabriel. We don't want an old one."

"It's not junk. It's in good condition. Even Henry said so."

"Henry? When did he see it?"

"I asked him to take a look. He said it's sound. He said it's Victorian. Mom likes that kind of thing."

Tommy was still skeptical. "I don't know. Maybe we should get her something for the kitchen. A pop-up toaster? A new tea kettle?"

"You heard her. She could really use a rocking chair. And I've found one. At least come and take a look at it."

"All right. But if it doesn't work out, we're going to scrap it and come up with a different idea."

"A different idea for what?" Lillian asked, coming into the room.

Tommy lifted his book to his face.

Lillian waited for them to answer.

"Tommy has to come up with a good idea for his French project with Amy."

Tommy lowered the book and picked up the thread. "A presentation. With instructions on how to do something – using sequences, time phrases, that kind of thing."

"That shouldn't be too hard." Lillian had noticed the subtlest shift in the friendship between Tommy and Amy. Amy had blossomed from the confident little girl with striped stockings into a willowy beauty. The round glasses she had always worn now added a hint of maturity to her that vanished when she burst into that contagious laughter of hers. She and Tommy seemed closer than ever. "Do you have any ideas?"

"Not yet. We're thinking about how to build something."

Gabriel ran to the radio and turned up the volume. "Here's your song, Mom."

Lillian smiled. "I think it's everyone's song this year." She pretended to take Charlotte as her dance partner, kissing her as she sang along. "*Kiss me once, then kiss me twice, and kiss me once again, it's been a long, long time.*" With each kiss to her cheek, Charlotte gurgled with her fist in her mouth. Lillian held Charlotte's little arm out, turned around again, and handed her back to Gabriel who was reaching up for her.

Still humming, Lillian skirted the partition that separated the kitchen and living room. She opened the oven and inhaled. "Mmm." The baked chicken glistened with butter and the scent of herbs and onion filled the small kitchen.

Tommy looked up from his homework. "I turned it on low about twenty minutes ago."

"Thank you, Tommy. It looks perfect." Was it her imagination, or was his voice beginning to change? That was the second time she had heard it crack. She took a closer look at him. He was almost fifteen. She wished she could slow everything down.

She walked back into the living room and sat on the couch. "Just think, boys – this will be the last year your father will miss out on your growing up. Soon, he'll be with us every day, and won't miss out on anything."

"Finally," said Gabriel. "A real Christmas, all together. With Charlotte."

Lillian gave a deep sigh. "At long last."

Tommy closed his book and set it on the coffee table. "So, they liked your drawings?"

Lillian tucked her legs beneath her. "So much that they gave me a similar assignment. But the big news is – " she waited for Tommy and Gabriel to look up – "I'm being considered for a five-book deal. An adventure story! And since the main character is a ten-year-old boy, I would be needing you two for all sorts of information."

"Sure, Mom," said Gabriel.

Tommy stood to take Charlotte. "My turn, Gabe."

Gabriel gave Charlotte a loud kiss on her cheek, causing her to laugh and grab onto his hair just as Tommy lifted her.

"Ow! Wait," cried Gabriel, following them with his head bent until Tommy sat back down. "She's got a strong grip. Let go!" he laughed, coaxing her fingers out of his hair. Then he reached for the baby blanket and tucked it around her.

Tommy cuddled her. "You look just like a little bird in a nest, Charlotte." He looked up at Lillian. "I can't believe Dad has never seen her. He's going to be so happy."

"I can't wait for him to see her," said Gabriel. "You think he'll make it home for Christmas?"

Lillian leaned her head in thought. "I just don't know. He's going to try – but with so many servicemen returning, it's hard to say with any certainty exactly when he'll be home." She smiled at Charlotte's gurgling. "I do hope so."

"*Operation Santa Claus* will get him home."

"Don't be so sure, Gabe," said Tommy. "Millions of people have to get back. You can only fit so many people on a ship."

"If not for Christmas, then soon after," Lillian said.

Gabriel raised his eyebrows at a happy thought. "When he gets back, do you think we'll go to Aunt Annette and Uncle Bernie's?"

"Not for a while, I'm afraid," said Lillian. "The trains are all tied up with returning servicemen. The delays are extensive. Perhaps in the spring. Charles will also want to visit Kate and her children in Illinois. Perhaps we'll all take a train trip. Wouldn't that be fun?"

Gabriel nodded at the thought. "Where do you think Dad is right now?"

Lillian leaned forward and took a chestnut. "I imagine he must be somewhere in the Mediterranean by now. He should arrive in London in a week or so. He'll send us a telegram when he does. Then, hopefully, he'll be able to set sail." For a moment, her eyes filled with worry, and she saw the image from a recent dream…

She wouldn't let her thoughts go in that direction. "I'm going to meet Izzy for lunch tomorrow. I'm so looking forward to it. It will be like old times." She took a bite of the chestnut and widened her eyes in delight.

"Do you miss her, Mom?" asked Tommy. "Meeting her for lunch like you used to?"

"I do. Though I've hardly had time to think about it, between Charlotte and my illustration work. But, yes, I do miss spending time with Izzy."

"Do you miss Rockwell Publishing?" asked Gabriel.

"No," Lillian answered without hesitation. "I loved my time there, and I learned so much – but working at home suits me better. It's been so nice this past year, being able to spend more time with you boys. And now, with Charlotte. I can't stand being away from her."

Lillian observed Gabriel stretched out on the couch, and then looked over at Tommy with his long legs draped over the side of the chair, cuddling Charlotte.

For being a half-sister, Charlotte looked so much like Tommy and Gabriel – and yet she had Charles's quiet intensity. Perhaps she would be a scholar, or an artist or – Lillian laughed away her thoughts.

No sense trying to predict the paths of children – they all go on their own journeys, answering to some internal prompting that tells them where to go and who to become. You can push and steer and encourage them in one direction, and then, one day, all on their own, they take an unexpected turn – following their heart's compass.

Like herself. Though it had seemed impossible, there was nothing that could have changed her path as an artist. Impractical, difficult, improbable – and yet it had happened. She had been true to her vision, and it had rescued her on many occasions.

She smiled indulgently at her boys. Tommy wore a red vest over his shirt. Gabriel had on his favorite blue sweater. She had to laugh to think that, after all these years, they still gravitated towards their favorite colors, red and blue. She inclined her head to look at Charlotte, dressed all in lacey white. Hmm, thought Lillian. We shall see.

Gabriel sat up and reached his arms out for Charlotte. "My turn."

Chapter 2

The cold winter predicted by the Farmer's Almanac was proving true in Illinois. More snow was in the forecast, though for the time being, cold temperatures were all Kate and her family had to contend with. Patches of snow lingered along the roads and ribbed the fields in white rows. On the north side of the farmhouse and outbuildings, the snow lay in cold blueish shadows until the sun rose high enough to turn it white.

Kate was using the afternoon to get a little baking done, and the kitchen filled with the comforting scent of cinnamon and buttery pastry browning in the oven. Ursula enjoyed the warmth emanating from the stove as she slowly stirred the pan of oatmeal for her baby. She held him on her hip, eight-month-old Francis James Gerhard – or Frankie, as he was called. His name held the memories of two uncles killed in the war – her brother Francis and Friedrich's brother Gerhard – and a third uncle, Ursula's brother Jimmy, very much alive somewhere in the South Pacific.

Ursula was still shaken by her run-in with Mr. Creight earlier in the morning. He was filling in for Otto who was down with a chest cold, driving several POWs to and from camp and the farms where they worked. Though Kate had invited him inside where it was warm, he shook his head and remained outside. Creight was a tense, angry man, who regarded the prisoners with contempt. Ursula hardly knew him, but she had been a classmate of his son who was killed in Germany in the spring. And so Mr. Creight hated Friedrich, and all Germans.

Ursula hadn't seen Friedrich in weeks. Though he had arrived in the morning, she knew that Ed planned to take him and Gustav to the Bloomfield's farm to help tear down an old shed. Love and longing had perhaps made her reckless. Earlier, while her brother Eugene was still upstairs, she thought she had seen Mr. Creight walk to the machine shed with Ed. But she was mistaken – it had been Gustav. Mr. Creight had returned to the barn and was there when she rushed in with Frankie and ran straight into Friedrich's arms.

They embraced, and Friedrich gathered his son in his arms, kissing him again and again.

"Friedrich, it's been so long. Every day I stand at the window, hoping that the truck will bring you – "

They heard a sound and whipped around – there was Mr. Creight, white-lipped.

"Friedrich!" came Ed's voice from the machine shed. "Bring the hand-saw with you."

Friedrich and Ursula held each other's gaze, and then parted. Friedrich waited until Ursula and Frankie were gone, and then left for the machine shed.

Ursula stood by the pump, making sure that Friedrich was safe with Ed. She watched them load up the truck and drive off to the Bloomfield's farm.

Suddenly, Mr. Creight was at her side, his face stiff with anger.

"My son wasn't good enough for you, was he? But you can take up with *that*!" He spat on the ground, and walked to his truck.

Ursula instinctively held Frankie closer, stunned by Creight's tone and words. What did he mean? She had known his son, Jeremy, since they were in grade school and had always been friendly with him. She watched Mr. Creight drive off and then hurried back to the house, hoping Eugene hadn't seen anything.

Eugene, her eldest brother, who had been stationed in England, had returned home a month ago – and was furious with her. Somehow he knew about her and Friedrich, and couldn't forgive her. Ursula could brave the anger of anyone, but the presence of her brother, and now Mr. Creight, prevented any chance of finding time to spend with Friedrich.

Ursula continued to stir the oatmeal and shifted Frankie to her other hip. She looked around, wondering where Eugene was. He had a restless energy about him. Sometimes she would see him staring fixedly at the floor, or out the window. Then he would jump up and find a task to busy himself with. Her heart ached for him – she wished she could speak to him and try to help him. But he wanted nothing to do with her.

She heard his footsteps coming down the stairs and kept her back to him. He cut through the kitchen, stopping on the back porch to grab his flight jacket on his way out.

Jessica had just returned home from student teaching at the town's elementary school and was describing her day to Ursula and Kate. She watched Eugene walk right past them. "Hello to you, too! There's no mail – I just checked."

"What do you call that?" Eugene closed the door behind him and headed down the lane to the country road. It was his habit to check the mail every day.

Jessica looked out the window at the mail truck that had just pulled up to the mailbox on the country road. "Well, it's late today. How was I supposed to know?"

Ursula stepped aside as Jessica cracked open the oven to peek inside.

Jessica inhaled the scent, but her smile shifted to a frown. "He's always mad about something."

"On the contrary," said Kate. "He's happy to be back. Happy to be alive. And leave the oven shut. They still need a few minutes."

Jessica leaned against the table and crossed her arms. "He was so nice when he first got home. Remember how happy he was to see us all? Four years away from us in the Army Air Forces. Now he barely talks to me."

Kate washed the mixing bowl and whisk and set them in the rack to dry. "Be a little understanding. The GIs have a hard time adjusting, especially the ones who have been gone for years, like him."

"So I've noticed," said Jessica.

"It's hard for them to do things that everyone else takes for granted. Like sleeping in. Like taking their time when they eat or take a shower. Not jumping at loud sounds. Give him time."

Ursula spoke softly. "It's my presence that sets him off."

"I think it's the mail, or lack of, that upsets him," said Jessica. "He's fine until he checks the mail. Have you noticed?"

Jessica pulled the curtain wide. She saw that Eugene stood next to the mailbox, sifting through the letters in his hand. He stared out over the fields, lowered his head a moment, and then walked back up the lane to the farmhouse. At a slower pace from when he left to check the mail.

"I wish she'd hurry up and write," said Jessica.

"Who?" Ursula asked, turning to her.

Jessica put a hand on her hip and gave a puff of disbelief.

"Oh." Ursula nuzzled Frankie and added a little sugar to the oatmeal. "Maybe. Who knows?"

"Well, don't antagonize him," said Kate. She patted Ursula to step aside while she opened the oven and lifted out the cookie sheet full of golden cinnamon twists. She placed them on the table to cool. "Whatever it is he's waiting for is troubling him."

"Those smell heavenly," said Jessica. She lifted a hot twist and bounced it from hand to hand. Then she blew on it and took a bite.

Eugene opened the door, stomped off the snow from his boots, and hung up his jacket.

"Any mail?" asked Kate.

He came into the kitchen and tossed a few letters on the table. "Here's a letter for the Blake Farm."

Jessica glanced down at it. "Maybe Mr. Creight can drop it off when he runs the boys back to camp."

Eugene's face darkened at the friendly tone used for the Germans. "The boys? They're war prisoners. And how much longer is Creight going to be here? He's like a black cloud hovering about. He's still sore we outbid him for that scrap of land. Five years ago!"

Ursula felt a flash of guilt. "It's not that. His son was killed, and it's been hard – "

"The war was hard on everyone." Eugene dropped into a chair. "No need to make it worse."

"Otto's on the mend," said Kate. "Shouldn't be much longer."

"Like they even need a guard," Jessica said.

"Someone has to drive them to and from the camp," said Kate. "I do miss Otto, though." She wanted to avoid any discussion of the POWs and went to the table, looking through the mail.

"Open this from my cousin," she said, handing an envelope to Eugene.

She made a sound of frustration at not finding any letters from Jimmy or Paul. "When your brothers finally make it home, I'm going to wring their necks! Why don't they write? Don't they know how I worry when I don't hear from them? Why has there been no word?"

"Paul wrote that he's on his way to San Diego," Ursula said. "And we know that Jimmy is headed for Hawaii."

"That was over two weeks ago!" Kate sat in the chair next to Eugene.

He handed her the opened card for her to read. "Mom, every sailor and soldier is trying to get home. It's chaos out there. I told you how we had hammocks strung all over the place on the ship heading back home – we had to sleep in shifts. Not to mention the pandemonium at chow. Mail is the least of their concerns."

"I suppose." Kate heaved a sigh. "I just want them home. Safe."

"They'll likely spend Christmas on ship," said Eugene.

"Listen to you!" Jessica said, sitting down. "And you say Mr. Creight is like a black cloud. They'll be home, Mom. Don't worry. But it could take a while. Jimmy's letter said that after Hawaii, he'll most likely go to San Francisco, and then take a train to Los Angeles. And then take an eastbound train."

"Goodness! Sounds like it could take months!"

"Once they're stateside, we'll hear from them," said Ursula, turning off the stove.

Jessica leaned forward on her elbows. "Remember, Mom – it was only a few months ago that Jimmy was in the Philippines, waiting for the invasion of Japan."

"Thank God, I didn't know that at the time. I wouldn't have slept a wink."

"And he'll be discharged effective New Year's Day! That's less than a month. And then – " Jessica beamed with excitement – "his wedding! I saw Gladys in town and you never saw anybody happier. She said Jimmy wrote that he would wear his dress blues for the wedding."

Eugene restlessly rose to his feet and went to the window with his arms crossed, staring out over the fields to the east. Then, just as suddenly, he dropped his arms to his side and sat back down.

Kate and Ursula exchanged glances at his sullenness.

Jessica lifted another twist and held it out to Eugene. "Still hot." She waited for him to take it. His habit of ignoring her hurt, and she responded by trying to coax him out of his mood. "Come on, Eugene, tell us why you're always checking the mail. Waiting to hear from a girl?"

He half-heartedly sorted through the Christmas cards from relatives and glanced at the red cover of *Yank* magazine. "None of your business."

"What am I supposed to tell everyone? All the girls are asking about you. Shirley says they're asking her the same thing – like she might have some inside information. What should we tell them?"

"Tell them to mind their own goddammed business." He waved aside the offered twist.

Jessica ate it, licked her fingers, and waited a moment. "Is she pretty?"

The scowl on his face caused her to throw up her hands. "All right, all right. Sorry I asked." She jumped up. "I'm going to change."

"Take these with you," said Kate. She went to the back room where the ironing was done and came back with a pile of neatly folded clothes.

Jessica took the clothing and ran upstairs. She was always careful to keep her school clothes nice. Though she was now in training, she insisted on feeding and watering the animals at end of day. Still, with Eugene at home, and Jimmy and Paul soon to arrive, she was happy that the burden of the farm would, for the most part, be off the shoulders of her, Ursula, and their mother.

Kate squeezed Eugene's shoulder. "I'll make us some coffee."

He raised his head and smiled, and tossed the letters aside.

Ursula set Frankie down and dished out the oatmeal into a bowl for him. Frankie crawled over to Eugene's leg and began to pull himself up, babbling in happiness.

Eugene pulled his leg away, grabbed the *Yank* magazine, and went into the living room.

Ursula's cheeks flushed at the rebuff. She swept up Frankie into her arms and pressed her cheek to his silky hair. "I'll feed him and give him his nap." She took the bowl and walked to Kate's room down the hall where a crib was set up for his naps.

Kate waited for the water to boil, made a pot of coffee, and took a cup to Eugene. "There's nothing like the scent of fresh coffee. Especially on these cold days."

Eugene sat up and took the cup. "Thanks." He frowned at Frankie's cries resisting sleep. Soon, the soft sounds of a lullaby were heard.

Eugene noticed that Kate remained standing in front of him. He raised his head to her.

"What?"

"I think this has gone on long enough. You've been home a month now and have yet to acknowledge Ursula's child."

"It's German," Eugene said dismissively, and took a sip of coffee.

"He's a baby!"

Eugene's head snapped up and he repeated firmly. "And German. I just spent four years of my life being shot at by Nazis."

Kate opened her mouth to respond, but they heard Jessica clamoring down the stairs. She had changed into dungarees and a flannel shirt. She came into the room holding a bundle of fabric in her arms.

"I was putting away Eugene's laundry and look what I found – another parachute!" She turned to Eugene with a mischievous raise of her eyebrows. "The one you gave us is more than enough for me and Ursula. We'll get several dresses out of it." She bounced on her toes, waiting for Eugene to explain the second bundle of silk. She cleared her throat.

"So who's this one for? The letter writer? Or one of your old girls from home?"

"I'll thank you to stop snooping around my room." He grabbed the folded parachute and set it next to him.

Jessica's fists went to her hips. "I wasn't snooping! I was just – " She caught the shake of head from Kate.

"Come help me with dinner. You can get started on the salad."

Ursula soon joined them in the kitchen. "Frankie fell right to sleep." She began rinsing and scrubbing the potatoes Kate had dumped in the sink.

Jessica sat at the table, slicing a few carrots for the salad. "I was *not* snooping."

"A good meal will set him right," said Kate. "Tell us about your plans for the school Christmas party. Are you sorry you volunteered?"

"I'm only in charge of first through third. I can handle that." When the telephone rang, she jumped up to answer it. "I'll get it!" She chatted for a few moments, then hollered from the hallway, "It's for you, Eugene! It's Burly!"

Eugene scowled as he took the receiver. "I could have heard you out in the fields."

"That wasn't loud," Jessica muttered as she sat back down at the kitchen table. She picked up a cucumber and began slicing it, then stopped. "Do I talk too loud?"

Ursula threw her a smile over her shoulder. "Of course not."

Jessica remained unconvinced. "I have to raise my voice so that the kids can hear me. Maybe it's becoming a habit."

"I've never noticed it," said Kate. "Don't pay any attention." She lifted her head and a light came to her eyes as she heard the happiness in Eugene's voice.

"Hey, Burly! Not much. What'd you say? *Clem's* home?" he shouted into the phone. "Yeah, put him on. Clem! You home?" He listened, his face transformed into happiness. "You bet! We sure as hell did. Home Alive by '45!"

Jessica sat immobile as she listened to Eugene.

"Sure. Stop on by. We'll go uptown and have a cold one."

Eugene stepped into the kitchen, all smiles. "That was Clem! He made it home!"

"Clem's home?" asked Jessica, her eyes brightening. "Clem Corrigan?"

"Thank goodness," said Ursula.

"He and Burly are going to stop by – then we'll go into town. I haven't seen him since he left. In early '42."

"That's wonderful news," said Ursula. "What a long time for you both to be gone."

"Indeed, it is," said Kate. She had noticed that anytime a local boy made it back home, Eugene visibly cheered. She was glad to see that his mood had improved. He had never been good at sitting still, and since his return, he hadn't yet fallen into a routine. Other than farm chores, he didn't know what to do with himself.

"Thank goodness I made the cinnamon twists. Let me see what else I can offer." Kate went to the pantry and took out a loaf of date bread.

"Don't fuss, Mom. It's just Burly and Clem. And we won't be staying long. We're going into town."

"I wish you'd all have dinner first," said Kate.

"We'll grab a bite in town."

Jessica finished slicing the last of the cucumbers. "When did Clem get back?"

"I don't know. Guess I'll find out. God, I'm glad he's home. He had a tough time of it, from what I hear."

Jessica's head snapped up. "What do you mean?"

Eugene didn't answer.

"I'll be happy to see him again," said Kate. "Don't keep him out late drinking, Eugene. He's going to need to catch up on his sleep and ease back into civilian life. It's taken you a good month."

"I know, I know. But we might be out late, so don't wait up."

Kate knew better than to object and was secretly relieved that Eugene had something to take his mind off whatever was bothering him.

"When are they coming?" asked Jessica, sliding the cucumbers into the bowl.

"They're on their way," Eugene called over his shoulder as he headed up the stairs.

"I guess he's going to change out of his work – " Kate stopped mid-sentence when she saw Jessica jump up from the table and run upstairs. "Jessica?"

"I'll make a little more coffee," said Ursula. She turned on the stove and took out the good teacups and plates from the hutch.

In a few minutes, Eugene came down and sat at the table. "He sounded good, Clem. The more fellas that come back... You hear things, you know, and you start to worry." He sat next to Kate and ran his hand through his dark wavy hair.

Kate took a moment to admire her eldest. He and Ursula looked so much alike – he was much more angular, but they both had the same intensity in their beautiful faces. Both with dark blue eyes that always seemed to have a storm at the back of them.

Eugene gave a wide grin. "And with Burly, well, it could get late, so don't go fretting. We're sure to see a bunch of the guys."

He sat up and jerked his head back when Jessica walked into the kitchen. She had changed into a yellow print dress and a blue sweater. And had tied a ribbon in her hair.

"Who're you trying to impress?" asked Eugene.

"I want to look nice for our returning servicemen."

"It's Burly and Clem! They couldn't care less what you wear."

Jessica went to the window and saw the truck trundling down the road from the next farm over. She watched it turn onto the lane. "They're here!"

Eugene stepped out onto the porch and ran down the steps to greet his friends. He was soon slapping them both on the back. "It's good to see you, Clem! Good to have you home. Come inside. Come on, Burly, just for a minute, then we'll head into town."

They walked up the porch stairs, to where Kate was holding the door open for them. "Welcome home, Clem! And in time for Christmas. Come in, come in!"

Jessica had moved to the kitchen table. Her hand gripped the back of a chair. "Hi, Burly," she said, looking past him to where Kate was welcoming Clem.

"Hey, Jessica, Ursula." Burly pulled out a chair at the kitchen table and began talking to Ursula as she set out calico napkins by their plates. When Clem made his way to the table, Ursula greeted him. "Welcome home, Clem!"

"Thanks. It's good to be home."

Jessica took a step forward, waiting for Clem to notice her. Her hands played with the hem of her sweater.

Clem turned and stopped on seeing her. "Jessica?"

"Hello, Clem."

He leaned his head back in disbelief. "You sure grew up fast."

She nodded, with a wide smile.

"I thought you were still a kid."

"Hardly! I'm seventeen and a half."

Kate pulled out a chair and gave Jessica a nudge. "Have a seat, Clem. Jessica, pour them some coffee."

The kitchen soon filled with Burly's booming voice and laughter, and talk about the guys who were back and those who were scheduled to return soon.

Jessica tried not to stare at Clem but her eyes kept going to him. She swallowed hard as she watched him talk, and carefully filled the other cups. She set the coffee pot on the table.

"Date bread?" she asked, moving the plate closer to Clem.

He shook his head, but Burly leaned forward and took a slice.

"Mmm, mmm. Mighty good," said Burly, and he was soon describing Shirley and Sue Ellen's holiday baking frenzy.

Jessica tentatively slid into the chair next to Clem. "How's Donny?"

"He's fine, fine."

"I'm student teaching now. So I see him now and then. At the school." She waited for him to say something, but he remained silent. "It's only three days a week. But it keeps me pretty busy."

He nodded, regarded her briefly, and faced the others.

"I was able to start teaching while I was still enrolled in the War Emergency Courses. Because of the shortage of teachers. I'll have my certificate soon."

She opened her mouth to add something, but Clem picked up on something Eugene said.

"Joe Madden? I haven't seen him since I left. It'll be good to see him again."

"He and Sue Ellen are married, did you hear?" asked Jessica. Her comment was met with no response from Clem. She pressed her lips together in frustration at his lack of attention to her.

Burly laughed. "I already told him – and about how me and Shirley will likely follow suit. We're two of the bravest men in the county marrying those two sisters. They can get us to do anything they want. Can't say I mind tasting their new recipes, but Shirley had me drive to Peoria so she and Sue Ellen could shop for trimming for their dresses. Lace!"

Jessica jumped up and took the coffee pot, topping the near-full cups. "A warmup, Clem?"

He shook his head, and laughed at Burly's comment. "So, Joe's all right. And married! Think we'll see him tonight?"

Burly shook his head. "Sue Ellen dragged him over to Jacksonville for a few days – to a cousin's wedding. Should be back on Saturday. Maybe we can all go out – "

"Joe and Sue Ellen are coming over here on Saturday," said Jessica, causing Kate and Ursula to look up in surprise. "For dinner. Stop on by, Clem." Clem started to decline but Jessica turned to Burly. "You're coming, aren't you Burly? I'm sure Shirley mentioned it to you. It will be so nice to have you all here."

Burly scratched his chin. "Huh. I don't remember her saying – "

Jessica turned to her mother and Ursula for help.

"Yes, please come," said Ursula.

"We'd love to have you," added Kate. "I was planning to make a pot roast."

"So, you'll all come?" Jessica asked with a smile.

Burly nodded. "Course we will."

Clem leaned back in his chair, but didn't respond.

Kate noticed he was toying with his coffee but not drinking it. "Clem, what are your immediate plans now that you're back?"

He shrugged. "For now, I just want to enjoy being back home. Spend some time with my dad and my nephew, Donny. First thing I need to do is get my truck worked on so I can get around. It's going to need an overhaul. I'll take it into town tomorrow."

"Friedrich can look at it," said Kate. "He's one of our POWs. He can fix anything."

Burly took another cinnamon twist and dunked it in his coffee. "He sure did a number on my truck. Runs better than ever since he worked on it."

"Friedrich's an engineer," explained Jessica.

Clem looked over at her, then down at his coffee. "I don't want to impose. I'll take it to the mechanic in town."

"Nah, bring it on by," said Eugene. "Let what's-his-name take a look. Might as well get work out of him while we can. He won't be here much longer."

Ursula winced at the words.

Eugene suddenly scooted his chair back and reached for his flight jacket. "I could use a beer. Come on. Let's go."

Clem stood and thanked Kate.

She placed her hand on his shoulder. "Please stop by anytime."

"It's good to have you back," said Ursula.

"Yes, it's good to have you back, Clem," echoed Jessica, standing next to him.

He smiled at Kate and Ursula. "It's sure good to be home." He gave a slight nod to Jessica, paused, as if to speak, but instead walked to the door.

After the door closed, Kate raised her eyebrows to Jessica. "Dinner on Saturday?"

Jessica shrugged. "It seemed like a good idea."

"You better call Shirley and hope they don't have plans."

"They'll come." Jessica stood and smiled. "I'll change and then feed the animals." She ran up the stairs, adding, "Poor old Clover will be wondering where I am."

Ursula cleared the table with Kate. "That cheered Eugene. Clem looks good, doesn't he?"

Kate nodded. "A little lean, maybe."

"He always seemed so much older than us. Jessica had a crush on him when she was younger."

"Looks like she still does. Not that I ever know what's going on with my daughters."

Ursula set the dishes in the sink, avoiding that topic. "So, his nephew still lives here. I know there was some talk of his moving to Chicago with relatives."

Kate nodded. "Can't uproot a child like that. Donny didn't want to go and I can understand why. Losing both parents to the flu like that. He's been a big help to Clem's father these past few years. The house would have been empty without Donny there. And Clem has been like a brother to him."

Ursula washed the dishes as Kate brought the rest of them to the sink. "It will be a happy Christmas for them all."

Kate stood silent for a moment. Then she nodded, as if confirming some internal dialogue she was having. "I like Clem. He's got a good heart. He's always been steady and hardworking."

"Yes, he has," said Ursula. She began drying the dishes. "I thought he seemed a little downcast. I remember him as being more cheerful."

Kate nodded. "You never know what goes on in a man's mind, after he's been to war. It changes him. Look at Eugene. He's struggling with something."

They left it at that, and soon Jessica was running back down the stairs and out the back door, humming a cheerful tune.

Chapter 3

∽

Lillian tightened her scarf around her neck as she walked to the restaurant to meet Izzy. The temperatures had dropped and more snow was in the forecast. She hoped it would snow for Christmas – a white Christmas would be wonderful.

She felt a burst of happiness at seeing Izzy sitting at a table in the window. She had only seen her old friend a few times since the birth of Charlotte, and always at home when Izzy visited. This did feel like their old times together.

"Izzy!"

Izzy jumped to her feet and embraced her.

"It's so good to see you, Izzy. I was just telling the boys how I miss our lunches." As usual, Izzy looked beautiful – dressed in a moss-green velvet suit with a white silk blouse.

"Ah, our old times together," Izzy said with a warm smile. "I have to admit that things are different with you gone."

After settling in, they took the menus offered by the waiter and ordered drinks.

"A martini for me. Shaken. For you, Lilly?"

"A cup of tea would be nice."

Lillian felt Izzy's eyes on her. "What is it?"

"Something I noticed the last time I saw you. A new expression playing about your eyes – rays of merriment at the corners, at some internal delight." Izzy leaned back. "My God, you're happy, aren't you?"

Lillian had to laugh at Izzy's comment. "I am. Sometimes I can't believe how happy I am. Sometimes I'm afraid that it's all too good to be true."

"It's true, all right. The war is over, and Charles will come home and see his new daughter. You're working as an artist." She waved to the poinsettias and pine boughs decorating the restaurant. "And it's Christmastime!"

The waiter returned with their drinks. Izzy lifted her glass to Lillian.

"To Christmas! To the war being over and to new beginnings." She took a sip of her drink. "What have you heard from Charles?"

Lillian stirred sugar into her tea and added a splash of milk. "Just that he's on his way back to England. Once he's there, he'll send a telegram to let me know when we can expect him. London – and then home! I'm sure he'll see Red – "

"How was your meeting? You've been able to keep up with the illustration work?"

"It's worked out so well, Izzy. Better than I ever could have dreamed. Mrs. Huntington allowed me all the time I needed, gradually giving me assignments to see how the arrangement would work out. She appreciates that I always meet my deadlines – and I love the assignments. They've assured me of as much work as I can handle. The predictions are that the children's book market will keep expanding."

"All those returning servicemen," Izzy said with a chuckle. "I guess we can expect a lot of growing families." She looked out the window and was suddenly miles away. Then she shook out her napkin, draped it across her lap, and folded her elbows on the table.

Lillian sipped on her tea, noticing the shifts in Izzy.

"And the boys are adjusting to having a little sister? What a change for them."

"They couldn't be happier."

"I remember when Lois had her last child – she said her youngest had a hard time. She said he felt like he wasn't important any more. That he had been pushed aside."

"The boys don't feel that way, I'm sure. They argue over who gets to hold Charlotte," Lillian added with a laugh. "And they're so busy with their own lives. They've really matured over this past year. Tommy loves having a job. Gabriel is busy with school and Scouts. He's involved in a class project that's really fired him up."

"And Mrs. Kunztman watches the darling when you meet with Mrs. Huntington?"

"Yes, if the boys aren't around. She's a god-send." Lillian took a piece of bread and began to butter it. "She watches her on our volunteer nights at the hospital, though it's only one day a week now. She still loves to cook for Tommy and Gabriel. And they love to help her – running to the store when she needs something, helping her peel apples or chop nuts. Though that's usually Henry's job."

"Henry Hankel! What a charmer. Does he still volunteer at the hospital?"

"Three nights a week! He's as busy as ever." Lillian bit into her bread. "Though his main duty now is to help Mrs. Kuntzman with her baking. He tracks down hard to find ingredients, rolls out her strudel, and is her official taster. Once a week they go out to dinner and a movie."

"Just like young love." Izzy looked down at her glass.

"Or like an old married couple who still enjoy each other's company. It's so nice to see. Life is full of surprises, isn't it?"

Izzy briskly opened the menu and they soon placed their orders.

"What about you, Izzy? Are you going to continue volunteering at the canteen?"

"The USO will keep the canteens open well into next year, if not longer, with all the service-men coming home." She gave a laugh. "One thing I won't miss is the letter writing." She flexed her fingers. "Give my hand a rest. Though it's sad to think how many never answered." She gave a deep sigh and gazed out the window. "It's all different now, isn't it?"

"It is. It's a different world," said Lillian. "FDR gone. Hitler gone. So much of the world in shambles. It feels like the old world order has come to a close and a new one has arrived. They're calling it the Atomic Age! I don't think I like the sound of that. It sounds ominous, doesn't it?"

Izzy gave a soft sound of agreement. "It feels like a sudden goodbye to the old world."

"It does, indeed. Though better times are surely ahead. Did you see that the United States will be the location for the new United Nations? The *United* Nations. That sounds hopeful."

Izzy buttered a slice of bread. "Do you think it will help?" There was a skeptical edge to her voice.

"Yes. I do. Well, I hope it does." Lillian remembered the same hope she had for the 1939-1940 World's Fair – the *World of Tomorrow* – with all the nations side by side. She brushed aside that thought and leaned forward in excitement.

"Last week I went to Charles's office to meet with Mrs. Sullivan, Edith, and Mr. Mason. They wanted to see Charlotte. And listen to this." Her eyes brightened. "Edith and Desmond are to marry in the spring!"

Izzy sank back in the booth. "I'm happy to hear that. Those two were meant for each other. And to think that I introduced them at the canteen – what, three years ago?"

"Desmond's still touring with the USO in the South Pacific, but he'll be home in the spring. Then they'll marry and move to Hollywood! Can you imagine? He's been offered some work in the movies, so he's going to give it a try."

Izzy put her chin in her hand and squinted at the vision in her mind. "I can see Edith in a cozy bungalow in the Hollywood hills. What an adventure it will be."

"Edith believes his heart is with the stage and that he'll miss New York City. But she's willing to give it a try, even if it's just for a few years."

"Sounds exciting. Everyone is moving on with their lives, leaping into the bright future." She took a slow sip of her drink.

"Don't you feel that way, Izzy?"

"I feel stuck. I can't explain it. It's like I don't know what I want." She gave a shrug. "And how about Mrs. Sullivan?"

"Down to three days a week and looking forward to retiring in the summer. She's training a new office manager – a returning soldier – to take over her role. She said Brendan was more than happy to vacate his position as machinist so that a returning GI could have his job. They have plans to travel."

"That's wonderful," she said, moving aside for the waiter to set down her dish. But her words of happiness did not match her tone.

"If I didn't know better, Izzy, I'd say your mind is miles away."

Izzy raised her head, surprised. Then she dropped the pretense and her shoulders sagged. "Sorry. I guess it is. I had a letter. I guess it's still on my mind." She picked up her fork and looked down at her food.

"From Red?"

Izzy nodded, and her brow wrinkled. "Now that we've exchanged a few letters – just as friends, you know – I can't stop thinking about him. Wondering how he's doing. And if I'll ever see him again." Her forked remained poised above her plate.

Lillian waited for Izzy to say more. "Do you think he'll be returning anytime soon?"

Izzy let out a deep breath and broke off a piece of sole. "Red's not in a hurry to come home. If he ever does. His last letter said he would stay in London for the transition. He feels that he's needed there. He's juggling his time between administration work at the U.S. office trying to get our boys home, and volunteering at a veteran's hospital as a sort of counselor."

"Do you – do you think – will he…"

Izzy raised her eyes and smiled. "That about sums up our position. All questions, no answers. It took a while for us – for me – to start writing back to him. But it's become a lifeline for me. Sometimes, I feel so close to him, and I forget the bad years. He filled something in me that has left a void. When he, when he – left – I was like an empty vessel clanging noisily at every bump. Now, even though it's just letters, I feel more complete, more rooted."

Lillian took a bite of her chicken and closely observed Izzy. She had often tried to ask about Red, but Izzy never wanted to talk about him. Lillian thought Izzy had closed that chapter and was somewhat surprised to find her still so preoccupied with him. She realized that Izzy wanted to talk about Red.

"Besides what was between us," said Izzy, growing more animated, "I've always found him so interesting – the way he sees things, the way he thinks. I've missed that. Our conversations, our long walks, our quiet times together..."

The sadness and longing in her voice was impossible to miss.

"So many things." Izzy looked out the window and a wistful smile came to her lips. "Red loved poetry and would read to me by candlelight." Her eyes filled with warmth. "Our nights were always magical – it was something we believed in."

Lillian was struck by the intimacy of the comment and realized how much Izzy had suffered over Red. And how much she still loved him.

"Maybe if you asked Red to come home? Maybe then you could – "

Izzy gave a hint of a shrug. "I've thought of every scenario. And I just don't know what to do. We had something so perfect. And it was broken. I don't know what I feel. In a way, I see it as a relic from the past – and it feels safe, protected there. Something wonderful that once happened to me."

Then, as if she had ventured into dangerous territory, Izzy waved her hand and gave a dazzling smile. "That's the past. I'm so happy for you that Charles will be home soon. Your first Christmas since having Charlotte. How absolutely marvelous!"

"I hope it's soon." Lillian understood that, for now, Izzy needed to come back to the present.

"Over the years, I've come to expect delays and disappointments. You know he was near Ceylon when Japan surrendered. It took so long for his ship to turn back. Once he arrives in London, he'll arrange for transport home. Of course, there will be delays. London is still in ruins."

They caught up over their meal, with Lillian answering Izzy's questions about Tommy and Gabriel. When they finished, they paid and slipped on their coats.

"Yes, I suppose I better be getting back," said Izzy, glancing at her watch. Lillian noticed that it was the watch Red had given her when they first met.

"How's life at Rockwell Publishing, Izzy? You haven't mentioned it once."

Izzy pulled on her gloves. "Good. Fine. A lot of men are returning, resuming their old positions. The place has a completely different feel about it now. Many, if not most, of the women have left. Which was to be expected. The returning soldiers need jobs, and Rockwell has rehired most of his former employees. The ones who came back."

They exited the restaurant and began walking down the crowded sidewalk towards Rockwell Publishing.

"I suppose the women were happy to leave?" Lillian asked.

"For the most part, yes. Though some were resentful. They gave it their all during the war, put in long hours, got paid less. And now they're told they're no longer needed."

"I understand how they must feel. I'm lucky to have my work. I think I would have been crushed if I suddenly had nothing."

Izzy agreed, and then stopped when they reached Rockwell Publishing. She glanced up at the building. "But it's not the same, Lilly. It all feels different."

"Even for you?"

Izzy gave it some thought. "It's funny. Now that I have a secure position, I find it doesn't matter much. I love my job, but something is missing. I'm not sure what. I used to feel that Rockwell and the company needed me. Now?" She gave a dismissive shrug as an answer.

Then she took hold of Lillian's arm. "Speaking of Rockwell," she said in her old playful tone, "he's hosting a welcome home Christmas party for all the returning soldiers."

"Really?" Lillian asked. "That must be the softening influence of his wife, now that they're back together."

"And he invited you."

Lillian turned her head in disbelief. "Did he really? I have to say I'm surprised."

"Well, his exact words were: 'Make sure you fill the room with plenty of good-lookin' dames,' and he mentioned you."

Lillian's mouth dropped open – and then she laughed. "That sounds more like him. I'd be delighted to come." She hugged Izzy goodbye, and waved at her as she pushed through the revolving doors and stepped into the lobby.

Chapter 4

❧

Kate and Eugene lingered over breakfast, while Jessica and Ursula sat at the other end of the kitchen table sorting through clothing for the Red Cross refugee drive. Next to Ursula, Frankie sat in his high chair playing with his stuffed farm animals that Jessica had made.

Kate pushed the platter of pancakes closer to Eugene. "How about some more? Or another helping of hash browns?"

Eugene smiled and shook his head. "You're spoiling me, Mom. I haven't eaten this good since I left." He raised his cup to the coffee pot she brought over from the stove. "Just a warmup – then I need to get back out there. Ed and I are going to the hardware store after the POWs leave and I need to get a few things done before then."

Kate saw the disappointment in Ursula's face. Friedrich was working on the farm today, but only for half a day. There was no denying, the POWs were at the farm less and less. The camp commanders were using them to assist with the loads of paperwork to be processed, utilizing Friedrich's knowledge of English. Though Ursula tried to hide her feelings, the increasing tension in her was noticeable. It was just a matter of time before Friedrich would be taken away.

Jessica picked up the stuffed rooster Frankie had dropped, and then addressed Eugene. "When will you go through your old clothes and shoes? You must have things you could give for the drive."

Ursula, in the habit of glancing out the window, sat up straight and narrowed her eyes. But the truck she saw out on the country road was the mail truck. She folded a sweater and placed it in the box at their feet.

"There's the mail truck," said Jessica. "I could do with a little break."

But Eugene had already jumped to his feet. "I'll get it," he said, grabbing his jacket from the back porch.

"I promise not to hide any letters addressed to you, Eugene. Even those from your girlfriend."

He slammed the door and Jessica rolled her eyes.

"Don't tease him," said Kate. "Perhaps he does have someone." She held up a pair of dungarees and assessed them. "They need a patch or two but they have a few more years left in them."

"Then why doesn't he just come out and say so?" Jessica lifted an old quilt to be added to the pile of items. "Why all the mystery?"

Kate leveled her eyes on Jessica. "Well, I can think of a number of reasons, and many that would only cause heartache. So watch your words."

The sharpness in her mother's voice caused Jessica to stop inspecting the quilt. She stared down at the floor, blinking in thought. "I didn't think of that."

"Apparently not."

Kate had moved to the window and was watching Eugene come back down the lane. He was walking briskly. She pulled the curtain wider.

"He's smiling," she said, causing both girls to look up.

They waited expectantly as he came inside.

"Good news?" asked Kate.

Eugene smacked the letter with his hand. "Just received my discharge papers!"

Kate hugged him. "I'm so glad to hear that. First Jimmy and now you – Paul is sure to follow soon."

"Earned enough points for a January 1st discharge." He turned away from the noise Frankie was making, banging his hands against his tray.

"That's wonderful, Eugene." Ursula smiled and waited for him to say something.

"Yep." He was soon on the telephone telling Burly his news.

Pain shot to Ursula's eyes. Eugene's coldness to her, and her baby, increasingly weighed on her. She lifted Frankie and spoke softly. "Time for your bath."

Jessica stood and glanced at the clock. She bunched up the quilt and took a spool of thread and a needle. "My program's on. I'll be in the living room mending this. I'll embroider over some of the worn spots." Music, talking, and laughter from the radio soon sounded, with an occasional chuckle from Jessica.

Kate brought the dishes to the sink, washed them, and set them in the drying rack. She was unsure what to do about Eugene's disapproval of Ursula. The word around town was that Ursula was married to a soldier who had not yet returned. But as the months wore on, the story was beginning to thin. Still no word? Had she been jilted? Some people hinted that her baby resembled the handsome POW who worked on their farm. Sooner or later, the truth would come out.

Kate touched the side of the coffee pot – still hot. She poured herself another cup and stirred in some milk. She couldn't blame Eugene. And yet Friedrich was not a Nazi – far from it. In fact, he reminded her very much of Eugene. Hard working, respectful, with a quick intelligence and a gentleness beneath a reserved demeanor – she stopped that line of thought. Eugene would be furious to know she was comparing them in that way.

She sat at the other end of the table and regarded the pile of clothes to be sorted. She lifted an old dress of hers that she had always loved but didn't have much occasion to wear. Blue-gray with a scatter of burgundy and white posies and gathered fabric at the shoulders. Perhaps a bit old-fashioned, but she always thought of it as her elegant dress. She spread it before her and briefly imagined it on some poor refugee in Europe. She folded it neatly and added it to the pile of clothes. She hoped the prettiness of it might bring a touch of pleasure to the woman who would wear it.

Kate imagined a thin, worn woman unfolding the dress – then she stood and went to the hutch, opening its top drawer. She took a pencil and a bit of paper and sat back down. Realizing that the refugee would most likely not understand it, nevertheless, she wrote: *With love, from America.* She folded it and tucked it into the dress pocket.

She took a sip of coffee and lifted another dress. Then she dropped it on her lap and stared out the window. It was hard to ignore the tension between Eugene and Ursula. She hadn't counted on Eugene figuring out the truth about Ursula and Friedrich so quickly.

Her plan had been to say nothing about the baby's father until after Friedrich was gone. She didn't want to burden Eugene with the information. And she didn't want to make any trouble for Friedrich. Or Ursula.

That thought made her even more downhearted. With Friedrich gone, what would Ursula do? Karl had already been taken away over a month ago. Friedrich and Gustav anxiously awaited the dates for their departures. They would likely be assigned to hard manual labor in a bombed-out Allied country. 'Payback,' as she had heard some of the townspeople call it.

A few snowflakes fell past the window and she let her gaze rest on the bare trees against the gray sky. Kate didn't know how Eugene had found out about Ursula and Friedrich, but he knew. After a few weeks home, he had figured it out. Of course Frankie looked like Friedrich, but it was more than that. Eugene had surely picked up on the little threads of connection between a husband and wife, between a father and his son. There was no hiding it.

Home for a month and Eugene had made the discovery that *she* – Ursula's mother, for God's sake – had missed! She shook her head at her own blindness during Ursula's pregnancy. All her thoughts were on Eugene back then – not knowing if he was dead or alive. And yet, as she thought back to a year ago, it was as if she *had* known, deep inside, but didn't know that she knew. She shook her head against such fuzzy logic and took a sip of coffee. The fact was, it had taken two wallops to the head for her to realize the truth.

She leaned back in the chair, remembering that day in January when the first, stunning wallop had come. Ursula had been doing the ironing. She stood at the ironing board and had pressed her hands to her lower back just as Kate came in. Ursula, with her back arched, stood in profile. Kate's mouth dropped open and her eyes widened in shock as it struck her – Ursula was pregnant! Reserved, aloof, mysterious Ursula – pregnant!

Kate now wondered if her exploding anger had resulted from the fact that Ursula had kept the secret to herself, or because *she* – a mother of six children and two miscarriages – had missed all the signs?

Ursula had hung her head. "Yes, mother," she said gently. "I'm pregnant. And, yes, I'm married."

"And – and you didn't tell me?" Kate could barely choke out her words.

"I knew you wouldn't approve."

"I don't approve. Of course, I don't! Why all this secrecy?" Kate racked her mind for a clue, any clue. "It's all that business in the fall, isn't it? Those trips to Peoria."

Ursula turned her head away.

"I should have known! A soldier?" Kate had demanded, remembering something about an officer.

Ursula had squeezed her eyes shut. "A soldier."

Kate had stormed out of the room and left it at that. Until the second wallop.

A month of coldness between mother and daughter followed, with Kate waiting to be confided in. She kept an eye on Ursula – half expecting the soldier from Peoria to show up at their door. But he never did. Then, surprising Kate, in the following month Ursula had grown happier instead of sadder. Her fretting and sorrow lessened, and Kate had caught her and Jessica whispering and smiling. The POWs had just arrived for the spring planting and there was a palpable buzz in the house. She felt it herself, delighted to have the same three POWs back with them.

And then all the pieces had fallen together, with such a loud and obvious bang that she felt it like a smack to the head. Of course! And all those little signs that had sat at the periphery of knowing had coalesced right in front of her in a silent explosion.

Ursula had been taking the laundry from the clothesline. Friedrich was passing by, walking from the barn to the machine shed. They didn't see Kate watching from the window. But she saw the soft smile that passed between them, saw the gentle stroking of Ursula's hand over her swollen belly.

"Friedrich!" Kate had whispered, staggering backwards and dropping heavily into a chair. And felt – what? Anger at the subterfuge. Outrage at the position it put them all in. Relief because it all made sense. And, God help her, trembling happiness. She had lifted her apron to her eyes and cried. She now understood the reason for Ursula's secrecy. And she realized the depth of their predicament and how they must have suffered. That was the moment she fully accepted the situation. The apron came up to her eyes again, only this time she was laughing-crying. Her first grandchild! She had never admitted it to herself before then, but she loved Friedrich almost like a son.

She kept it to herself and played along with the soldier story. After all, he was a soldier, she admitted, finding herself suddenly in Ursula's camp. It all began to make sense. Ursula's distance, her sorrow, the tension – good God, even the arguments with Jimmy the previous Christmas! Could he have possibly known? And Jessica? Suddenly, she was sure they knew, were in on it. She could feel it in her bones. I've raised some wily children, she thought – though a smile played about her lips.

Kate kept the secret that day, and for many weeks later. And though she was happy, it was mixed with worry – what on earth were they going to do?

Kate now let out a sigh, folded the dress on her lap, and sorted through a few more clothes. She glanced at the time – she would have to get busy with baking the bread soon. Yet she took a minute to finish her coffee, not ready to leave those days back in the spring.

She gave a self-satisfied smile at her own duplicity, on remembering the day of the birth in April. Ursula had gone into labor in the morning. The baby had been born at the house, late at night with the midwife in attendance. Ursula was sleeping the following morning when Ed arrived with the POWs. Kate remembered how pale and drawn Friedrich looked, as if he hadn't slept.

Ed had come up to the porch, waiting to hear the news. He stood just inside the front door, twisting his hat round and around until Kate and Jessica came down the stairs.

Jessica ran to Ed and embraced him. "It's a boy, Ed! A healthy, sweet, beautiful baby boy. They're sleeping now."

Tears welled up in his eyes. "Opal said it would be a boy. Though I don't know how she reckoned it. I told her there's no way in heck she could know. She knitted this here blanket in white." He gave the bag to Kate. Jessica uttered a gasp of delight at the sweet baby blanket. "Then to prove her point, she made this." He handed over a pale blue baby sweater and matching booties and hat, eliciting another cry from Jessica.

"Oh, how lovely!" said Kate. "Wait until Ursula sees these."

Out of the window she saw Friedrich, Gustav, and Karl, awaiting Ed's instructions for the day. Friedrich held on to the wagon, as if for support. Kate had to smile.

"Jessica, you go on and get some sleep. You were up all night. Go on."

Jessica nodded. "I think I will just lie down for a few minutes. While they're sleeping."

Ed grinned from ear to ear. "A boy! Well, that's something." He put his hat back on his head. "Can I bring Opal round in the evening?"

"Of course! Ursula will be expecting you both."

Kate walked with him out to the porch. Rather than look at him, she kept her eyes on the horizon. "Ed, I was thinking today might be a good day to get some of those supplies you've been talking about. You can take Gustav and Karl with you. I – I have a few things that I'd like Friedrich to take a look at."

Still grinning, Ed nodded. "While I'm at it, might as well swing by the hardware store over in Greenfield and pick up a few things."

"Greenfield? Won't that be out of your way – " And it hit her – Good God, Ed knows! And he's playing along with me! The twinkle in his eyes confirmed it.

"We'll most likely be gone the better part of the day," he said. He also looked at the horizon, and pulled his hat down. "Even an old head like mine occasionally puts two and two together. Though it takes a while."

Kate placed a hand on his arm and her eyes filled with gratitude. "You've always been a good friend to us, Ed. And a second father to Ursula." Her voice cracked and she lifted the knitted goods. "I look forward to seeing you and Opal this evening."

"Well, best be going."

Ed walked down the porch stairs. All three prisoners waited for the news. Karl smiled in anticipation. Gustav finally asked, "Vell?"

Ed smiled proudly. "All's vell! Come on, boys. We got our work cut out for us. Be gone most of the day. Mother and son need to rest."

Friedrich's knees buckled on hearing he had a son and again he gripped the side of the wagon.

Karl and Gustav began laughing and talking in German as they walked back to the truck. Friedrich's eyes traveled to the upstairs window. He slowly turned to join the others.

Ed headed to the truck and spoke as casually as he could manage.

"Karl, you squeeze up front with Gustav. Not you, Friedrich," he said, causing Friedrich to halt. "Kate needs you today. The water heater is making a funny sound or something. Go on." He waved him over to the house, got in his truck with the others, and drove out onto the farm lane.

Friedrich stood frozen, an expression of confusion in his eyes. He looked from Kate to Ed's departing truck, and back to Kate.

Kate opened the porch door. "Come inside."

He walked up the porch stairs, trying to decipher the look on her face.

A tiny cry came from upstairs and tears shot to Friedrich's eyes. He brought his hand to his mouth and turned away. He began to walk to the basement.

Kate placed a hand on his arm and smiled gently. "Go on upstairs. Your wife and son are waiting for you."

Friedrich took a step back in utter surprise, then clasped her hand with both of his. "Danke!" He ran up the stairs, taking them two at a time.

Kate hummed as she put together a tray crowded with eggs, buttered toast, muffins, and coffee – for two. She took it upstairs and set it on the trunk at the foot of the bed.

Friedrich was kneeling beside the bed, one hand linked with Ursula's, the other touching the blanket around his son. Friedrich's cheeks were wet with tears though his smile couldn't be any wider.

Ursula's mouth trembled as she met her mother's eyes.

Kate leaned over her grandson and beamed. Then she stroked Ursula's hair. "I'll try my hardest not to check up on you every ten minutes. Ed and the others will be gone for most of the day." She turned to Friedrich. "I'll be downstairs if you need anything."

Kate then went out onto the front porch to enjoy the mild spring day, leaving the door open. She sat in the rocker, gazing out at the budding trees, the first green, new beginnings. Then she stretched her hands around the curved armrests and began to rock lightly. She looked up at the trees to see which bird was making that wonderful warbling. There – at the top of the ash tree. A robin singing its heart out. Lines from her bedside book of poetry that she hadn't opened in years suddenly filled her mind. What was that poem? – "*all's right with the world*" – something about "*God's in his heaven – all's right with the world.*" Kate smiled. For this spectacular moment, all was right with the world.

She wished her husband were there to share it with her. Then her eyes rested on the farm all around her – their farm – and she smiled. I suppose he is, she decided, and continued rocking.

Kate was brought back to the present by a burst of laughter from Jessica in the living room. The sweetness of memory shifted to ache – it was cold December, not gentle spring. The winter winds were blowing, the fields were white with snow.

She wanted to cup a protective hand around the past, to shield it from what was coming. An unspoken dread thickened the atmosphere of their home. Friedrich would be taken away soon. Every week they breathed a sigh a relief that another week had gone by without word. She didn't want him to go. She wanted him to stay with Ursula and their son. Sorrow filled her face at the idea of the impending separation. She could scarcely imagine what Ursula must feel. She had tried to comfort her daughter and convince her that after he left, they would find out where he was, and would make contact. And would wait for him to return. Though in her heart, she knew that his return, if ever, would take years.

Jessica turned off the radio and came back into the kitchen. "There. All patched." She handed the quilt to Kate. "It will keep someone warm."

Kate inspected the embroidery and smiled. "Very nice, Jessica." She placed it next to the pile of clothes.

Jessica stretched her legs in front of her and brushed at the worn knees of her dungarees. "One of the things I like best about teaching is that I can wear dresses." She pulled out the front of her flannel shirt and frowned. Then she sat up and leaned forward on the table, her eyes brightening. "I'm thinking of dying the silk from the parachute red for the Christmas dance. Or do you think green would be nicer? I can't decide."

Eugene came down the stairs and into the kitchen, holding a pile of clothing. He handed a jacket to Kate, along with a few shirts and a pair of boots. "There. You happy, Jessica? That's all I got."

Jessica jumped up and hugged him. "Yes, I am happy."

A horn tooted from outside, causing them to look up.

Eugene moved to the window and grabbed his flight jacket. "That's Clem and Burly dropping off Clem's truck."

Jessica jumped to her feet. "You didn't say they were coming – look at me!"

Eugene shook his head. "They don't care about the appearance of a kid like you." He walked out to the porch and greeted them.

Jessica slipped on her coat and followed Eugene. She waved at Burly as he shut off his truck and opened the door.

"Hey, Jess! Dropping off Clem's truck for Friedrich to take a look at."

"Hi, Burly. You'll be coming to dinner tomorrow, won't you?" She watched Clem drive his truck alongside the machine shed where Eugene was motioning for him to park.

Burly shoved his hands into his coat pocket. "Sure thing. Me and Shirley'll drive Clem over. If his truck's ready by then, he can drive it home."

Jessica walked with Burly over to the machine shed where Clem and Eugene stood next to the truck.

"Hello, Clem. You're looking well." Jessica took a step towards him.

He gave a quiet hello and raised the hood of his truck.

Jessica stood next to him. "How's Donny?"

Clem nodded. "He's fine. I'll tell him you asked about him."

Ed came out of the machine shed with Friedrich and introduced him to Clem. Eugene kept his back to them and leaned on the fence talking with Burly.

Jessica saw that Clem was civil to Friedrich, and even shook his hand. She moved back to the porch steps, sat down, and watched Clem as he discussed the truck with Friedrich.

After a few minutes, Friedrich closed the hood, and said a few more words to Clem. He then walked over to Gustav, just as Mr. Creight pulled up to take them back to camp.

Jessica waved goodbye to the POWs and walked over to Clem. "Well?"

Clem kept his eyes on the truck as he answered. "He thinks it just needs a tune-up. Says he should be able to do it tomorrow." Without saying anything else, he walked over to Burly and Eugene.

Burly rubbed his hands together against the cold, got into his truck, and let it run. Clem and Eugene exchanged a few words as Clem opened the door to Burly's truck.

Jessica waved after them. "See you all tomorrow!" She tried to catch Clem's eye, but he looked away.

As Eugene came up the steps, Jessica smiled. "Friedrich will have Clem's truck running like new."

Eugene bristled at the pride she always showed when it came to the POWs. His eyes followed the truck as it drove down the farm lane. "Don't be surprised if Clem doesn't stay for dinner."

Jessica opened her mouth. "I would be surprised. He knows we're expecting him." She tried to interpret his expression. "What?"

"Nothing. But it can take a guy some time to get used to things, after just coming back. That's all I'm saying."

"Other than being moody, you seem to have adjusted."

"Like hell. One minute I'm fighting Germans, the next minute I find I'm related to them." He glared over at the barn where Friedrich and Gustav stood talking with Ed. "And don't tell me you didn't know about it."

Jessica knew better than to respond. She lifted her chin at the truck that was just turning onto the country road. "Clem will come."

"To see Joe and to pick up his truck. Don't you go pestering him."

"I don't pester people!"

"You're still a kid to him, Jessica. Don't be getting any ideas."

"I'm not getting any ideas! And I'm almost eighteen!" But the only response from Eugene was the door as it banged shut. Jessica looked back out at the truck as it got smaller in the distance, and then ran up the stairs and into the house.

Chapter 5

❧

Gabriel dashed out of school, his book strap slung over his shoulder, and sprinted down the sidewalks. He dodged a delivery man, wove in and around a few pedestrians, and just missed bumping into a mailman as he rounded a corner in his excitement to get to The Red String Curio Store.

When he pushed open the door, the little silver bell above it rang. He cast his eyes up at it and gave a short nod, as if the bell had personally greeted him. Then he smiled and took in the sounds and smells and liveliness of the shop. Christmas music played from the radio behind the counter, and the old grandfather clock in the back chimed. Several people browsed the aisles, searching for the rare and unusual. The proprietor, Mr. G, waved to him from the side of the store, where he and Junior were studying the empty frames on the wall, tilting their heads this way and that.

Gabriel stepped behind the counter and placed his books and coat on the bottom shelf beneath the cash register. Then he lifted his dark green shopkeeper's apron from the row of hooks and secured it around his waist. Lastly, he tucked a small notebook into the front pocket of the apron, and slid a pencil behind his ear. He was ready for business.

Mr. G strolled over to the counter. "Greetings, Master Gabriel! Punctual, as usual."

Junior trailed behind, his cane tapping against the wooden floor with every other step. He held a small frame at arm's length, assessing the dull gold vines twining around the edges. He gave a decisive nod.

"This is the one," Junior said to Gabriel, as if he had been in on the decision. "I see moonlight and dreams and long-buried wishes. Ideal for O'Shaughnessy." He handed it to Gabriel and pulled on his long, gray beard – his Tennyson beard, as Dusty, another regular, referred to it. "Now, use your imagination, Gabriel, and tell me what you think." He hooked his cane on the counter top and cleared his throat. Mr. G stood next to him in deep concentration, his knuckle crooked on his chin.

Gabriel divided his focus between the emptiness inside the frame and Junior's recitation. The old man was a born performer, his voice rich and melodic, his gestures fluid and natural as he swept his arms to the ocean in his mind's eye and lifted his gaze to the beauty of the moon.

We are the music makers,
And we are the dreamers of dreams,
Wandering by lone sea-breakers,

And sitting by desolate streams;
World-losers and world-forsakers,
On whom the pale moon gleams:
Yet we are the movers and shakers
Of the world for ever, it seems.

"That was real nice, Junior. I'll add that poem to my General Knowledge notebook." Gabriel ran his fingers over the wooden frame and positioned it in front of him. "And this is the frame for it. I can see it and it will be the perfect match." Gabriel opened his notebook and Junior obliged him by reciting the lines again. At the last word, Gabriel added an emphatic period.

"There's more, of course," said Junior, pulling on his beard again. "But to my mind, the first stanza's the best. Besides, the rest won't fit."

Mr. G lifted the frame, nodded in agreement, and handed it back to Gabriel. "An excellent choice, indeed! Gabriel, can you wrap this for Junior? I must attend to Mrs. Cranford. I've left her deciding between three lace tablecloths."

"Sure." Gabriel soon had the frame wrapped in brown paper tied with the store's trademark red string. "There you go!"

"Should have it ready next week." Junior tried to flex his gnarled, arthritic hands, tucked the package under his arm and thanked Gabriel. He turned around at the door and tipped his hat. "Then it's on to Shakespeare. The sonnets. Perfect for holiday gifts, don't you think?"

"And they'll fit in almost any frame!" said Gabriel.

Junior gave him a wink in understanding and left the shop.

Gabriel waved goodbye and wended his way down the labyrinthine aisles. He stopped to assist an elderly customer, Mrs. Peasley, find just the right gift for her husband. After listening to her describe her husband's interests, Gabriel tapped his cheek a few times. Then he held up his index finger and led her to a display of items related to coin collecting, and another section on birdwatching.

The next hour passed agreeably for Gabriel. He heard the cash register ring with sales, accompanied by Mr. G's hearty exclamations to customers and their appreciative remarks. The little bell tinkled in the background as customers came and left.

Mrs. Peasley finally decided on the items for her husband and Gabriel carried them to the counter for her. He froze in his tracks when he heard Mr. G say, "Greetings, Tommy! Came to see the rocking chair, eh? There's Gabriel, over by the assortment of globes."

Gabriel stood rooted to the floor as Tommy walked up to him. "Hi, Tommy. I – I thought you were coming tomorrow."

"I was at the soda fountain with some of the fellas so I decided to look at the rocker today." He took a step closer, wondering at the apron Gabriel was wearing, the pencil behind his ear, and the items in his arms. "What are you doing?"

Mrs. Peasley patted Gabriel on his shoulder. "Thank you, young man. I couldn't have made up my mind without you. Chester will be delighted." She held up the items for Tommy to see. "An illustrated Audubon book – and binoculars! I can hardly wait until Christmas to give them to him." She gave a small chuckle as she headed to the counter. Then she turned around. "I'll be back next week. Let's see what we can find for sister Lobelia. She collects bluebirds. And bells. Small ones."

Gabriel whipped out his notebook and jotted down the items. "I'll start my search today."

Tommy's eyes widened. "You're *working* here?"

Gabriel winced and nodded.

"And you didn't tell Mom? You're in big trouble."

"I couldn't tell her. She wouldn't like it. But I'm not doing anything wrong. I'm sure of it!"

"That's not the point, Gabriel."

Mr. G walked up to them. "Now, shall I show you my collection of rocking chairs? All in excellent condition, I assure you."

"Sure." Tommy gave Gabriel a sidelong glance and followed the store owner.

Mr. G made a left, a right, and another left. "Here we go. One, two, and three." He placed his hand on each one, setting them rocking.

"This is the one that caught Gabriel's attention. A lovely Victorian. In rich, deep oak." Mr. G hooked his thumbs behind his red suspenders and rocked on his heels. "I'll let you boys try them out. Just holler if you need anything."

Tommy looked at the rockers, then back at Gabriel. "How long have you been working here?"

"About a month. Or two. It depends how you count. It just kind of happened."

"Jobs don't just kind of happen, Gabriel."

"It did, honestly. I like to stop by now and then, just to look around, and to talk to Mr. G and his friends. Junior teaches me how to do calligraphy. And Dusty shows me pictures of the Great Pyramids and the Sphinx in some of the books here. And Mr. G teaches me how to find the marks on pottery to tell where they're from. I brought Henry in and now he's a regular too. It's fun, Tommy. And I'm not lying – it *is* my project." He patted his trusty notebook.

"But it's not a school project."

"It's related. It's about learning things. Mom would approve of that. Mr. G has one of those colossal dictionaries on a tall stand – you've seen it, right by the counter. When it's slow we take turns discovering new words."

"Colossal," Tommy echoed with a shake of his head. "So that's why you've been sounding like an old man lately." He scrunched up his mouth, giving the situation some thought. "I don't think it's a good idea."

"Aw, Tommy, give me a break. I love it here! Like you love working at Mancetti's."

"I'm stocking shelves, sweeping, dusting. What are you doing here? Learning words?"

"Sometimes I dust and sweep. But mostly I help people find things. They get happy. Like when we help the wounded soldiers at the hospital write letters or tell them jokes. Please don't say anything, Tommy. At least not yet. Wait until after Christmas."

"I'm not going to lie for you."

"I'm not asking you to. Just don't say anything." He pointed to the rocking chairs. "Take a look. That's one of the best things about working here. I get to see merchandise as it comes in. Like these rockers. This is the one I think Mom will like."

Tommy looked at the tag. "It says SOLD."

"I put that there," Gabriel said with pride. "Until I could show you."

Tommy flipped the tag around and gaped at the price. "We can't afford that!"

Gabriel beamed. "Employees get a discount. Mr. G said I could have it at cost. That's half."

Tommy sat in the chair and rocked. "I don't know…"

"And he said I can work most of it off. So it won't cost much at all. But I'd have to work for a few months."

Tommy continued rocking but his eyes narrowed with worry. "I don't have a good feeling about this, Gabe. Mom would be furious."

"But I'm not doing anything unethical."

Tommy stopped rocking. "Unethical?"

Gabriel took out his notebook, flipped through a few pages and placed his finger on a word. "Unethical. Wrong."

"So just say 'wrong' – why do you have to make everything complicated?"

Gabriel gave it some thought. "I like having more choices."

Tommy rolled his eyes and continued rocking.

"It's comfortable, isn't it? Admit it, Tommy. Mom would love it. It's a beaut."

"All right, all right." Tommy jumped out of the rocking chair. "You're right about the chair. But you have to tell Mom about the job."

"I will. But I have to find the right time."

"Come on. I have to get home. And so do you."

The boys walked to the front counter. Gabriel slipped off his apron and hung it on the hook. "Tommy agrees about the rocking chair, Mr. G."

"A wonderful Christmas present, indeed!" Mr. G made out a bill of sale and slipped it into the cash register. "You've made an excellent choice. A little sanding, a judicious touch of stain here and there, and light coat of oil. Henry said he'd be happy to help you with this."

Tommy gave another indignant look to Gabriel. "So you already have it all planned?"

"Henry was here yesterday and I asked his opinion about it. He said we can store it down in Mrs. Kuntzman's basement. And he'll help us deliver it for Christmas."

Tommy leaned on the glass display case, staring at the jewelry arrayed on the top shelf.

"*And*," Gabriel continued excitedly, "Billy thinks his Dad has the stain and oil. From when they worked on that cabinet over the summer. He'll let me know and bring it here. So we're all set!"

Tommy listened but his eyes kept going back to the jewelry.

"Something catch your fancy, Tommy?" Mr. G asked.

Tommy began to crack his knuckles. "Can I see that necklace? The round one."

"Ah, the locket. Lovely, isn't it?" He took out the pale blue box with the locket and set it before Tommy. "A circular pendant. I'd say 18 karat gold, with a small opal in the center. Victorian."

Tommy gently lifted it. "Everything's Victorian," he muttered.

"That's because Queen Victoria reigned for almost sixty-four years! 1837-1901, to be exact."

Gabriel whipped out his notebook and jotted down the information.

Tommy opened the little locket. "I think Amy would like it. What do you think, Gabriel?"

"She's like Mom that way. She loves all the old-time things. The opal really sparkles, like there's a little fire inside."

Mr. G pointed to the opal. "Curious thing about opals. While it appears that a bit of fire has been trapped inside the stone, just the opposite is true. It's water that gives opals their fire!" He chuckled at the paradox. "I have a book on minerals somewhere here…" He fumbled around a stack of books behind the counter. "Hmm. I'll have to locate it later." He turned to Tommy and Gabriel. "More vital intel anon."

Tommy turned the box over and saw the price, gulped, and pushed the locket towards Mr. G. "Thanks. I'll think about it."

"Of course. There's still plenty of time before Christmas."

An old pendulum clock on the wall behind the counter began to chime. Gabriel saw Tommy's confusion as he glanced from it to the mantel clock on the counter.

Gabriel pointed to the wall clock. "That's the only clock in the shop that's set at the real time. That way, people can hear the chimes of the different clocks better." He slipped on his coat, and lifted his books.

Tommy blinked at the explanation, but his mind was still on the locket.

"Well, my shift is over. See you tomorrow, Mr. G."

"Au revoir, Gabriel. Arrivederci, Tommy!"

Tommy opened his mouth to answer, but settled on a wave.

The boys left the shop and walked a few blocks in silence, with Gabriel looking at Tommy's frown now and then.

"You're not sore, are you? Aren't you happy about the present for Mom?"

Tommy nodded.

"Then why are you so quiet?"

"I'm thinking about the locket. I know Amy would really like it."

"So why don't you get it for her?"

Tommy screwed up his mouth. "I don't know. You don't think it's too – romantic?"

"A locket? I don't see how."

They walked a few more steps and Tommy stopped.

Gabriel had been studying the clouds and bumped into him. "What?"

"I know it's the perfect gift for her. Did you think it was nice?"

"Sure. Why didn't you have Mr. G hold it for you?"

"I wasn't sure." Tommy began cracking his knuckles again. "What if it's gone when I go back?"

They stared at each other, spun around, and ran back to the store, just as Mr. G was flipping the CLOSED sign around.

Tommy explained that he wanted to buy the locket for Amy and would pay a little bit each week.

"Fine, fine," said Mr. G, making out another bill of sale. "And since you're the brother of my favorite employee" – he gave a little chuckle, since Gabriel was his only employee – "you can have it at a discount." He showed Tommy the revised price.

Tommy's face brightened as he looked from Mr. G to Gabriel and back. "Thanks. Thanks a lot. That's swell!"

"That's just dandy, Mr. G!" added Gabriel.

"And you can pick it up whenever you like."

They were soon on their way again, running now that they were late for dinner and the day was growing dark.

Tommy and Gabriel sprinted up the stairs and into the apartment. "Hi Mom – " Gabriel dropped his voice when he saw that she was pointing to Charlotte asleep in the bassinette.

Lillian looked up at the clock when they arrived. "Where were you boys? I was starting to get worried."

"Sorry, Mom. We were…" Tommy was unsure of how to answer.

"We were looking for Christmas presents," answered Gabriel.

"I thought you were with Mickey and Billy."

Tommy washed his hands in the bathroom, listening to Gabriel's answers.

"We decided to shop for some presents. Tommy found something for Amy. A locket."

"A locket?"

Tommy nodded, coming into the kitchen. "Just something I think she'll like. It has a little opal in the center. It's Victorian."

"It sounds lovely," Lillian said.

Gabriel ran to wash his hands and was soon seated at the table. He helped himself to a big scoop of mashed potatoes with butter melting on top.

Lillian noticed that a notebook had fallen from Gabriel's pocket and she reached to pick it up.

A flash of fear crossed Gabriel's face. "I could have lost it! All the information I've gathered!" He set it next to him and placed a hand over his heart in relief. "It would take months to recreate it."

Lillian smiled at Gabriel's dedication. "I don't think I've ever seen you so enthused over a school project. Which class is it for? You never told me."

Tommy looked at Gabriel.

"I call it my General Knowledge notebook."

"May I?"

Tommy exchanged a nervous glance with Gabriel and got up to get more milk.

"Sure."

Lillian flipped through the pages, landing on the most recent pages. Her brow furrowed on reading the miscellany of words. "Bluebirds. Bells. Small ones. QV... Opals. Water makes the fire. More vital intel anon." She looked up at Gabriel.

"That's what Mr. G always says. 'More vital intel anon!'" Gabriel said with a flourish. "He has some more information on opals for Tommy." Gabriel took a bite of mashed potatoes and closed his eyes in delight. "Mmm."

Lillian turned the page back and uttered a soft surprise. "*We are the music makers?*"

"That's part of a poem by Arthur O'Shaughnessy."

"Why, Gabriel! That was my mother's favorite poem! I used to read it all the time." She gestured to the bookshelves in the living room. "It's in that red and gold book on the top shelf."

"Swell! I'll copy out the rest after dinner. Add it to my notes." Gabriel patted his notebook and gave Tommy a small smile of assurance.

Chapter 6

❦

Mr. Creight arrived late afternoon to take the POWs back to camp. As always, Kate asked him to come inside. As always, he declined. He tended to arrive early and wait for the POWs outside in the cold, sometimes sitting inside his truck, sometimes walking around the farmyard. Time on his hands weighed heavily, and he did his best to stay busy. He kept to himself and resented any intrusion into his misery.

Kate and Ursula sat at the table writing a few Christmas cards. Frankie had been fed and now sat in his high chair, playing with animal crackers. From time to time, Ursula walked to the window and looked out over the farmyard. Ed had taken Friedrich and Gustav to the meadow to reinforce one stretch of the fence. She had hoped they would return before Mr. Creight arrived. A few words in the morning was all she had managed to have with Friedrich.

Kate glanced over at Ursula, understanding her disappointment. "Ed said Otto's on the mend and is eager to get back to work. Abe Creight won't be here much longer. I think we'll all breathe a sigh of relief. It's hard to be around such bitterness."

"I don't blame him," said Ursula. "I was bitter for a long time after Francy's death." As if just realizing something, Ursula looked up at her mother. "You never were, were you? I know you were heartbroken. Bereft. But you were never bitter."

Kate signed the Christmas card and put it inside the envelope. "I didn't want to be. The weight of grief is heavy enough without adding anger to it. Does no good. But I had dealt with grief before."

"Mr. Creight lost his wife a few years back. Like you did with Dad."

"Well, we all deal with pain in our own way, but sometimes it takes over. It becomes stronger than anything we can control." She selected another Christmas card, and sighed at the image of a cheerful family seated around a table. "I hope his pain lessens. Jeremy was his only son. And his youngest child. His daughters are all grown and married." Kate shook her head. "Poor man. At least I had my children with me."

Ursula looked out the window and saw Mr. Creight stroking one of the cows near the fence. She could see his suffering in the way he stood, the tension in his shoulders, his gazing out at the bleak snow-covered fields. He wore his sorrow like a dark cloak gathered tightly about him – the only vestige of his beloved son. He raised his face to the heavy, gray winter sky and moved to the entrance of the barn, rubbing his hands together. Ursula felt a wave of sadness. He looked so cold and alone out there.

"I think I'll take him some coffee," she said.

Kate jumped up to answer the telephone and was soon discussing yet another drive with Mildred Bloomfield, while Ursula prepared the thermos. Kate motioned that she would keep an eye on Frankie.

When Ursula walked into the barn, Mr. Creight noted her arrival, and turned away. "He's not here. They're out in the meadow with Ed." He shoved his hands in his pockets and moved back to the entrance, his eyes locked on the steely gray sky.

Ursula hadn't expected him to refer to Friedrich. There was pain in his voice but not malice.

"I came to see *you*, Mr. Creight."

He bristled at her words. "I got nothing to say to you."

Ursula walked up to him. "Mr. Creight, Jeremy and I were friends since grade school. I always liked him. But there was never anything between us. Only friendship."

Bitterness filled his voice. "You were blind to what he felt."

Ursula's brow creased as she tried to recall the last few times she and Jeremy had spoken. In general, she was quiet, not one to have a large group of friends, and had recognized the same in Jeremy. It had made them quiet allies in a way. "I – I think Jeremy and I were friends because we were alike. But he never spoke to me in any way except as a friend. Truly, Mr. Creight."

The rigidity in his shoulders lessened. "Well, he wouldn't, would he? Not without any encouragement from you."

Again, Ursula played back their time in high school. Jeremy was always courteous, friendly. But nothing more.

Mr. Creight let out a deep breath and put his foot on a bale of hay. He leaned forward on his knee and crossed his arms against it. He kept his eyes on the ground. His voice dropped into gentleness. "I had no right to speak to you the way I did the other day. Jeremy would be furious with me."

"No," Ursula said with a gentle smile. "He often spoke of you. Always lovingly."

She lifted the thermos and he gave a slight nod. She opened the lid and poured him a cup of steaming coffee.

He accepted it and nodded his thanks. He took a sip. "The truth is, he didn't tell me how he felt about you. But I saw it. I pieced it together. Especially once he was called away. His letters always mentioned you. He said if I saw you in town to say hello for him."

"I would gladly have written to him. Had I known."

"He had too much pride for those kinds of letters, the kind the other girls wrote to the GIs. All fluff and talk about them coming home."

They stood silently for a few moments.

"I felt so sad when I heard about his death. I lost my brother in the war. I know what that pain is. That loss. I'm so sorry."

Mr. Creight finished his coffee and shook out the drops from his cup. His face had hardened, and Ursula understood that pity was the one thing he couldn't go near. It would surely break him.

He straightened and his chest puffed out as if it were a shield. "I'll be fine. I'm a practical man. A farmer. We understand life and death better than most people. Are forced to accept it." He handed her the cup. "Thank you for the coffee."

Ursula nodded. She realized that the door to his heart had clicked shut and now he just wanted to be alone. He turned and walked to his truck.

The others were now coming back from the meadow, and Ursula returned to the farmhouse.

She lifted Frankie from his highchair and carried him up to her room where she stood before her bedroom window. This was their practice – so that Friedrich could catch a glimpse of his son. Gustav got into the truck, and just before Friedrich slid into the seat he raised his eyes to her window. He took a moment, as if to adjust his jacket, and his face showed a glimmer of a smile.

Ursula watched the truck drive down the lane and turn onto the country road. She followed it until she could no longer see it. She had barely spoken to Friedrich, and it could be days before he was back again. She never knew when he would arrive.

She pulled the lace curtain across the window and then gave Frankie a bath. After he was dried and dressed, she combed his hair and then settled him on the bed. She laughed at the neatness of his hair.

"You look older with your hair combed." She stretched out next to him and propped herself up on one elbow. She ran her hand over Frankie's cheek, his dark hair. "You're going to look just like your papa, do you know that?"

Frankie's attention was caught by the amethyst earrings she always wore. He reached up to one.

"Oh, no you don't! Last time you pulled it." She playfully nibbled his tiny fist, which set him laughing. He wriggled for more, giggling in anticipation. "You want to play, but it's time for you to sleep, my darling."

She began to sing a lullaby, and Frankie's focus shifted to her mouth. His blinks became slower and longer, and soon he was asleep.

Ursula pulled the quilt over her and tucked it around Frankie. She thought of the longing in Friedrich's face as he looked up at them. She curved herself more closely around Frankie, fearing what lay ahead for them all.

With a flood of longing, she remembered how happy she had been in the spring, with the return of Friedrich and the birth of Frankie. They had enjoyed a few moments of pure bliss – moments when she was sure that everything would work out for them, somehow.

Then the slow crumble came, the disintegration of their happiness. It began, oddly enough, with the fall of Germany. May 8th, Victory in Europe. She had been thrilled and allowed herself to believe in a future for them.

But V-E Day had changed people in unexpected ways, especially as more details of the war were made known, and as more servicemen returned home with information. The attitude towards the POWs shifted, hardening. Stories began to spread about how poorly the Germans had treated American prisoners. People, tired of the rationing, resented giving up their share of food to the enemy. Within weeks, the POWs experienced a drastic reduction in their food.

The news from Europe changed the POWs, as well. Gustav was not the same since the bombing of Dresden. A beautiful city, flattened. Obliterated. The jewel of Germany crushed, civilian life stamped out. Gustav had insisted that his wife and children go there and stay with his wife's family, believing that they would be safer there. That had been in February, and still there was no word. It was almost certain that his family had not survived. His grief affected Karl and Friedrich.

As more images of the destruction of Germany filled the newspapers and magazines, the POWs realized that there was no home to go back to. The thin thread of hope they had so desperately clung to had frayed, then snapped. All they had was loss and a desolate future.

Like Ursula, the POWs had discounted the rumors of the Nazi concentration camps as propaganda. The barbarity reported in the newspapers and radio could not be true. It was not humanly possible. But after Eisenhower and Patton visited the camps and gave testimony, and once photographs and footage were released, the truth became irrefutable, the evidence sickening.

The friendliness between the POWs and their guards disappeared, along with the ease between the prisoners and the townsfolk – replaced by disgust. Aversion towards the Germans turned into hatred.

The day came when Friedrich and the others in the camp were forced to watch footage of the concentration camps. She heard through Otto that what the POWs saw was even worse than what she had read about. Karl had gotten sick and had to leave the room. Gustav refused to believe the images. Many of the POWs believed that the emaciated bodies were those of Germans, and that the scenes had been staged by the Soviets. There was no other way to make sense of it.

Friedrich had met enough hard-core Nazis to know what they were capable of. But he could not fathom that such evil existed on so massive a scale. As more information was made known over the next few weeks, and more films were shown to the POWs, he slowly understood the truth. He and the others were stunned into silence, withdrawing into themselves.

Friedrich's beloved Germany of Beethoven and Goethe and Schiller – the Germany of his parents – had been replaced by a different one, by a culture twisted into deformity. All his memories, all his connections to home were contaminated by this monstrous horror, a blight on his soul. Not only did he have no family and no home to return to, there was now no association, no memory to take refuge in. Evil had worked its way into everything, leaving only a deep sense of revulsion, loss, and shame.

He told Ursula that he would be forever tainted. Besides feeling a profound sense of betrayal, he realized that he had been a part of it. Like a good soldier, he had done what he was told to do.

Ursula had tried to convince him that there was no way he could have known what was happening. That he was in Africa when the horrible crimes were beginning to take place. And that people kept silent out of fear and in order to protect their families.

But Friedrich took responsibility for the part he played and fell into a deep depression.

Ursula had read about other camps where the atrocity films were shown. In one camp, a thousand men had burned their German uniforms. Many other POWs, to show their disavowal of their homeland, requested to fight the Japanese. As with Gustav, others refused to believe the films. They could not accept that their country, their friends and neighbors and family, were complicit – or worse, actively took part in – the horror.

Friedrich had stayed away from her, avoiding her when she sought him out. Weeks turned to months, with only a few glimpses of him. He had volunteered for administration duties at camp, leaving him only an occasional day now and then at the farm.

When Ursula finally found a few moments with him, she saw that he had changed. He had grown gaunt and dark circles ringed his eyes. In part, this was due to the reduction of food at camp, but mostly it was due to sleepless nights. Though Friedrich didn't want to speak about what he was feeling, he told her about how it all began for him.

"My father said that after we were defeated in the Great War, the nation's spirit had been broken, and we wanted our honor back. We had been humiliated and had nothing. People clung to the hope that the fatherland would stand proud once again. That was the allure of Hitler. But the ugly signs of where Germany was heading became increasingly clear.

"The schools became breeding grounds for Hitler's way of thinking. Jews were banned from teaching. Several of my father's friends at the university lost their posts and were replaced by Nazis. To protect me, my father sent me to school in London, where two of his friends had moved. He said fear was in everyone's heart and he urged me to be careful. Not to speak of anything political in my letters. I was there for almost four years.

"Then I was summoned home. At first, I was happy at the thought of being closer to my parents and my little brother. But I rarely saw them. I served the required six months in the Labor Service, and then entered the military. I became part of the Afrika Korps. Germany once again became a distant home."

He shook his head at the thoughts that filled his mind, and his eyes hardened. "My father was involved in some activity that cost him his life. On my only visit home, my mother whispered to me that he had died protecting the old Germany he so loved."

Ursula had held him tightly in her arms. There was so much she wanted to say to him, to try to lessen his anguish. But after that day, he was gone again for several weeks.

Then, after the surrender of Japan in August, there was finally talk of the POWs returning home. But soon a harsher reality made itself known. For most prisoners, immediate repatriation would be combined with a minimum of six months of required labor in Allied countries. The POWs would be used to help rebuild Europe. A grim-faced Gustav had said, "Our war is just beginning."

Ursula felt helpless. She couldn't get through to Friedrich. He was struggling day to day in deep pain. She tried to imagine the emptiness he must feel.

And then, the additional blow in September. Just when she sensed that Friedrich was coming round and tentatively reaching out to her again, he had been caught at camp trying to falsify papers. At first, she couldn't believe it. It was out of character for him to do anything underhanded. But he admitted his guilt and lost all privileges for a month. When she finally was able to see him, he didn't want to speak about it. When she pressed him, he said only that he had tried to change Karl's place of origin.

Frankie stirred in his sleep, shifting Ursula's thoughts back to the present. There had been some healing, some change in Friedrich recently. As if he knew their time together was limited and he wanted their last weeks or months to be as good as possible for them.

Shadowy evening settled in the room, and a heavy weariness overcame Ursula. She wiped away her tears and kissed Frankie's forehead. Then imagining that Friedrich was curved around the other side of their baby, his hand linked with hers, his eyes filled with love, she closed her eyes and succumbed to sleep.

Chapter 7

~

Lillian brought a few library books to the kitchen table to be returned. Though she tended to use Charlotte's nap time to work on her drawings, she still found time for a little more reading now that she was at home more. She realized how much she missed it.

She glanced out the kitchen window to see if Gabriel was on his way home from school. He was getting home later and later, but today he promised to be home early. She felt the need for a little distraction. There was still no word from Charles, and even though she knew the lines of communication were jammed, part of her feared that he had gotten sick again, or something worse. She couldn't bear the thought that something might now befall him. She had heard of such things. Boys finally home from the war – then killed in an accident on an icy road. Or in a train wreck. Or succumbing to pneumonia. She squeezed her eyes shut – she would not entertain such thoughts. Charles would come home. He would get word to her as soon as he was able.

She was somewhat concerned that Gabriel was spending more and more time away from home. She supposed it was just a part of growing up. Though now that she thought of it, he did seem a little distracted lately. Izzy's comment about how the youngest child often feels neglected when there's a new baby came to mind. Perhaps she should have a talk with him. He was so independent that she sometimes forgot there might be things that troubled him.

As she bundled Charlotte in her jacket and booties, she heard Gabriel running up the stairs.

"I'm home, Mom!" he said, stepping inside and wriggling out of his coat.

"Don't take your coat off, Gabriel. I thought we could walk to Mancetti's to pick up a few groceries. Do you mind?"

He shrugged. "No. Hello, Charlotte." He bent over his little sister. "Did you miss me? I thought so." He made faces and noises to make her smile.

"I need to get a few ingredients to start my holiday baking. And I'd like to stop by the library. I'm in the mood for a little Dickens."

"I think what you really mean," Gabriel said with a sly grin, "is that you want everyone in the neighborhood to see Charlotte."

"Well, it's supposed to get colder, so I thought I should take a stroll while I still can." Lillian adjusted her hat in the hall tree mirror. "And I do have a few books to return to the library."

Gabriel smiled at her explanations.

She chucked him under the chin. "And, yes, I want everyone to see how much she's grown. And what a delightful baby she is!" Lillian lifted Charlotte above her head, causing her to smile and open her eyes wide.

Gabriel laughed. "I like showing her to everyone, too. People become instantly happy when they see her, did you notice? And Tommy will be glad to see her."

"If we go to the library first, maybe he'll be finished with his work by the time we get to Mancetti's and can walk home with us."

Gabriel put his coat back on and brought the baby carriage down the steps, while Lillian followed with Charlotte. He patiently waited when the elderly woman on the first floor stepped out to see Charlotte.

"I heard you coming. I just want to take a peek at little Charlotte. Oh, my goodness! She's grown so much! May I?" she reached out her arms and held Charlotte, then bounced her gently on her hip. "Hello, little one! Look at those beautiful curls! Oh, she's adorable. Just adorable." She handed Charlotte back to Lillian.

"Thank you, Mrs. Gibson," Lillian said smiling at the remarks. "Yes, she's really growing."

"How wonderful to have two older brothers to help out!" She patted Gabriel's head. "You're no longer the baby, are you?"

"I haven't been that for a long time," said Gabriel. "I'll take the carriage outside, Mom." He made his escape through the vestibule and opened the carriage on the sidewalk.

Lillian said her goodbye and was soon nestling Charlotte in the blankets. "You're a good older brother, Gabriel."

They hadn't even made it to the end of the street when they ran into another neighbor.

"Why hello, Mrs. Wilson!" said Lillian. "What a nice surprise. I feel like I haven't seen you in ages. I don't get out as much as I used to."

"Not with a baby, you don't." Mrs. Wilson leaned over the carriage and gave a gasp of amazement. "How big she's grown!" She put her arm around Gabriel's shoulder and squeezed. "I expect you'll be seeing me more often – now that I've abandoned my position with the Transit Authority."

Lillian raised her eyebrows at the news. "I thought you loved your job there. And weren't you recently promoted?"

Mrs. Wilson tightened her head scarf and gave a shrug. "The returning men are all desperate for work." She leaned over the carriage and smiled at the baby. "Yeeees, they are," she said, tickling Charlotte under the chin. "So, I'm back to volunteering – or as Harry puts it, working for free. Ah well, we must all do our part. What is she now, two months?"

"Three!" Lillian pulled back the carriage top and repositioned Charlotte's hat. The baby began to kick her arms and legs.

"Hello, sweetheart!" Mrs. Wilson's expressions shifted back and forth as she held a conversation with Lillian and then engaged with Charlotte – offering a concerned expression to Lillian, and then smiling and wiggling her fingers at the baby. Gabriel looked on, amused.

Mrs. Wilson clasped her hands. "Oh, that little dimple when she smiles. What a darling! Just seeing her warms the cockles of my heart."

"The *what*?" asked Gabriel.

"Any word from your husband?" Mrs. Wilson briefly shifted to a serious mode.

"Only that he's on his way to London. I expect to hear from him soon. Any day."

Mrs. Wilson considered Lillian's words. "I'm sure you will. Though he'll have a devil of a time getting back home." She went back to cooing. "Oh, what a big girl you are! Yes, you are!" She straightened and faced Lillian. "All the ships are full to capacity – the voyages to victory!" she said with a fisted swing of her arm. "Twelve thousand troops on the *Queen Mary* alone. I can scarce imagine it! Is there any hope he'll make it home for Christmas?"

"It's possible. But if not for Christmas, then soon after," said Lillian

"He'll do his best, I'm sure." She leaned over the baby carriage. "To see his little angel, yes, he will!"

Mrs. Wilson pinched Gabriel's cheek. "Feeling a little lost these days? With all the new changes?"

"Not really…"

Mrs. Wilson took Lillian's arm and whispered. "It can be hard on the youngest, whatever the age."

Lillian glanced at Gabriel who was looking up towards Billy's apartment window. "He's been a little distracted lately with school and all, but he loves having a little sister."

"Mark my words, he's feeling the change. He just needs a little reassuring." Mrs. Wilson leaned over one last time to fuss over Charlotte. "Well, I promised Harry a baked chicken tonight. Best be on my way."

"Say hello to him for me. It was so nice seeing you."

"Goodbye. Ta-ta, little one," she said, wiggling her fingers to Charlotte. "Ta-ta! You take good care of your little sister," she added to Gabriel, pinching his cheek again.

Gabriel smiled as she left, and then leaned over Charlotte. "Don't worry. It won't always be like this." He rubbed his cheek and frowned. "Except for the pinching."

Similar conversations took place at the library and the grocery store, the longest with Mrs. Mancetti, who gathered Charlotte in her arms and walked around the store with her, leaving Mr. Mancetti to ring up the customers and bag their groceries.

Gabriel saw that Tommy was up on a stepladder restocking the shelves and ran over to him. Then he noticed that Amy was standing there with him.

"Hi, Amy!"

"Gabriel! You have to help us! We're still trying to find a theme for our French project." She flung back her head and groaned in frustration. "I just can't think of anything! We must include sequences, numbers, transition words. We thought of explaining how batteries work, or radios, or talking about stamp collecting, but nothing feels right. Have you thought of anything else, Tommy?"

He shook his head.

"Well, don't give up. We have to submit our idea by Monday. Put on your thinking cap, Gabriel."

"Okay. We'll figure something out."

Lillian had retrieved Charlotte from Mrs. Mancetti and turned onto the aisle. She saw Amy looking up at Tommy, her schoolbooks in her arms. Her long wavy hair hung down to her waist.

"Hello, Amy."

Amy spun around and her eyes brightened at seeing Charlotte. "Hello, Mrs. Drooms. Oh, can I hold her?" She set her books at her feet.

"Of course." Lillian lifted Charlotte out of the carriage and handed her to Amy.

"Oh, I would love to have a little sister like this. I just adore her!" She walked up and down the aisle, prattling to Charlotte. "When you get older, I'll buy paper dolls for you to play with. And I'll teach you how to make a sailboat out of newspaper, and…"

Lillian smiled and turned to Tommy. "Are you almost finished, Tommy? Oh, I'll take one of those."

Tommy handed her a can of condensed milk. "Once these boxes are empty, I'm done."

"Good. Then we'll wait for you at the counter. I'll just finish my shopping."

"Amy! Come along!" cried Mrs. Little from the counter.

"My mom's calling me." Amy handed Charlotte back to Lillian. "Look – her eyes are starting to close."

Lillian smiled and gently placed Charlotte back in the carriage. "You have the magic touch, Amy."

Amy glowed with pride, then turned to Tommy. "Let me know if you think of anything, Tommy. You too, Gabriel. Bye!" She blew a kiss to the now-sleeping baby and ran to the front of the store.

Lillian turned down another aisle, humming as she looked at the spices.

Tommy put away the rest of the cans of milk, but held on to the last one, staring intently at it. "Gabriel!"

"What?" Gabriel wondered at Tommy's fixation with the can. "What is it? Do you need help? Do you feel all right?"

"Food! Baking!" cried Tommy. "For our project!"

Gabriel's face lit up. "Like how to make something? A recipe! Dessert!"

"It'd be easy. Lots of instructions, time phrases and numbers. I think Amy would like it."

"And you could pass out the results to the class. They'll love it!"

"Let's go tell Amy!"

Tommy jumped off the stepladder and he and Gabriel ran down the aisle and out the door to catch up to Amy.

When they came back, Lillian was at the counter paying, and was surprised to see the boys coming in the store. "Where – "

"We'll explain later," Tommy said. He quickly finished emptying the last box of canned goods, with Gabriel at his side.

All the way home, they described their ideas about the project to her. "Do you know any French recipes, Mom?"

"I made crepes once. Maybe Mrs. Kuntzman can give you some ideas. Amy must have been happy with your suggestion."

"She sure was," said Gabriel. "She slapped me on the back and said 'good work!' and she gave Tommy a kiss on the cheek."

"Shut up, Gabe."

Lillian turned her head to hide her smile.

As they passed the brownstone where Mickey and Billy lived, she heard the second-floor window open and saw Billy waving at them.

"Hey, Gabriel! I got the stuff!" He made several gestures with his arms, pointing, and motioning for Gabriel to come up, until Mickey appeared next to Billy and pulled him inside. Mickey waved at them and then closed the window.

"What was that all about?" Lillian asked Gabriel.

"Well…"

Lillian leaned down and sniffed at him. "You and Billy better not be smoking cigarettes again!"

"No! I told you I just did it once and didn't like it."

"What 'stuff' is he talking about?"

"Can I go and see? Could be something for my project."

Lillian glanced up to the window, then down at Gabriel. "All right. But I want you home for dinner."

"Sure, Mom," Gabriel called over his shoulder as he ran off.

"Do you know what that was all about, Tommy? Is there anything I need to be worried about?"

"Nah. That's just Gabriel being Gabriel. You don't have to worry about him, Mom. He would never do anything – unethical."

Lillian gave a puzzled look at Tommy's choice of word. "No, I don't think he would. But he's been acting differently lately. I'm a little worried that he might be feeling left out. I haven't been spending as much time with him since Charlotte was born. Or you," Lillian said, placing a hand on Tommy's shoulder.

"You don't have to worry about that, Mom. We're not little kids anymore. Besides, Gabriel's different. Sometimes I think – "

Lillian looked over at Tommy. "What? What do you think?"

He pinched his eyebrows in thought. "I don't know. Sometimes I think – even though I'm older than Gabriel, he's strong, in a way that I'm not."

"Why, what do you mean, Tommy?" Lillian stopped, surprised at his words.

"In a good way. He just plows ahead and knows that things will work out. He isn't afraid of things." Tommy twisted his mouth, knowing he wasn't explaining himself very well.

They continued walking down the sidewalk. "Can you give me an example of what you mean?"

"Like at the hospital. I watch him sometimes with the wounded soldiers. Even the quiet ones get happy when Gabriel is there. He gets them to laugh and talk."

"But so do you, Tommy."

"It's different. When I help a patient write a letter or hold one for him to read when – you know – they can't hold the letter or see, I feel so bad and I try so hard not to look at – the missing part. But Gabriel doesn't even seem to notice. He talks to all the men like there's nothing wrong with them. Like it's just a part of them. I think they like that."

"That's very perceptive of you, Tommy." Lillian mulled over his words. "Everyone connects with people in different ways. But you're right. Gabriel has always been very accepting of people. He's always been at ease with all kinds of people."

Tommy began to crack his knuckles. "Do you think I'm helping them? I know I'm not making them better – sometimes even the doctors can't. But do you think I'm helping them?"

"Of course, you are, Tommy. You have a quiet way of bringing them comfort and encouragement. It's good for the patients to have a variety of personalities around them. You and Gabriel, Henry and I, and the other volunteers all bring something different to them. But I've observed the patients and I think they all feel especially safe with you."

Tommy gave his half smile. "I hope so."

Lillian's heart clenched. Sometimes she was overpowered by the love she felt for her children.

When they reached their brownstone, Lillian gently lifted Charlotte so as not to wake her. Tommy ran ahead and opened the door for her. He then brought the carriage inside, put it under the stairs, and checked the letter box.

Lillian held her breath as Tommy sorted through the cards and bills. "Anything from Charles?"

He shook his head. "Sorry, Mom."

"Well, with everyone sending letters home…"

"Here are some Christmas cards," Tommy said cheerfully. "A card from Aunt Annette. And look – here's a letter from Jessica."

Lillian had to smile. Jessica was turning out to be the letter writer in Kate's family. "Oh good, I look forward to reading them."

Tommy gathered the groceries and books and followed Lillian upstairs.

Inside the apartment, Tommy waited for Lillian to put Charlotte in the bassinette. "Want me to do anything for dinner?"

"You can put the casserole in the oven to warm – that would be a big help. I think I'll make myself a cup of tea."

Tommy turned on the oven and set the casserole inside while Lillian put the groceries away and made a cup of tea. Once she was resting on the couch with her letters, Tommy sat next to her. Then he jumped up and turned on the lamp. The apartment filled with a golden glow.

"Ahh. How cozy! Thank you, Tommy." She pulled the afghan over her legs and smiled out at the room.

"Do you mind if I go see Mickey? Then I'll bring Gabe home with me."

"Of course not. Dinner won't be ready for another hour or so."

"You sure? Do you need anything?"

"No, everything's all set. Dinner is in the oven, Charlotte is sleeping – and I have my tea and letters."

"Swell. See you, Mom!" Tommy grabbed his coat from the hall tree, and ran down the stairs.

Lillian opened the letter from Jessica and a few photographs spilled out. There was Jessica smiling widely, standing outside the school. What a lovely girl – she appeared a little older, but still so sweet and innocent. Another photo of Kate on the front porch – her smile didn't hide the worry in her eyes. Lillian knew that until all her sons were home, Kate wouldn't have any peace.

Lillian lifted a photo of Ursula holding her baby. My God, she was more beautiful than ever. Her direct gaze into the camera revealed an inner sorrow. No one had mentioned the fact that Friedrich was the baby's father, but Lillian had pieced together bits of information that had trickled in through the letters – that Ursula had married last Christmas, the baby had been born in the spring, cryptic hints from Kate that when the war was over and things had settled down, she would tell Lillian more. And the letters from Ursula, speaking her heart without ever using Friedrich's name. Lillian understood that they were not at liberty to put anything in writing.

Ursula had written a few letters about how happy she was with her baby, that she was so grateful the war was over and that her brothers would be home in the coming months. And that maybe soon her life would begin in earnest. There was the unspoken hope that with the war over, she and Friedrich could live openly as husband and wife. Ursula had mentioned that she expected to be temporarily separated from her husband because of the war, and that when he finally returned, they would perhaps move to Chicago where he could find work.

Lillian took a sip of tea and looked out at the empty fireplace. That had been in the summer. Ursula's letters had grown infrequent, and the optimism was no longer there.

She unfolded Jessica's letter and read that Eugene was slowly adjusting to civilian life, and that Paul and Jimmy were on their way home from the Pacific. Jessica wrote about the challenges and rewards of teaching, and commented on how the town had changed with so many boys and men returning home. She ended with the hope that perhaps *this* was the war to end all wars.

Lillian smiled at the young woman's words. That sentiment was fueling the pervasive euphoria

– evil had been defeated. Fascism was shattered. Nazism was destroyed. But Lillian couldn't rouse her earlier optimism. Not after these four years and with the news that was coming out about the horrors that had taken place. She felt it as a stain on her own soul – the knowledge that human nature was so much worse than she had ever believed. She feared that the dark force was like a geyser – erupting into violence and then retreating underground. With the pressure always building for another burst of evil.

Lillian looked down at Jessica's words and felt protective of that youthful optimism. In spite of everything, Lillian wanted to believe that the nurturing of such a hopeful view might, one day, bring it about.

She thought of Charles, and worried about the effects of two world wars on him. There couldn't possibly be another one in his lifetime – could there?

All she wanted was to hold him. Again, there was the almost unbearable ache, the fear that something would happen to him. After all, President Roosevelt hadn't lived to see the end of the war. And many soldiers had been killed just days before the war ended. Life could be cruelly ironic.

She buried her face in her hands, haunted by the image from the recurring nightmare she'd been having. That Charles's ship had been hit by a torpedo. And he was thrown into the dark waters, floating away from her…

She refused to look at that image. Charles would make it home – and she would never let him go. Lillian rose to her feet, wanting to keep busy. She went to the kitchen and began to make a salad for dinner. She turned on the radio as she bustled about the kitchen, humming along with the music. Her mind filled with Charles and she found herself smiling as she imagined their long-awaited embrace.

Chapter 8

Ursula stood at the living room window in the late afternoon. Sometimes she felt that her life was being lived while looking through windows – watching, waiting, hoping.

She saw Eugene wave goodbye to Ed as he drove off. They had tended to the animals all day and made a few repairs to the grain bin, while Friedrich worked on Clem's truck. Ursula suddenly became aware of how quiet it was. Gustav had not come to the farm today, and Mr. Creight hadn't yet arrived to take Friedrich back to camp. She had just put Frankie down for his nap, and her mother and Jessica were busy in the kitchen with last minute preparations for the dinner party. Her heart began to quicken – Friedrich was alone.

Ursula listened as Eugene came inside and sat at the kitchen table. But when Jessica offered him a cup of coffee, he declined, saying that he was going to shower. Ursula heard him go up the stairs – she could hardly believe her good fortune.

She pulled her sweater tight and ran out to the machine shed. Friedrich had just stepped inside and was putting away the tools when Ursula called out his name and ran to him.

At first, he was fearful and hesitated in embracing her.

"It's all right. They're all inside. But we don't have long."

They held each other tightly, neither of them speaking. Then Friedrich sat down on the bench by the door and pulled Ursula onto his lap. He cradled her in his arms and kissed her face, her hair, her hands, her lips.

"Oh my God, it's been weeks since I held you, Friedrich!"

He looked around and then took her hand. "Ursula, listen to me."

Her face tightened at the seriousness of his tone.

"Gustav is going to be moved back to the base camp. Soon."

She stiffened. "Are you sure?"

"We are never sure. But one of the camp administrators told him that. Back to Camp Ellis, and then transferred out west somewhere to another camp. They are closing the branch camps. My time here is short."

Ursula shook her head. "No, Friedrich. The camp is fuller than ever, and they need you because of your English. To help process all the prisoners. They won't send you away. Not any time soon, at least."

"We don't know what they will do, Ursula. Everything is changing quickly now."

She stood and began to pace. "I was so sure it wouldn't happen until spring or summer." She sat back next to him. "We'll have several months, surely."

Friedrich saw the tentative hope in her eyes. "We must be prepared, my love."

She passionately embraced him. "I can't bear it. I can't bear to think you will leave me."

They both jumped to their feet when they heard a truck driving up the lane.

Ursula went to the entrance. "It's Burly."

Friedrich embraced her one more time. "I will try to find out more information. But nothing is certain anymore." They separated, but Friedrich held onto Ursula's hand. "We must speak, Ursula. About what will happen when – "

She kissed his words away and ducked out the back door. Then she leaned against the shed and tried to steady her breath. She couldn't think about it. The only way she could face his leaving was to push it out several months.

Burly gave a quick toot on his horn announcing his arrival.

While Ursula was outside, Frankie had begun to cry. Kate now held him as she tried to turn down the potatoes that were boiling over. "Ursula! Jessica!"

Eugene walked in, his hair still wet from his shower. Kate shoved Frankie into his arms. "Take him! He didn't sleep a wink. I have to tend to dinner and the girls are getting dressed."

Eugene scowled and held the baby at arm's length. He searched for a place to put him and walked with him into the living room. He sat on the couch and set Frankie next to him.

Frankie pulled himself up and leaned against Eugene. Then he smiled and grabbed at Eugene's mouth.

Eugene jerked his head back. "Cut that out!"

Frankie laughed and tried it again.

"I said – Aw hell, come here." He positioned Frankie next to the couch. "You're always trying to walk. Use this," he said patting the edge of the couch. Frankie tried to balance himself and walked sideways holding onto the couch, then fell. Eugene stood next to him. "If you're going to walk, then walk. Not like that."

Frankie babbled in earnest as he tried again to pull himself along the couch.

Eugene held out two fingers for Frankie to hold. "Come on. You can do it." He walked backwards slowly as Frankie lurched forward one step at a time, prattling in delight. "You see? Good! There you go – "

"Frankie?" Ursula, always afraid that Frankie had crawled into mischief, rushed into the living room – and halted when she saw Eugene with him.

Eugene's scowl reappeared. He lifted Frankie and handed him to Ursula. "Here. Take him." He left the room abruptly and was soon outside greeting Burly and Clem.

Jessica threw a jacket over her yellow and blue floral dress and went outside to join them.

"Hi, Burly. Hello, Clem." She turned to Burly. "Where's Shirley?"

"Hey, Jess," said Burly. "She's coming later with Joe and Sue Ellen. They're fussing over a cake that's still cooling."

Jessica flashed a smile to Clem, but he looked away. Yet every time she turned towards him, she caught him looking at her. She felt encouraged and couldn't keep from smiling.

"Thought we'd come early and check out Clem's truck while your POW is still here." Burly and Clem walked over to where Friedrich stood. He had propped open the hood of the truck and was listening to the engine running, using a cloth to dab at and polish a few places.

Clem looked inside and showed his surprise. "It's never sounded this good. Or looked this clean."

Friedrich gave a slight shrug as if to say it wasn't much.

"What do I owe you?" Clem reached for his wallet, but Friedrich put up his palm.

Burly gave a light chuckle and slapped Friedrich on the back. "The only money these boys get is script."

Clem took a step back. "But I can't accept – "

Eugene walked up. "No need, Clem. That's his job." He walked over to Burly. "Come on inside. We'll wait for the others where it's warm." He led the way to the farmhouse.

Friedrich lowered the hood and used the cloth to wipe his hands.

"Much obliged," said Clem, offering his hand to Friedrich. "I can see that you put more effort into it than you had to. Thank you."

Friedrich shook his hand. "Let me know if you have any problems with it."

Mr. Creight was just turning into the lane. Friedrich hurried back into the machine shed and stepped out the back door, his eyes going to Ursula's window. There she stood with Frankie. Friedrich gazed up at them, his heart filled with longing, until Mr. Creight's horn forced him away.

"Bye, Friedrich!" Jessica called out to him. She remained with Clem, who had just turned off his truck. His eyes followed Creight's departing truck.

"That's not right," said Clem. "He did work for me and I should pay him."

"But you can't, Clem. It's not allowed. He fixed it, right?" asked Jessica. She leaned forward so that he would have to look at her. Their eyes met briefly.

Clem nodded. "He must have spent all day cleaning it and changing out the parts."

"He did. He likes working on things. You'll need your truck now that you're back, won't you?"

Jessica hoped he would respond with an invitation, but she felt that perhaps he was shy. Clem hesitated, but remained silent. Then he looked away, down the road. "Here comes Joe now." He started to move away.

"Clem!" Jessica said, taking his elbow. "I have something for you. Here." She handed him a photograph of her taken at her graduation.

He held it, studying it for a few moments. "Nice picture."

"Thought you might like to have it. To remind you that I'm not a kid anymore." She stood before him, smiling expectantly.

He looked at her and turned the picture over. He saw the words *To Clem, from Jessica*. He tucked it in his pocket and spoke quietly.

"You passing around your photograph to all the fellas?"

Jessica's eyes widened and a jolt of red shot to her cheeks. "I haven't given it to anyone! But if you don't want it – " She made a grab for it, but he had already turned away to catch up with Eugene and Burly. Joe Madden drove up the lane with Sue Ellen and Shirley and parked next to the barn. Clem waited with the others on the porch for them.

Jessica spun around, regretting her offer. What had she been thinking! Of course, he wasn't interested in her. Still, it was an unkind thing he said.

She ran up the porch stairs and Clem opened the door for her. She blinked away the tears, refusing to look in his direction. Behind her she could hear the happy greetings to Clem from Joe, Sue Ellen, and Shirley. Joe gave Clem a hearty embrace, and everyone began talking at once, while Eugene ushered them all inside.

Jessica was still bristling from Clem's words as she bustled to and from the kitchen to the dining room.

"There you are," said Ursula to Jessica. "Thank goodness Frankie fell right asleep. Hello, Sue Ellen! Shirley. Come in."

Kate and Ursula greeted the group as they congregated in the kitchen and admired the decorated cake that Sue Ellen carried in.

"Read it!" cried Sue Ellen, setting it in the center of the table. "We made it specially for you, Clem!"

Clem came to the table and looked down at the cake. He read the words written in blue icing. "Home Alive in '45!"

Joe slapped him on the back. "I knew you'd make it. Bet you're glad it's all over."

Clem nodded. "That's real nice. Thank you, Sue Ellen."

She waved away the compliment. "We would've been here sooner but Joe kept messing up on the numbers. I finally had to do it myself."

"I told you to do it yourself," Joe said. He looked at Kate and laughed. "She knows I can't compete with her in the kitchen but likes to remind me of it every now and then."

Sue Ellen took his arm and nestled her head in his chest, laughing as if she had never heard anything funnier. "It's true! I always try to get him to do something he doesn't want to do." She kissed him on the cheek. "You're a good sport, Joe!"

Shirley walked over to Jessica and caught the aroma of the soup. She lifted the lid to the pan and peeked inside. "Looks like your tomato soup turned out well. Can I help with anything?"

"No, no – just go ahead and all have a seat in the living room. We'll get you some drinks. She felt Clem's eyes on her but avoided looking at him.

Jessica went to the bathroom to splash cold water on her face. She could feel that her cheeks were still hot and didn't want Clem to think that his words mattered to her. She took a deep, calming breath and went back to the kitchen and ladled out the soup into a tureen. Laughter and conversation floated in from the living room.

Eugene opened the refrigerator and reached for a few beer bottles. "Clem can't stay for dinner," he said to Jessica.

"That's his business," she replied. "He can do whatever he likes."

Kate exchanged a surprised glance with Ursula.

"We're going to meet over at Burly's later for a game of cards," Eugene explained. "Petey and Bob are coming over."

"But surely he'll stay for dinner, now that he's here," said Kate, as she arranged the pot roast on a platter.

Eugene left with the beers and handed them out to Burly, Joe, and Clem, while Ursula offered a few choices to Sue Ellen and Shirley.

"Cider for me," said Shirley.

Sue Ellen gave it some thought. "I wouldn't mind some of your elderberry wine."

"I'll get it," said Kate, "and will join you with a glass."

They all sat around swapping stories and catching up. When Jessica brought the cider for Shirley, Clem went up to her.

"Can I help you with anything?"

"Nope." She turned and went back into the kitchen. She and Ursula went from the kitchen to the dining room with utensils and dishes for the table.

Clem sat back down in the living room. Though he smiled and nodded at the conversations, his eyes followed Jessica as she moved about, and his fingers nervously peeled the label off his beer bottle.

"So, you heard that me and Joe got married?" Sue Ellen asked.

"I sure did," said Clem. "Over the summer, wasn't it?"

"A June wedding. And these two are next," Sue Ellen said, pointing her thumb to her sister and Burly. Burly grinned and took a long swig of beer.

"First, he has to officially ask me," said Shirley, giving Burly a playful punch on the arm.

Kate had to laugh at Burly's discomfort. She leaned back and took a sip of her wine. "You know Jimmy and Gladys are getting married, just as soon as he returns. I guess we'll be having a winter wedding."

"No point in waiting," added Shirley.

Ursula gave a nod to Kate, indicating that everything was ready in the dining room.

"Everyone's getting married," said Sue Ellen, getting to her feet. "And starting families and…" Her voice trailed off as Kate waved them into the dining room.

Clem stood. "Well, I best be going."

Sue Ellen grabbed his arm. "You just got here and you're already talking about leaving? You can't leave before dinner!"

Clem hadn't planned on Sue Ellen's insistence. He appeared uneasy as she pulled him into the dining room. "Look, a place has been set for you. Now you have to stay," she said, laughing.

Kate noticed Clem's reluctance. "Whatever you want Clem, don't feel that – "

"Nonsense!" said Sue Ellen. "Look at the beautiful spread. Come on, Clem! Have a seat." She pulled out the chair next to her and patted it. "Besides, you have to tell me what you think of my cake."

"Of course." He sat down and tried to smile.

Kate placed a hand on his shoulder and sat down next to him. "Donny must be beside himself with joy to have you back home."

Clem nodded. "He's got all kinds of plans for fishing and fixing up the yard. He wants to build a treehouse in the spring."

"You're a good uncle, Clem," said Kate.

"And you'll make a good father, one day," Sue Ellen chirped in.

Clem took a sip of beer and looked down at his plate.

"There's no getting around it, Clem. A good-looking guy like you will be snatched up in no time!" Sue Ellen laughed at her own words. "Look at that spread! Oh, Ursula, those rolls smell heavenly! Absolutely heavenly. Don't they, Clem?"

He looked out at the bread basket and agreed.

They were soon seated around the table in animated conversation. Jessica made sure everyone had a drink at their plate and then sat down.

Ursula went around with the soup tureen and began to ladle out the soup. When she came to Clem, he put his hand up. "No soup for me, thanks," he said with a forced smile. His mouth twitched subtly. "Never was one for soup."

Jessica gave a puff of annoyance at his response. "How can you say that? You might not like a certain kind of soup, but you can't say that you don't like soup in general."

"Besides," said Shirley, "this is Jessica's famous garden tomato soup. You *have* to try it. She made it special, she told me so."

Jessica pressed her lips together and passed around the hot rolls. Clem gave a small nod to Ursula and she ladled Jessica's soup into his bowl.

"If a guy doesn't like soup, he doesn't like soup," said Eugene, growing sullen. "Eat what you want, Clem. Don't let them nag you into eating something you don't want."

Everyone began to butter their rolls and sample the soup.

"Isn't it just delicious?" asked Shirley. She gave Burly a sharp elbow in his side.

"Mmm-mm," he said. "Pretty tasty."

Clem lifted his spoon. He stared at the red soup and blinked hard a few times.

"Jessica, it's better than ever. I don't know how you do it!" said Sue Ellen, waiting for Clem to taste it.

"Soup is soup," muttered Eugene.

Jessica regretted making the soup and would be glad when the dinner was over. What a terrible idea it was!

"Cooking is so much easier now without the rationing, isn't it?" asked Shirley.

"Yes. Thank God, the war is over," Ursula said.

Eugene asked mockingly, "You think a piece of paper is signed and war is over? It doesn't work that way."

Ursula set the tureen in the middle of the table and took her seat.

"China, Java – they're still at it," he continued. "Not to mention the retaliation going on in Europe."

Kate gave Eugene a look of warning. "Well, I for one, am happy that a piece of paper has been signed and that my sons are coming home."

Shirley looked up from her soup. "Do you think they'll be here in time for Christmas? Wouldn't that be wonderful!"

"This will be the happiest Christmas in years!" said Sue Ellen. "Have you seen all the lights in town? The town square has never looked so bright and – "

A small tapping sound caused the conversation to stop.

Clem's hand was shaking, causing the spoon to rattle against the inside of his soup bowl. He tried to steady his right hand with his left and over-corrected himself. A splash of red landed on his shirt.

Jessica's mouth dropped open.

Kate jumped up. "Come into the kitchen, Clem. I can help with that. A little baking soda should do the trick."

"Excuse me," he said. His face flooded with shame as he stood and followed Kate.

Eugene, Joe, and Burly began to talk loudly about some incident that happened last time they went to town, covering the awkward moment with noise and laughter.

Jessica rose to her feet and followed Clem into the kitchen.

Kate finished brushing at his shirt. "There you go," she said, as if nothing had happened. "Shouldn't stain. Just come on in when you're ready." She returned to the dining room.

Clem nodded and made a few more wipes at his shirt.

He didn't look up as he addressed Jessica. "I hope you enjoyed the spectacle."

Jessica wrung her hands before him. "I'm sorry, Clem. I – I didn't know."

"Well, now you do."

She saw the open pan of soup on the stove and feared that the color or smell had triggered some terrible memory. She hurried over to cover the soup and, in her haste, dropped the lid. It landed on the stove top with a bang and then clanged noisily to the floor.

Clem jumped at the sound and held his head. "I can't do this." He threw the rag in the sink, grabbed his coat and ran out the door.

"Clem!" Jessica called and started to follow him.

Eugene came into the kitchen and grabbed her arm. "Let him go. I told you to leave him alone."

Jessica raised questioning eyes to her brother.

"There are plenty of guys like that. Never order soup because their hands shake so bad. Just leave him be." He walked back into the dining room.

Low murmuring filled the table, then a few attempts at normal conversation. "These rolls are light as cotton," said Shirley.

Sue Ellen took a helping of buttered carrots. "Ursula, did you see the new bolts of fabric at Arnold's?" Seeing that Ursula had left the table, she directed her conversation to Shirley. "There's a bolt of satin the color of raspberry jam and – "

"I was there with you!" protested Shirley. "Don't you remember? I was the one who pointed out that fabric to you."

"Carrots?" Sue Ellen snapped, annoyed that Shirley misunderstood her ruse to cover the tension. She spooned a large helping onto Shirley's plate.

"Looks like it's fixin' to snow," said Joe. Burly and Kate took up the thread with talk about the storm moving their way.

Jessica stood at the kitchen window watching Clem drive away. She felt Ursula's arm around her shoulder.

"Oh, Ursula," said Jessica. "I shamed him! I didn't mean to."

"Of course, you didn't. He knows that. Come back in, Jessica. Put on a brave face – for his sake."

When they went back to the table, Sue Ellen was saying that most of their POWs were already gone. "We're down to one! We hoped we could keep the other two into the new year. She turned to Kate. "I don't know what we're going to do in the spring. At least you'll have your sons to help."

"We couldn't have survived without our POWs. It's been two months now without Karl and I miss him terribly."

Shirley looked up. "What have you heard from him?"

Kate's face darkened. "We've only had the one letter through the Red Cross. That was over a month ago."

Eugene gave a snide laugh. "You won't be hearing from him anytime soon."

Ursula was growing angry with Eugene's spiteful words. She was determined not to be beaten down by him. "Karl was working on a degree program offered through the camps. He hopes to return in the next year or two."

Eugene set his fork down noisily, disbelief and derision filling his face. "That was a war we fought! You talk like they were all here on vacation."

Ursula ignored his words and held her ground. "He hopes to be reunited with his – "

Eugene stabbed at his food. "Ed said Karl's from eastern Germany. Now controlled by the Soviets. You better pray he doesn't get handed over to them."

Ursula blanched at his words. She suddenly understood why Friedrich had tried to falsify Karl's papers.

"Trust me," said Eugene. "No German POW will be coming back anytime soon."

Joe had quietly followed the exchange. "The War Department announced that many of them will have to put in six months or more of reparation work. Hard to know where they'll all end up."

Eugene reached for the bowl of potatoes. "Six months won't make a dent in Europe. It's been blasted to rubble. Those POWs will be doing some backbreaking work for a long time – for a change. And they won't be coming back."

Ursula's lip trembled.

"At any rate, Eugene," Kate said with a hint of sternness in her voice, "we can hope for the best."

"Amen to that," said Shirley. "I hope ours get home safely and can reunite with their families."

Eugene opened his mouth to speak but saw that Kate was staring him down.

Joe took another slice of pot roast and smiled out at the table. "Isn't this what you missed most,

Eugene? Home cooking? I've been home for two years and I still think I'll never get my fill of it."

"Not with Sue Ellen's cooking, you won't," said Kate.

Sue Ellen grabbed at the opening and was soon describing the dishes she planned to make for the Christmas dance in town.

*

Later that evening, Eugene sat in the living room, finishing up a letter. He and Joe and the others had decided to put off the card game until the following week. The incident with Clem had affected them all. He stared ahead, added another line, and then sealed the envelope and leaned back.

Music followed the news report on the radio, scratchy but soothing. Ursula had fed Frankie and was now gently rocking his cradle, and Kate sat next to her, knitting a baby blanket. Jessica rested her elbows on the living room desk as she graded papers, but her attention was on the conversation that began between her mother and brother.

Kate held out the pale yellow blanket and finished the row. "Clem has a lost look about him."

"He's doing all right," said Eugene. "Better than a lot of guys."

Kate raised her head, waiting for an explanation.

"We saw Sparky Evans uptown the other night. You remember how lively he used to be? Always up for a good time." Eugene shook his head. "All his spirit's gone. You ask him a question and all you get out of him is – 'I guess so, I don't know, I don't care,' or silence. Like there's a big emptiness inside him. Sometimes he just stares out at nothing."

Kate's hands stopped. "Perhaps he needs some care."

"He's got his family."

Kate knitted in silence for a few moments. "Has he said anything?"

Eugene tried to remember. "He doesn't say a whole lot. Never complains. I asked him if he was sleeping. He shrugged and said, 'I'm having nightmares, so I must be.' Eugene looked out at the floor, squinting in thought. "The guys on the ground had it bad. Close up, you know. Most of what I saw was from the sky – which was bad enough. But the infantry…" He shook his head. "I don't think the war will ever be over for some of those guys."

Kate and Ursula looked over at him with anxious eyes. They waited to see if he was going to say anything else. They worried constantly about the effect of war on Paul and Jimmy. One of Paul's best friends had been lost in the USS *Indianapolis* tragedy in July, and Jimmy had experienced several close calls himself.

Eugene became aware of the silence. "Paul and Jimmy are fine. Don't you go worrying about them. And Clem's okay. A bit lost, but he'll be all right. It'll take him some time to find himself again. Something we all have to go through. Some more than others."

Jessica's eyes filled with tears at the idea of Clem suffering. She tried to imagine the conditions of war. As bad as the newsreels were, she knew they didn't capture the real horror.

From the radio, came the lighthearted voice of the announcer. "Private Calhoun said the best Christmas gift ever was stepping onto U.S. soil. Yes, siree, *Operation Santa Claus* is going to make a lot of families happy this Christmas!" The cheerful contrast was almost jarring. But welcome, all the same.

Ursula had been watching her mother and read the worry in her eyes. "Paul and Jimmy should reach California any day now. We should hear from them soon. They could still get here in time for Christmas."

Kate took a deep breath. "They're not letter writers, those two." She sniffed and took up her knitting. "All I want is them home safe. And I hope to God Charles is on his way home. He's been gone for most of the war. It would mean so much to him and Lillian."

Eugene leaned towards the radio and adjusted the dial until he found some music.

"Especially now that he has a baby," continued Kate. "A child of his own that he's never seen! I can hardly imagine it."

"That's true for a lot of the men returning home," said Eugene. Some dark thought filled his mind and he scowled. "Not like these POWs who sat out the war in comfort. Well fed, cushy conditions, earning college credits – "

Ursula snapped. "They were captured, for God's sake. Why can't you just leave it alone?"

"It's just not right," he said.

Ursula lifted Frankie from the cradle. "A lot of things aren't right, Eugene." She left the room and went upstairs. They heard the door to her room close.

Kate gave a deep sigh. "There's no point in tormenting her. Ursula has suffered enough. So has Friedrich."

"They don't know what suffering is. And I hate being lied to. Why didn't you just come out and tell me?"

"I told you why. For everyone's sake we're keeping it quiet for now. Anti-German sentiment is high."

"For good reason. Now the whole world knows what the Nazis are made of. When were you going to tell me?"

"At a later time. Your attitude proves me right. For God's sake, we don't know how much longer Friedrich will be here. It could be any day. Karl is already gone. You never met him. He was a lovely boy. Some mother's son."

Eugene ran his hands through his hair and let out a deep groan. "I hope he can stay out of the Soviet's hands. I wouldn't wish that on anyone. The Russians and Germans – the things they did to each other – they're vicious animals. I hear some of the German prisoners are committing suicide rather than go back to what awaits them at the hands of the Soviets."

"God protect him," said Kate, her face filling with fear for Karl. A cheerful young man who had helped her so much on the farm the past two years. She missed him and his wide grin and ready laughter. She rubbed her forehead. "We were lucky to have him. All three of them. And Friedrich – he's a good man. You realize he may never come back. He could be killed. Or disappear or God knows what."

"Can't be helped."

"No, but your attitude can." She set her knitting down in exasperation. "He and Ursula are husband and wife. That child is my grandchild!"

Eugene stared out at the floor. "I can't help what I feel." He left the room.

Chapter 9

❧

Charles waited in line at the telegraph office in London, remembering the old Central Telegraph Office from the first World War. Reduced to rubble in the Blitz. What a waste. So much destruction.

He was exhausted from his prolonged voyage to England, but he couldn't rest until a telegram went out to Lillian. A smile came to his lips to think that he was actually in London now, one step closer to being home.

In his mind, he was adding to the letter he had started to Lillian. There was so much to tell her, things he had suppressed all these years. He had never written about his plans for the future, all the trips he wanted to take with her and the boys, and perhaps moving to a bigger apartment, or even a house somewhere. He had never wanted to talk about the future, in case…

But now the war was over, and he was going home. He had the freedom to dream about their future lives. He could hardly wait to continue his letter to tell her how much she meant to him. How he couldn't wait to hold her in his arms. How he still couldn't believe they had a daughter.

He looked around him. Most of the men in line appeared happy, though a few wore sad and weary faces. He had heard of the thousands of young Brits growing angry at the endless delays, stuck in India or Burma or some far-flung place while young men who had only recently been sent to war were already home with their families. The logistics of returning all the servicemen was proving to be a tangled endeavor for everyone. And yet it was taking place and soldiers were returning home. Just as the rubble was slowly being cleared from the London streets and communication lines were being re-established.

Charles thought back to V-E Day, May 8th. He had arrived London on the 10th and the celebratory mood was something he would never forget – the wild euphoria, the jubilation. He had caught the spirit and began to hope that the war with Japan would soon be over.

But his optimism had vanished when he had to set sail again, this time for the Pacific. He would be stationed near the India-Burma waters. His heart had sunk. It meant long months of grueling fighting. Perhaps years. With estimates of Allied losses at fifty percent. Back in those days, he wondered if he would ever see Lillian again. That was early August – Lillian was due the following month and he was desperate to be there with her – an impossible wish. Instead of being home with his wife for the birth of their child, he was on his way for the invasion of Japan.

Then came the shocking news – destructive bombs, atom bombs, had been dropped on Japan, unleashing unheard of death and destruction in a matter of seconds. It remained unimaginable to him, but it had brought Japan to its knees and the unconditional surrender soon followed. V-J Day, August 15th. He had reeled from the news and scarcely believed it. Feared he was dreaming. The war was over!

A few weeks later, he had received a telegram from Izzy informing him that he had a baby daughter! His world had shifted seismically – towards happiness. All that forward momentum of pushing on to Japan had halted. It took weeks before decisions were made that redirected the ship to London but, finally, he left the India-Burma theater of war, and all war, for good.

Charles straightened his shoulders and looked around him again. The faces were gaunt, the figures thin, but there was hope in the eyes and the sound of laughter. Lives that had been put on hold could now be resumed, dreams could now be pursued. He would let Lillian know that he had arrived in London and would try his hardest to be home for Christmas. Whenever he thought of it, tears shot to his eyes. Home to Lillian and the boys – and to his daughter. He had a daughter!

Some young soldier, having just sent a telegram, slapped him on the back, and smiled, full of joy and wanting to share it with a stranger. Charles responded with a broad happy smile of his own.

*

Lillian was bubbling with joy as she dressed for the party at Rockwell Publishing. The telegram from Charles had propelled her into boundless happiness. Perhaps the next time she dressed up, it would be with Charles!

She carefully pulled on her stockings and fastened them. Finally, nylon stockings were available again. She ran her hand over the silkiness as she read his telegram once more. He sent his love – could hardly wait to hold their daughter – was meeting Red the following day – and had a transport appointment in two days.

She jumped up and opened the closet door. She had splurged on a few new dresses in anticipation of Charles's coming home. She decided to wear the shimmery deep blue dress with the matching jacket – because it so beautifully matched the sapphire ring Charles had given her last year this time. She looked down at the ring on her finger and twisted it to catch the sparkle.

She called out to Tommy and Gabriel to hurry and get ready. She had arranged for the boys and Charlotte to spend the evening with Mrs. Kuntzman and Henry.

As she finished dressing, Lillian had to laugh – all those years of Tommy rebelling against having a babysitter. Now that he didn't need one, he sought her out! As did Gabriel. They were looking forward to having dinner with their old babysitter, especially since Amy would also be there.

When they walked down to the brownstone on the corner, they saw Henry just coming up from the basement. Lillian wondered at the exaggerated wink he gave the boys – a sort of vaudevillian stage wink.

"Martha's been cooking up a storm all day. Hope you boys are hungry!"

"Starving!" They ran up the steps and were greeted by Mrs. Kuntzman. Lillian handed Charlotte to her.

Mrs. Kuntzman took a closer look at Lillian and then at the boys. "Such bright faces!"

Henry also stood before them and noticed their wide smiles. "A merry group, indeed. Good news, is it?"

Mrs. Kuntzman gave a light gasp in anticipation.

Lillian nodded. "Charles is in London!" Her eyes teared up just saying the words. Then she laughed at herself.

"Dad sent a telegram!" cried Gabriel. "He's on his way home."

"Dang, if he won't be here for Christmas!" said Henry, beaming.

"We plotted it out on the calendar," said Tommy. "We figure Dad could be home anytime between December 22nd and January 20th. It will depend on the ship and the weather. It will probably be early January."

"But that's still next month!" exclaimed Lillian.

"We'll have a celebration dinner tonight!" said Mrs. Kuntzman. "Bring out all the goodies we can find! And as we have our dessert, we will discuss recipes. Tommy and Amy can make decision for their French class project."

Mrs. Kuntzman rocked Charlotte in her arms and kissed her cheek. Then she followed Tommy and Gabriel into the kitchen, laughing at their guesses as to the aroma filling the small apartment.

"Fried chicken and mashed potatoes?"

"Meatloaf? Bratwurst?"

She smiled at their hopeful faces and announced one of their favorites. "Chicken pot pie!"

Lillian took her leave, seeing that all three children were in for a merry evening.

She walked to the avenue and hailed a taxi. She was soon stepping into the lobby of Rockwell Publishing where she had spent a good part of the past five years. She hadn't been back since she had left at the beginning of summer. She pushed through the revolving door and took a moment to admire the tall Christmas tree and the holiday decorations in the lobby. She had a rush of nostalgia for the place – not that she missed it or wanted to go back, but because it had played such a pivotal role in her life.

She took the elevator to the main office and smiled at the music and laughter pouring forth from the open double doors.

"Lilly!"

And there was Izzy, just like old times. She wore a new red dress with green piping – perfect for the occasion. An enamel brooch of holly sat at her collar.

"Look at you!" cried Izzy. "You're brighter than the lights! Any particular reason?"

"A telegram from Charles! He's in London." Tears shot to Lillian's eyes. "He's safe, Izzy."

"Thank God." Izzy put her arms around her friend and smiled. Tears welled up in her eyes, too. "Look at us. We're supposed to be celebrating!"

Lillian nodded and took a hankie from her purse to dry her eyes. "I'm so happy – I don't know why I'm crying."

"To the punch bowl!" Izzy took her arm and they made their way to the table laden with food and drinks. Lillian was greeted by a few old colleagues and Izzy introduced her to several new and returning employees. Before they could get their drinks, Izzy gave a light groan on seeing Mr. Rockwell. She leaned into Lillian. "We might as well get this over with."

They walked over to Mr. Rockwell, and Lillian was surprised by the spontaneous embrace he gave her. "Mrs. Drooms, so glad you made it! I don't think you've ever met my wife. Barbara, this is Lillian Drooms. She was one of my top artists. My wife, Barbara."

Lillian exchanged a few pleasantries with his wife, a tall, attractive woman dressed in an elegant beige dress that set off her sparkling jewelry. Lillian took in the woman's style and noted the diamonds at her ears, neck, wrist, and fingers. Even her belt sparkled – and her shoes! She was one glittery woman, and Rockwell couldn't have been prouder.

Mr. and Mrs. Rockwell were soon pulled away by other employees and Izzy took the opportunity to escape back to the bar. With glasses of punch in hand, they meandered through the crowd.

After another hour visiting with old friends and colleagues, Izzy and Lillian sat at a table along the back wall, away from the dancing and party atmosphere.

"I thought you'd want to dance, Izzy."

Izzy threw her hands up. "The irony! The war's over, everyone wants to have a good time – and I'm not in the mood!"

"I've noticed that. Your mind is elsewhere these days and it isn't with Rockwell Publishing." She waited for Izzy to speak.

"No." Izzy watched a few people on the dance floor, then looked down into her glass. "I sent him a letter."

"Red?"

Izzy nodded, suddenly vulnerable. "I wrote to him, but now I don't think I should have. I don't know."

"But you said you've been writing to him these past few months."

"Yes, but not about us. Not about what happened. We were skirting the issue, avoiding any mention of it, and finally I just couldn't take it any longer." She lifted the glass to her lips and took a long drink. "I have to know."

Lillian had never seen Izzy so unsure of herself. "What did you write this time that was different?"

Izzy swallowed. "I asked him point blank – did you love her?"

"Oh. I see. And now you're afraid of how he might answer."

"Yes. Either way. If he says yes, I'll be devastated. If he says no, I'll be confused and angry. There's no good answer. And in the meantime, I'll be tormented by the wait."

"You did the right thing, Izzy. You have to know the answer to that question. It's the holidays – just keep busy and enjoy yourself. You said Lois and Sonny are coming up soon. Set the issue aside and do what you always do."

"You're right. No point in fretting about something I have no control over. I'll be volunteering a few extra nights at the Stage Door Canteen during the holidays. And Lois will be up next week." She nodded tentatively, as if trying to convince herself.

Lillian accepted another glass of punch by one of the waiters passing out drinks. "You know, Charles said he'll see Red while he's in London."

"Good. Good. I'm glad to hear that. And I'm so happy for you that Charles is on his way home." Izzy drained her glass and snatched another from the waiter. She raised it to Lillian. "To Christmas!" she said, back to her old playful self. "Come on. Let's go raid the hors d'oeuvres – I'm starving!"

Chapter 10

❧

Ursula sat at the kitchen table sorting through the potatoes, choosing the smallest ones for dinner – buttered with parsley. She heard Frankie laughing in the living room. No one could make him laugh like Jessica.

Kate stood at the stove, carefully following a new recipe from Mrs. Bloomfield. "I'll practice making this for Jimmy and Paul – a tropical cake! Won't they be surprised?" An open can of pineapple slices sat next to her mixing bowl. She read the directions aloud to herself. "Line the sliced pineapple rings on the bottom of the baking dish."

Just then, Jessica ran down the stairs, having changed into her work clothes. "I'll check the hens. Then I'll help with the baking." She tilted her head at the pineapple slices as Kate arranged them in the dish. "You think that's going to taste good?"

"Well, that's the point, isn't it?" Kate asked rather sharply. "I want to have a few new dishes to make when your brothers get home. After I wring their necks for not writing, I'll make them all their favorite dishes. Along with a few new ones."

Surprised that Jessica was not with Frankie, Ursula walked to the living room, about to call out to him. But on hearing Eugene's voice, she stopped, and glanced around the corner.

Frankie had just pulled himself up and was leaning on the couch, triumphantly standing.

Eugene laughed, and motioned for him to walk over to him. "Come here, you little tyke. You just don't give up, do you? That's good. You gotta be tough in this world."

Frankie toddled two steps and fell down with a laugh. He raised his arms to be lifted.

Eugene swept him up and when Frankie tried to grab his mouth, Eugene pretended to bite at his fingers. Frankie gurgled in laughter, fixated on Eugene's face.

Eugene walked around the room with him. "So, you gonna like sauerbraten? And wiener schnitzel? You think that's funny? Weiner schnitzel, wiener schnitzel," he said exaggeratedly, causing Frankie to almost choke in laughter.

"You probably will. It's pretty dang good. That's gonna be our secret. You hear?" Eugene walked from window to window, pointing to the cows beyond the fence, the windmill, the barn. Frankie laid his head on Eugene's shoulder. "You gonna help me on the farm when you grow up? Hmm?" Eugene gazed down at him and patted his back. "Getting sleepy, are you?" As he rocked side to side, he suddenly became aware of Ursula watching him.

She walked up to him and looked at Frankie. "I think he's asleep. I'll put him down for his nap." She reached out to take him.

"No sense waking him. I'll put him in the crib."

Just then Jessica burst into the room. "Ursula, where's the egg basket – "

"Shhh!" Eugene said with a scowl. "We don't want him bawling again." He walked down the hall with him to Kate's room.

Jessica raised her eyebrows to Ursula.

"Come. It's on the porch."

Jessica nudged Ursula. "We all have to say how delicious the pineapple cake is. Mom's putting her heart into it."

Ursula laughed and showed her where the egg basket was. Then she sat back down at the kitchen table and finished selecting the potatoes, smiling to hear her mother humming happily.

Half an hour later, the potatoes were boiling, and Ursula was setting the table. Kate opened the oven to take yet another look at the cake.

"It smells good," said Ursula.

"It does, doesn't it?" Kate said with a touch of surprise. "Everything's ready for dinner. Why don't you take a little rest before Frankie wakes?" She heard a truck coming up the lane, and she pulled the curtain aside. "Eugene! Clem's here!"

Jessica was just gathering the last of the eggs when she saw Clem's truck coming up the lane. Her heart lifted – but then she pushed it back down. She was nothing to him – worse, she had unintentionally hurt him.

From the side of the chicken coop, she watched him. The truck stopped, but Clem remained sitting inside, his hands on the steering wheel. What was he thinking? Why did he sit there?

"Oh, Clem," Jessica sighed. He was so handsome and kind. She felt she could spend all day gazing into his deep green eyes, listening to his voice. She had convinced herself that he must have someone – maybe even a fiancé in Europe. She had been too impulsive and hadn't even considered such a thing until she had made a fool of herself, shoving her photograph in his hand. As she watched him sitting there, her heart went out to him, but she vowed to hide her feelings.

She saw Eugene walking towards the truck and calling to him. "Hey, Clem! Come on inside."

Clem stepped out of his truck. Jessica watched them speak for a few minutes, then she went up the back-porch steps and carried the egg basket into the kitchen.

"Clem's here," Ursula said from the living room. She sat at the piano, picking out a melody. "Did you see him?"

"Yes." Jessica set the eggs in the pantry. "Eugene is out talking to him."

Just then Eugene came in the door. "Where's Jessica?"

She poked her head around the pantry door. "I'm here. Do you need something?"

Eugene pointed his chin to the open door. "Clem's here. Wants to see you."

Jessica stared at him a moment. "Me?"

"Go on." Eugene hung up his coat and went into the living room, taking the newspaper with him.

Ursula went into the pantry and took the egg basket. "I'll put these away." She smiled at Jessica's hesitation. "Don't keep him waiting. See if he wants to come inside."

Jessica went to the door, without straightening her hair or giving a thought to her dungarees and heavy shoes. She walked outside to where he was leaning against his truck.

"Hello, Clem," she said.

He straightened and put his hands in his coat pocket. "How are you doing, Jessica?"

Her heart gave a little flutter to hear her name on his lips. She looked at his mouth, his eyes, then away. "I'm fine. And you?"

"Fine." He turned his eyes to the expanse of snowy corn stubble on the other side of the lane where a few crows hopped around and cawed. The birds suddenly lifted and flew up to the sky.

Jessica watched them blend into a group of bare trees, hopping and fluttering until they settled. She turned back to Clem and waited.

He held her gaze. "I just wanted to apologize for the other evening."

Jessica started to shake her head, but he wanted to speak.

"I should have told you why I didn't want to stay for dinner. I'm sorry that happened."

Jessica took a step towards him. "You don't have to apologize for that. I'm sorry I was so rude. I should have been more sensitive or aware or something." Her face twisted as she tried to put her feelings into words. "Clem, you – guys like you, you're our heroes. You don't have to apologize for anything, ever!"

He gave a wry smile at the word 'hero.' "You sound like the doctors. That's what they told us, you know, in the hospital. That we had no reason to be ashamed."

"*Ashamed?*" Jessica leaned back in disbelief. "How can you possibly think that? It will take time, Clem, that's all. That's what Eugene said. That it takes a while to get used to being back home. I'm sorry I didn't understand that. I didn't mean to make you feel bad, Clem. That's the last thing I would ever want." She placed her hand on his arm.

Clem watched her closely as she spoke. "I know that." For a moment, she thought he might take her hand, or even give her a hug. But the moment passed, and he looked back out over the snowy fields, the bare hedgerows. "Well, that's all I wanted to say." He opened his truck door.

"Clem – I know I'm being rash and unladylike and all sorts of things, and I know this is improper of me to ask, but – " She bit her lip and then pressed ahead. "Do you have someone? A girlfriend? Or a fiancé or something?"

He gave a light laugh. "No, Jessica. I don't have anyone."

Her face brightened. She leaned in and kissed him on the cheek.

Clem pulled back in surprise.

"Then can't we – spend some time together and get to know one another? Now that you're home?"

His eyes hardened and he stared out at the cold and barren fields. "You're a real sweet girl, Jessica. But no. We can't." He got into the truck and was about to close the door, but Jessica held onto it.

"But why?" her voice trembled.

He started the truck. "You're going to make some lucky guy very happy."

Jessica folded her arms. "But not you." She grew angry that he didn't deny it and wouldn't look at her.

"Goodbye, Jessica." He closed the door, started the engine, and turned onto the farm lane.

She followed him a few steps, then watched him drive away.

*

After dinner, Kate sat in the living room patching a few clothes while she listened to the radio. Her sewing basket sat next to her. She had plugged in the Christmas tree lights and now took a moment to admire the tall pine tree decorated with shiny ornaments and a tinsel garland. A few days ago, Eugene, Ed, and Jessica had gone out to the woods to find a Christmas tree. It had been a happy day for them all, setting up the tree and decorating it.

The scent of pine filled the air, and the colored lights gave a festive and cozy cast to the room. A cup of hot cider sat on the side table next to Kate, along with a slice of the pineapple cake, which she thought had turned out rather well. She showed some surprise when Eugene came in and sat down next to her.

"I thought you were going out tonight."

"Nah. Think I'll turn in early."

"How about a slice of cake and something hot?"

He shook his head.

Kate lowered her sewing. "What's wrong with all of you? I sliced the up-side-down pineapple cake, thinking it would be a nice evening for us to sit together – and you all turned it down. Ursula went up early with Frankie – probably to stay out of your way." She looked at Eugene over her glasses. "Jessica's gone upstairs to do her schoolwork. She didn't say a word at dinner. And now you? Where's the Christmas spirit in this house? I'll be happy when my two rabble-rousing sons are home."

"So will I, Mom. So will I." Eugene reached over and lifted the shirt next to Kate. "Wasn't that Francy's?"

"You remember?" she asked, pleased. "Yes, it was. I tightened the buttons and patched the elbows. For the Red Cross drive. And I've decided we can part with this." She lifted a woolen quilt and chose a spool of brown thread to make a few repairs.

They sat in silence for a few moments.

Kate looked over at the tree. "I still feel Francis with me all the time. It's strange – sometimes I know he's gone and I accept it. Other times, I feel him right here with me – bringing me comfort and a smile just like he always did." Not getting any response from Eugene, she glanced over and saw him staring fixedly at the floor.

"Something on your mind, son?" She watched to see how he would respond and noted the tightening of his eyebrows.

Eugene leaned forward and linked his hands, then opened them.

"No. It's just – now that I'm officially discharged, I need to start thinking about the rest of my life. What to do with it."

"Good gracious, you're finally home from four years of fighting and you're already thinking about what to do next. And you don't sound too happy about your prospects."

"It's tough, Mom. A lot of guys have come home and they find their girls have married someone else. A good many can't find work. Jobs are scarce."

"But those things don't apply to you. You've always loved the farm. I assumed you'd want to carry it on, with your brothers."

"I don't know what I want." He leaned back and his linked his hands behind his head, then dropped them to his side.

He appeared lost and it broke Kate's heart. Her eldest had always been the strongest, inside, but now he looked utterly vulnerable.

"Sue Ellen said all the girls are asking about you. There's a dance coming up. Why don't you invite Ginny? or Doris? You used to like to spend time with her." Kate made a few stitches and looked up to see how he was reacting to her suggestions – and was shocked to see tears brimming in his eyes. "Eugene!" She reached over and pressed his arm. "What is it?"

He pressed the heels of his hands to his eyes. "I just can't stand it anymore. I don't know why she hasn't written. I'm so afraid something's happened to her. Or maybe she's moved on and has forgotten me. I don't know what to think."

"Who, Eugene? Who?"

His shoulders dropped and he spoke in a tender voice. "Edna." A sob escaped him on saying her name. He took a deep breath. "Edna Kinnan. A nurse from Iowa I met – over there. I should have heard from her by now."

Kate set her sewing down and leaned closer to Eugene. "Tell me."

He let out a groan and took another deep breath to steady himself. "I met her when I was in the hospital – last year. She was with the Red Cross. She was there for D-Day. She's strong, Mom. My God, she's strong. In the middle of all the carnage and turmoil, she'd patiently take care of us. Make us laugh. Yet she's also soft, gentle. Kind. At first, I thought she felt sorry for me. When I was shot down she took good care of me, of all of us. I think we were all in love with her. Or maybe I couldn't imagine anyone not feeling like I did."

Kate watched him. He seemed to be far away, a look of hope in his eyes. Then it left.

"Anyway, I got released from the hospital. We promised to keep in touch, to write. I thought she probably said that to all the guys. We exchanged a few letters. Then we lost touch – and that's when I knew. I loved her." He looked up, as if surprised to have discovered such a thing. "I was so afraid something happened to her."

His face brightened somewhat as his memory shifted. "Then, in the summer, by a miracle chance, I saw her when I was in Paris – and she saw me – and we ran to each other. There was no mistaking the look in her eyes. I kissed her and I held her tight. We had a few days together. I wanted to marry her right then and there. She said she would come visit, and meet you and everyone, and see the farm. Then she was whisked off to some emergency. We barely had a chance to say goodbye. Again, we promised to write. I've written and written to her through the Red Cross. And I sent a letter to her home, but…"

"Good heavens! No wonder you've been so tense. I wish you would have told me sooner. Listen Eugene, it could be a simple mail delay, or lost mail, or who knows what."

"I know. I keep telling myself that." He put his hand over his mouth and stared hard at the floor.

"Don't give up hope, Eugene. Given the situation, with so many men returning, it's delaying everything. The newspapers are full of all the interruptions, trains and flights canceled, traffic jams all over the country. I'm sure I read something about all the mail delays, too. That's all it is."

Eugene turned to look at his mother and slowly nodded. "I'm sure you're right." But his face remained shadowed by concern.

"Be patient, son. There could be so many reasons. You don't even know if she's home, or if your letters have gotten through. You've only been back a month yourself. Give it some time."

He gave a small smile. "You're right. It's only been a month. It just feels like so much longer." He placed his hand on her shoulder. "I think I'll turn in."

Kate rested her hand on his. "Get some rest, son. Things will look brighter in the morning."

She listened to him as he went up the stairs, each slow step pressing on her heart.

Chapter 11

Lillian kept glancing at the clock. The table was set, the meatloaf was ready, even the milk was poured. As she set the salad on the table, she spoke aloud in frustration. "He's getting later and later. I don't know what to make of it."

Tommy was in the living room, playing with Charlotte, glad that his back was to the kitchen. He too kept checking the clock. Then he breathed a sigh of relief as he heard Gabriel's running steps on the stairs.

Gabriel burst into the apartment. "Sorry I'm late! What smells so good?" He tossed his coat on the hall tree and stepped out of his shoes.

"You're an hour late, Gabriel! Hurry and wash up. We've been waiting for you."

Gabriel hollered as he washed his hands in the bathroom. "I didn't know it was so late. All of a sudden I saw the time and I ran home as fast as I could."

Tommy put Charlotte in her bassinette and took his seat at the table.

Gabriel stopped to see Charlotte. "Hello, Charlotte! Did you miss me?" He rubbed noses with her and laughed when she smiled at him. He pulled out his chair, sat, and scooted it up to the table. "Smells good, Mom."

Lillian studied Gabriel's face. His behavior had slightly changed, but try as she might, she saw no signs of him looking as if he were being neglected. If anything, he appeared happier than usual. Still, she would make sure that nothing was troubling him. As they dished out salad and meat-loaf onto their plates, she broached the subject.

"You know, boys, we've never talked about it before, but a new baby brings about a lot of changes in a family."

Both boys nodded enthusiastically.

"It sure does," said Gabriel. "It's hard to imagine how it was before Charlotte."

"Yes, well," continued Lillian, "roles change, duties shift. Sometimes it seems like there's less time for everyone."

Tommy raised his face to her, concerned. "Is there anything you need, Mom? Anything we're not doing?"

"Just ask us," added Gabriel. "We can help with anything."

"No, no – you've both been such a big help. I don't know what I would have done without you."

They both smiled at her, Gabriel chewing, Tommy taking a drink of milk.

She tried again. "They say it's normal for siblings to feel a little pushed aside with a new baby."

Gabriel looked at Tommy and shrugged. "We don't feel that way, do we Tommy?"

"Not at all. We love having a baby sister."

"And I love being an older brother," said Gabriel. "I think it suits me."

Lillian had to smile. "It certainly does. So, it doesn't bother you that so much of my time is spent with Charlotte?"

"Heck no, Mom," said Gabriel. "It's not like we're five years old."

"I thought maybe that's why you've been staying away so much."

A flash of guilt filled Gabriel's eyes. "Gosh no! I didn't know that's what you were thinking. It's just that – I have Scouts one night a week, the hospital another night, and –"

"And your school project. You've yet to tell me what it's about. You used to like to discuss your school work with me."

"Well, this is different. It's a different kind of – project." Gabriel played with the food on his plate.

Lillian began to eat her salad, observing Gabriel closely. "Why do I get the feeling that you're not telling me everything?"

Gabriel kept his head down but raised his eyes to Tommy as if for guidance.

Lillian looked from Gabriel to Tommy and back to Gabriel. "Gabriel? Is there something you're hiding? Gabriel!"

He threw up his hands in defense. "Nothing nefarious, Mom, I promise."

"Nefarious?" she asked, surprised by the word. "That means – "

"Gabriel, I know what it means. But I've never heard you use – oh, never mind. What is it you're not telling me?"

Gabriel heard the edge to her voice and winced.

"Are you and Billy up to something? You're not playing that crazy daring game again, are you? Or smoking cigarettes?"

"No. Nothing like that! It's nothing wrong."

Lillian pressed her lips together, waiting.

Tommy had also stopped eating. "You better tell her, Gabe."

Lillian's head snapped to Tommy now. "You're in on it?"

Gabriel jumped in. "He only just found out. And he told me he wouldn't lie for me."

Lillian set her fork down. "That's it. You're going to tell me this instant."

Gabriel took a deep breath, held it, and exhaled his response. "I have a job."

Lillian sat back in her chair, her mouth open in surprise. "A *job!* Where?"

"At The Red String Curio Store."

"The – " Lillian looked out at the room, wondering how she could have missed it. She fixed a stern eye on Gabriel. "For how long?"

Gabriel raised his eyes to the ceiling, calculating. "Two and a half months."

"You mean all this time I thought you were at Scouts or with Billy, you were at The Red String Curio Store – working?"

"Yes and no. I mean, I still go to Scouts. And I still see Billy. He likes to come into the store. He's a regular. So is Henry."

Lillian opened her mouth to say something, then changed her mind. She pressed her fingers to her temples. "So the 'general knowledge' project doesn't even exist, does it? That was just a ruse to fool me."

"No, Mom. I didn't fool you. I would never do that." Gabriel jumped up, and ran to his room.

Lillian's gaze fell on Tommy.

He fidgeted with his fork. "I know what you're thinking Mom, but – "

Gabriel came back to the table with his notebook. "This is my project. You saw my notebook. I wasn't hiding it." He pointed to the titled and read: "*General Knowledge*. See? I've added two pages since you saw it."

"But it's not a school project."

"No. But learning is learning, isn't it? You'd be surprised at all the things I'm learning at my job."

Lillian raised her eyebrows in skepticism. "Such as?"

Gabriel sat down at his seat again. "Well, Junior and his poems, for one thing. He writes them out in calligraphy. That's fancy handwriting – "

"I know what calligra – oh, go on."

"Then there's Dusty. He was a professor of archeology. He's always talking about Egyptian artifacts, Chinese dynasties – and art!" Gabriel hoped the last word would score him a nod of approval, but Lillian's face still registered anger.

"And then there's Mr. G himself. Henry says he's the most knowledgeable man he's ever met. That the slightest bump to him sends information spilling out of him. About the Napoleonic Wars, or opals, geography, the history of ship building. He knows all the big rivers and mountains of the world. And he knows lots of foreign words. Like *Auf Weidersehen*! And *donde esta el mercado*? And *prego, signora*." With each pronunciation, Gabriel mimicked the accent.

The crease between Lillian's brow was slowly deepening – in puzzlement that Gabriel so clearly enjoyed such an environment.

Gabriel took a bite of meatloaf, his enthusiasm increasing. "And when it's slow, we go to his dictionary, one of those big ones. He said we have Doctor Johnson to thank for that. Then he says – 'Gabriel, will you do us the honor?' Then I close my eyes, flip through the pages, and land my finger on a new word."

Lillian remained speechless and looked from Gabriel to Tommy. Tommy shrugged and kept eating. "But what exactly do you do there?"

"Help people. Well, at first, I was just sweeping and dusting and putting new merchandise out. But then I helped a few people to find things and Mr. G said he'd like to keep me on, after the holidays. Says I have a real knack for it. It's fun to help people find things – it's like a treasure hunt."

Lillian had only been in the shop once or twice but was drawing a blank as she tried to imagine Gabriel working there. "Find what kind of things?"

He opened his hands. "It could be anything – a doorstop or candleholder, a lampshade – with or without fringe. An Edwardian cigar cutter, sheet music. An Aladdin's lamp. Cut-glass water pitchers. Old buttons, vases, books. I know where everything is and can always help people find the perfect gift."

Lillian cast a concerned look at Tommy. He nodded. "It's true. I was there when a lady thanked him for helping her find an Audubon book for her husband."

"And binoculars," Gabriel pointed out. "I thought it would make a nice set. I learn all kinds of things without even trying. There are maps and globes and history books all over the place. There's a periodical chart on the wall I'm trying to memorize, and posters on travel. Mr. G loves opera and plays them on the phonograph and tells me what happens in them. And old porcelain. Mr. G teaches me how to look on the bottom of them for marks – and you can tell where they were made. The place is full of treasures, Mom. Full of information. Mr. G says when I'm older he might even take me scavenging with him. Thinks I might have an eye for it. Modern day rag-and-bone men, he said."

Worry flashed in Lillian's eyes as she imagined Gabriel sitting atop a rickety cart pulled by a poky old horse, scouring the city for the unusual and the curious…

"And the people who come in to shop – actors and stage managers from the theater. Collectors and artists and – "

"Gabriel!" Lillian shook her head as if clearing it. She took a deep breath. "That's enough for now."

She slowly buttered a slice of bread and wondered what to do. "The fact remains that you lied to me."

Now it was Gabriel's turn to be upset. "No, I didn't! I might have prevaricated, but I didn't lie. Not once. I was careful not to."

"You lied by omission."

Gabriel sat back in his chair, rubbing his chin as he puzzled out the concept. "Lying by omission? Huh. I didn't know there was such a thing." He tilted his head, and slowly nodded. "Makes sense, though." He opened his notebook and made a note of it. "I'll have to ask Mr. G about that."

"Gabriel, you're not taking this seriously."

"Yes, I am."

"Why didn't you just ask me if you could work there?"

"Because I knew you'd say no. Please don't make me quit, Mom! I love it there. I can't explain it. It's my favorite thing I ever did!"

Lillian was astonished to hear the passion in his voice.

"Please, Mom." Gabriel clasped his hands in supplication.

She tried to think it through rationally, but with Gabriel nothing was ever straightforward. He was honest in his way and tried to do the right thing. He just *marches to the beat of his own drum*, as her mother would have said.

"What do you think of all this, Tommy?"

Gabriel shot him a look of hope.

"Well, at first I was kind of against it. But everything he says is true. He's helping people. He's learning a lot. And he's making money." He shrugged as if it were all simple. "Plus, isn't it better that he's at The Red String instead of wandering around Central Park like he used to do?"

Gabriel nodded vigorously, wondering why he hadn't thought of that point.

Lillian couldn't deny Tommy's argument. "Let's be clear on one thing – no more secrets."

"Scout's honor!" Gabriel said, giving the three-fingered salute. "So, I can I keep my job?"

"You can work through Christmas as long as it doesn't interfere with your homework. Then we'll discuss it with your father once he's here."

"Thanks, Mom." He bit off a piece of bread with gusto and exchanged a smile with Tommy.

*

On Saturday, Charles took the Underground to visit Red. Though Red worked five days a week in London, he chose to lodge in a rooming house on the outskirts of the city, close to the veterans' hospital where he volunteered most nights and weekends. Charles found it quieter than the city proper, though still bustling and its streets alive with the post-war activities of cleaning and rebuilding and getting on with life.

Charles met Red at the hospital, and Red showed him around. They walked through floor after floor of wounded men in various stages of recovery, along with a good many who would never recover. Except for the new men being admitted, all the patients knew Red. In addition to helping process papers for the Yanks and Canadians, Red served as a volunteer counselor, encouraging the men, listening to them, offering advice and, when that failed, comforting them with gentle words.

It was obvious that Red was well-loved, and Charles understood what important work he was doing. Life-changing, perhaps even life-saving. He saw the shift from despair to hope when the patients saw Red.

Compared to them, Red was strong and vibrant. A slight limp was the only external sign of his previous injury, and now and then his eyes bothered him – he would stop in the middle of talking and rub them. Though he appeared cheerful and had a ready smile, Charles knew that he suffered from some unspoken sorrow. If he happened to catch him unawares, Charles noted the faraway look, the ever so slightly pinched eyebrows, as if trying to figure something out. The war affected men differently, depending on individual experiences. Red had a tough time of it in '41 and '42, losing buddies and being wounded.

Charles suspected that Red was also still grieving the loss of Izzy. They had touched upon the subject over a year ago and Red had shared his regret, but he was a private person and tended to keep personal matters to himself.

Rather than dwell on what he didn't have, Red kept busy and experienced the euphoria of going home through the other men. He said his purpose now was to help the U.S. and Canadian boys get back home. Charles knew that Red had signed up with the Royal Canadian Airforce before the U.S. entered the war. It was obvious that he had maintained a strong bond with many of the Canadians.

They concluded the tour and stepped out into the welcome sunshine and bracing air. Charles filled his lungs and exhaled deeply, happy to have made it through the war, through his bouts of pneumonia and other illnesses. Happy that he had a wife and family to go back to.

Red took Charles to a small pub for lunch, not far from the hospital. They made their way through the crowded front, with several men stopping to say a few words to Red.

One young Yank with a Brooklyn accent slapped him on the back but addressed Charles. "How'd you get this bum to drink with you? He always turns us down." Then he turned to Red, throwing his hands up. "What are we, chopped liver?"

Red laughed at the taunt. "Another time. I promise."

They found a table in the back, hung up their coats on the hooks of their booth, and settled in. Before they could order anything, a waiter arrived with two pints of ale.

The waiter hooked a thumb over his shoulder. "From the Yanks," he said, and walked off.

Red raised his glass in thanks to the men at the bar.

"You're well-loved, Red. You're making a big difference in a lot of lives."

Red shrugged off the comment and took a swig of ale. "I miss being around guys like that. The typical New Yorker. It took a while for some of the Brits to warm up to me. You remember what they used to say about us Yanks."

"That you're 'overpaid, oversexed, and over here,'" Charles said with a chuckle. He took a drink of ale and looked around the pub. It was full of good-natured soldiers, a few civilians with their wives or girlfriends, and several elderly people with worn faces. At the table by the window sat a family with a small boy and girl. "Ah, there's nothing like an English pub."

"Except maybe an Irish one," Red said with an easy laugh.

Charles observed the groups of men at the bar. "An interesting mix. Brits and Yanks drinking together with…" He cocked his ear, trying to make out the accents.

"Poles and Czechs, for the most part," said Red. "A few French."

They ordered sandwiches and filled each other in on the past year.

"Do you have a picture of your daughter?" asked Red.

Charles showed him the photograph Lillian had sent of her holding Charlotte with Tommy and Gabriel on either side of her, all with wide smiles. "I can hardly believe it, Red. Sometimes I think I've been dreaming, sure I've made it up – then I get out the photo to reassure myself. I can't wait to see them."

They were soon talking about the possibilities of Charles getting home. He had an appointment to sign up for transport on Monday.

"Let me know what you find," said Red. "You'll get passage on one of the ships, but it will take weeks. Not in time for Christmas."

"I expected as much." After all he had gone through, this was a small setback. "Well, the new year then." He took a bite of his sandwich and then lifted his ale.

Red stared down at the table, turning something over in his mind. "I don't want to get your hopes up, but there's a chance I might be able to find you a flight – if you don't mind a cargo plane."

Charles stopped mid-sip and looked up in surprise. "A plane?"

"To Canada – Nova Scotia, most likely, but at least you'd be on American soil. Then hopefully, you could catch another flight to New York."

"That beats waiting for several weeks to set sail and then another ten to twenty days at sea. My God, Red, do you really think there's a chance?" His heart beat in excitement. He had never considered being able to fly home.

"I can't promise anything. Let me look into it. I've gotten a few men home that way. The only thing is, you wouldn't have much notice."

"I'll be packed and ready to go at a moment's notice. Thanks, Red. Even if it doesn't work out, I appreciate the effort."

As they finished their sandwiches, the conversation shifted to the work Red was doing in London, Charles's time in Ceylon and his trip back to England, and the attempt to get as many men home in time for Christmas.

"Everyone's hopeful of *Operation Santa Claus*," said Charles. "Part of *Operation Magic Carpet* they formed in the fall."

"Such light-hearted names," said Red.

"Now that the war is over, I guess everyone wants a bit of magic and playfulness. And everyone wants to be home for Christmas."

"True. A lot of Yanks are spending Christmas with families here. The Brits are opening their homes to them. They don't have much, but what they have they're willing to share. It's the next best thing to being home."

"What about you, Red – any chance of you coming home soon? It looks like your work here could last years."

Red took a drink of his ale. "I'm not sure what I'll do, to tell the truth. I'll stay as long as I'm needed and then – I guess I'll go home. Take advantage of the GI Bill, finish my degree. Work at the family business or something else."

Charles accepted the fact that Red didn't want to discuss Izzy.

After talking about the rationing that was still going on in England, and the refugees all over Europe, Charles glanced at the clock. "You probably need to be getting back."

Red finished his ale and nodded. "They'll be expecting me for the afternoon round."

They stood and put on their coats and hats.

"It was so nice seeing you," said Red as they stepped out into the street.

"Depending on what transportation I find, I could be here for a few weeks," said Charles, "or longer. If I am, we can hook up in London next time."

"I'd like that. And I'll let you know as soon as I hear anything about the flights. But get your name down for transport all the same. The cargo flight is a long shot, I'm afraid."

Red watched Charles leave. Visiting with him had been like a bit of home – the ease of conversation, the familiarity with common things, the connection, however indirect, to Izzy.

Red completed his afternoon rounds, and then, as he did every evening, he walked to a little park along the river, down from the main street.

There was a bench where he usually sat, a peaceful spot set back under the trees. It was his favorite place to let go of the war years and enjoy the sunset. At this time of year, the sun sank just over the arched stone footbridge. He sat down and awaited the closing of day. The low clouds tonight would ensure a beautiful sunset. A few birds flocked around the water's edge. People walked along the river path, some hurrying, others strolling. A few crossed the bridge to the other side.

It had been good to see Charles. To see someone, a friend, who had made it through the war. Who had a family waiting for him back home. A slow ache filled his heart – he could be going home now too, to Izzy. But he had destroyed that possibility.

What bothered him most about his marriage to the nurse, was how little he remembered about that month and a half. He remembered getting out of the hospital. Attending a service. Living in the back of a little house on a cobblestone street. But he didn't remember his life there. He could barely remember her face. Red rubbed his eyes, his neck. He had been in a bad way at that time. Still, he should have known better. Done better.

A single leaf drifted from above him and landed on his lap. He picked it up. A thin yellow spear. He wasn't surprised when the marriage ended. It had never been right. He was going along with some wave that carried him along, barely keeping his head above water. Not long after the divorce, Myra had stopped by to say she was marrying someone from her old neighborhood. Red had felt relief. A chapter that could now be closed. He didn't have to do anything. Make anyone happy. Shoulder anyone else's pain.

As he often did when he sat at the bench, he looked back at his time with Izzy – what they had, how they met, their recent letters. Sometimes, he would softly say her name aloud – "Izzy." It made her seem more real.

There was a place inside him reserved for her. If he was honest, all of it was for Izzy. He protected it by not letting anything else enter that sacred space. On the outside, he kept busy with his job and his duties at the hospital. Work, letters to his family, volunteering with the patients. Then, as if he were a husband going home after work, every evening he returned to Izzy.

The trees rustled across the water, sending a few more leaves drifting down. Some landed on the water, others on the faded grass. The temperature was dropping. He tightened his scarf around his neck. The sun had dropped behind the clouds, turning them shades of pink and orange and a grayish purple.

His mouth lifted into a smile. He often thought that Izzy would like this place. It was quiet in a way that she would like. Kind of a busy quiet. That was Izzy's way. She would look at the trees leaning over the water, the ducks and birds. She would wonder where everyone was going at end of day – to families? To jobs? Out with a loved one to dinner, perhaps? Dancing? Yes. She would like it here.

It had been good to see Charles, he thought again. A good man. An honorable man. He represented what they had all been fighting for – decency, kindness, family.

Red made it his mission to get Charles home in time for Christmas. He sat up straight, infused with a new source of energy. He would use every spare minute to make telephone calls, talk to people, and call in as many favors and pull as many strings as necessary to make it happen. Charles deserved it. And there was the thread of connection. To Izzy. Charles's happiness would spread to Lillian. And her joy would touch Izzy. An indirect way of adding to her happiness.

Red leaned forward with his elbows on his knees and rested his head in his hands. The war. God, he was glad it was all over. Charles had asked him about going back to New York. He would return home. But first he wanted to see the poor Brits get on their feet a bit. He wanted to see the rubble cleared, the orphans sheltered, and the fields once more full of crops. He wanted to see the shoreline cleared of barbed wire, and the waters cleared of mines. Like a sick, wounded, trashed-out body that needed help. He desperately needed to see that the world had righted itself. He couldn't bear to think about the continent. Or Japan. Those were nightmares he could not yet look at.

And if he was honest, another part of him was desperate for home. The part that wanted to forget about the war and misery and destruction. To be around happy, well-fed people, and green fields. And the future. That was it. He wanted to be around people who had a sure foot in the future. In tomorrow.

He looked out over the river. The sun was sinking behind the footbridge, bathing it in diffused gold. He ran his hands over his eyes. His vision had never fully recovered. He didn't need glasses – but sometimes his vision would suddenly blur, and it would take him a few seconds to rub his eyes in order to see clearly again. There was no explanation for this – and no remedy.

He rubbed his hands together against the chill. What would he do with the rest of his life? Stay here? Go home? His family awaited him in New York, the family business awaited him there – all with open arms. Should he return?

No. Not yet. He would help the veterans. Right now, that was the only source of meaning he could find. Guys who, when they finally did make it home, would have to learn how to live. Young boys who would never walk again. Some who were blind. Many who were maimed, who had lost legs or arms, hands. Husbands who would never be able to embrace their wives again, or touch them, feel the sweet softness of the woman they loved. Never touch her silky skin, run their hands through her hair…

He rubbed his eyes. He couldn't think about all that. He had to cheer the men on, give them hope, convince them that they would find happiness again.

The sun was almost gone now, leaving the sky lavender gray, slowly darkening. This was the time of day he most felt Izzy. The last, excruciatingly beautiful moment of the day, before night covered it with blackness. He allowed himself a few minutes to torture himself. A few minutes for his heart to ache with longing, to imagine her in his arms, to remember her laughter, her expressions, that look of love in her eyes.

He reached inside his inner pocket and pulled out an envelope with a worn photo inside. A close-up of Izzy. A moment he had captured with her camera, with her looking suddenly at him, questioning eyes, her lips the moment before they burst into a smile. On the back she had written lines from Auden, a poem they used to read together by candlelight.

> *but from this night*
> *Not a whisper, not a thought,*
> *Not a kiss nor look be lost*

Red wouldn't allow himself to grieve. At least he had known love. At least he had been given that chance. So many young men would never know what he had once known. And yet – what he wouldn't give for one more night in her arms.

He took a final look at the photo and then tucked it back inside the envelope and into his pocket. He swallowed hard and straightened his back. There – it was over. Night had descended, and day was gone. He stood, gave his leg a moment to adjust, and walked down the lamplit path back to the boarding house.

Chapter 12

❧

Kate and Ursula finished packing a basket of molasses cookies and a tray of Christmas sugar cookies for the refreshment table at the American Legion Hall.

Kate tossed a glance over her shoulder at the boxes Eugene and Jessica were stacking next to the kitchen door. "How we managed to make up four boxes of clothes and blankets is beyond me," she said. "Feels good to clean out things that are just taking up room."

Jessica and Ursula exchanged glances. They knew it had been hard for their mother to part with Francis's clothes, shoes, boots, and his good overcoat.

"At the rate you're going, our closets will be empty by spring," Eugene said, adding the last box.

"Nonsense," Kate answered with a laugh. "But if we can help those poor people in Europe, then we must do what it takes."

"All the same, I'm keeping my flight jacket close at hand."

Kate gave a grocery list to Ursula. "Here's what I need for the pantry."

Ursula tended to avoid going into town and now she had second thoughts. Perhaps it was better to stay home. "Are you sure you don't want to go, Mom? I can stay and watch Frankie."

"No. You need to get out a little more. I was just in town. And I want you children to have lunch while you're there," she added, pressing a few bills into Ursula's hand.

When they arrived in town, they saw that the Red Cross drive was going to be a huge success. The American Legion Hall was already crowded.

"You girls go on in with the food," said Eugene. "I'll bring in the boxes."

Jessica and Ursula were greeted by the Bloomfields. "Over here!" Shirley called out, waving them over. Mrs. Bloomfield and Sue Ellen made room for the cookies.

"It's quite a turnout," said Mrs. Bloomfield. "I think everyone feels particularly generous this Christmas."

"It's a good thing we made extra coffee and hot chocolate," added Shirley.

Sue Ellen picked up a molasses cookie and bit into it. "Oh, my word! I need your recipe, Jessica. Mine never turn out like this."

While they compared recipes, Ursula looked out over the hall and saw different labels above the tables. She saw Eugene stacking their boxes by the tables for clothes.

"I'll go help Eugene unpack," said Ursula. "It looks like they want things sorted by category."

Mrs. Arnold from the dry-goods store directed the flow of items being carried in. "Men's clothing over at those tables, blankets on the corner table, and women's clothing here. And there's a station for children's clothing..."

While Eugene went to get another box, Ursula began to unpack a box of men's clothing – most of which had belonged to Francis. At the table next to her, Ursula saw three of her old schoolmates. Trudy Trumble had been fiercely jealous of Ursula all through high school. Though Trudy had primped and flirted and strutted, the boys had always favored Ursula, and Trudy was not one to forget it.

"Why hello, Ursula," Trudy said, sidling next to her. "We don't see you around these days, do we, girls?"

Ursula smiled a hello at the group but kept her attention on the clothes.

Trudy eyed the items Ursula was placing on the table. "Hmm. Some of these look pretty worn," she said, lifting a pair of overalls.

Ursula bristled at the criticism of Francy's clothes and pulled them away from Trudy. "Someone will be happy to have them." As she continued to empty the box, she heard a snicker and the words "German baby."

Ursula's eyes flashed in anger, and when she whipped around to confront Trudy, she saw that

Eugene was standing just behind the group, holding a box. She hoped he wouldn't say anything.

Trudy followed Ursula's gaze and, seeing Eugene, patted her hair. She ran a finger along the sleeve of his flight jacket.

"Why, hello, Eugene! I heard you were back. I must say you're looking handsome in your – "

Eugene raised his chin. "You got something to say about Ursula?"

Trudy was momentarily taken aback at being called out. "Of course not, I was just – "

"Or about her baby?"

Trudy turned to her friends and raised her eyebrows.

Eugene dropped the box on the floor, causing several people to look. "Because if you do, you say it to *me*." He thumped his thumb on his chest. "You understand?"

Trudy widened her eyes. "I don't know what you're talking about."

"If there's one thing I learned to despise in this war," he looked around at anyone who was listening, "it's cowardice. Spiteful, self-righteous cowardice. People who stab their friends and neighbors in the back. The Nazis and Fascists love those kinds of people." He returned his glare to Trudy. "I despise them."

Trudy's lip curled in a sneer and she walked over to her friends. "Come, girls. Time for some refreshment."

Eugene's challenging stare caused the onlookers to turn away. Ursula continued unpacking as if nothing had happened, but her cheeks burned.

Sue Ellen spotted Eugene and made her way to the table. "Joe could use your help, Eugene. He needs to make a run out to the Olson farm to pick up some boxes. Can you give him a hand?"

"Gladly," he said angrily.

"I can help Ursula." Sue Ellen bent down to lift a few items out of the box.

Eugene leaned into Ursula and spoke in a low voice. "Don't you take any guff from anyone. Especially from the likes of Trudy Trumble."

Ursula raised her head high. "I can fight my own battles."

"Like hell. This is a family matter. Don't go thinking you have to do everything on your own. That's just stubbornness."

Eugene spun around to leave, almost bumping into Mr. Creight who had just arrived at the next table. Both men bristled.

Mr. Creight gave an almost imperceptible nod. "Eugene."

"Abe."

Ursula feared another confrontation and was relieved when Eugene made his way to the front door.

"Mornin', Ursula."

"Good morning, Mr. Creight." She was about to say more to him, but he turned his attention to the bag of clothing in his arms. He didn't want to be bothered. She folded the items that Sue Ellen placed before her.

"There!" Sue Ellen lifted the last of the items and set them on the table. She looked up and gave a huff of exasperation. "Oh, honestly!"

Ursula saw that Shirley was waving Sue Ellen over to the refreshment table.

"I'm gone two seconds and – "

Ursula smiled. "I'm all right, Sue Ellen. I'll just finish up here." She folded a few more clothes, watching Mr. Creight as he pulled out shirts, sweaters, and a jacket. She was sure they were Jeremy's.

Mr. Creight slowly folded the clothes. He stood looking at them and rested his hand on the jacket, lost in the corridors of memory. Then his hand clutched the fabric and Ursula saw his mouth tremble. He slowly opened his hand and released the jacket. He gave it a final caress and abruptly left, bumping into people as he made for the side door.

Ursula hesitated a moment and then followed him outside. She found him leaning with all his weight against a pole on the small porch. He straightened when she stood next to him. He briefly turned to her and then looked away. She saw tears in his eyes.

"Mr. Creight, I know how hard that was for you."

He kept his eyes fixed on the horizon. "He won't be needing them. Someone else might as well get use out of 'em."

"We – we brought the rest of Francy's clothes. Part of me didn't want to. It felt like saying goodbye to him all over again."

He took a deep breath and let it out. "No point holding on. I'm a practical man. I packed up his clothes and – " His voice cracked and he brought his fist to his mouth.

Startled, Ursula saw that he had broken. His body shook and tears streamed down his weathered face.

His strong voice quivered in pain. "People tell me that life goes on, that the pain lessens. And I nod and go along with them." His hands clenched at the rail. "But inside, I rage." He turned his ravaged face to Ursula. "How can this still be called *life* – without my boy?"

Ursula's eyes brimmed with tears. She rested her hand on his arm.

His fist went to his chest, pressing on his heart with each utterance. "He was my son! My boy." His voice lost strength, his shoulders sagged. Then as suddenly as he broke, he composed himself. He took out his hankie and wiped at his eyes, blew his nose. "We had three girls, and then Jeremy. I thought I'd always have him near me."

They stood in silence, staring out at a world grown cold and empty.

Mr. Creight looked at Ursula, then back at the horizon. "You were a kindness to Jeremy. That means a lot to me."

Ursula raised her eyes to him. "He was a good person, one of the best."

He nodded and wiped his eyes with his rough sleeve jacket. "Some of the girls made fun of him, because of his stutter. You never did. I thank you for that."

"Jeremy and I were always friends, since we were little. He was always kind to me – we were partners in our eighth-grade science class. He always talked about you and said how much you helped him with his school work. I saw him shortly before he left. He told me you had cooked his favorite meal for him."

Mr. Creight looked down at Ursula. "He told you that?" A faint smile came to his mouth.

"I told him he was lucky to have a father like you, and he said he knew it."

His mouth twitched and he blinked hard. He gave two quick pats to Ursula's hand that still rested on his arm. "My boy chose well. He was made of finer stuff – and recognized the same in you."

He tried to stand tall, his barrel chest puffed out, his face hardened. "I'm not the only one who has lost in this war. I'm just glad his mother didn't have to see it. Maybe they're together now."

They stood silently for several moments. Then he took a deep breath and let it out, his breath white in the cold air. He turned to Ursula.

"I'll be all right," he said. "I'm a practical man. Life does go on. Whether we want it to or not." He gestured to the door. "Go back inside, dear. Where it's warm."

Ursula was reluctant to leave him with his heart so full of anguish.

He forced a smile, as if to say he would be fine, and opened the door for her.

Ursula stepped inside the doorway and watched him walk to his truck. A weather-beaten farmer – broad shoulders, rough hands, a determined gait. And inside, a tender heart breaking from unbearable loss.

She closed the door, and stepped inside the noisy, warm hall.

"Ursula!" cried Jessica. "I've been looking for you. Come join us at the refreshment table. And warm up with something hot – you look frozen."

For the next half hour, they filled cups of coffee and hot chocolate for the people coming and going, and served cookies and cake. Jessica gave a small gasp when she saw Clem come into the hall with Donny. She watched them take three bags to one of the men's clothing table. Donny was soon talking with his friends. Clem said a few words to him, and then began to walk to the door.

Jessica knew she should leave things be. She didn't want to look like a little puppy always trailing after someone. And yet when she saw that he was leaving, she grabbed her coat and caught up with him.

"Hi, Clem!"

Clem spun around, his face flushing on seeing her. "Hello, Jessica." His eyes searched for something else to look at but kept returning to her face.

"You're not leaving already, are you?"

"No. Just have something to deliver to someone, then I'm coming back."

"Someone special?" Jessica blurted. Her eyes filled with hurt – so he did have someone after all.

Clem saw her disappointment and smiled. He lifted a record. "Not that kind of special. I have something for Mrs. Fletcher."

"Mrs. Fletcher?" Jessica couldn't hide her surprise.

"You know I was in class with her son. Martin. You know he was there for D-Day."

"Yes," she said. She well remembered the lists of names that appeared in the newspapers during that dark time.

He nodded, and they were silent for a few minutes.

Jessica bit her lip. "Can I walk with you a bit? It's kind of stuffy inside."

"Sure."

They walked down the sidewalk and crossed the street.

"Now that you mention it, I haven't seen Mrs. Fletcher for a while."

"I don't think she goes out much. Martin was her only child. I've heard she's having a hard time with it."

Jessica silently berated herself for not reaching out to the woman. Even though she didn't know her well, she could have done something, brought her some cookies or…

"Her husband died young. Martin was all she had."

Jessica let out a sigh. "How terrible for her. Even though the war is over, there's still so much sadness, isn't there?" She looked down at the item tucked under his arm. "What is it you're bringing her?"

"Nothing much. Just something I thought she might like."

"A record?"

Clem nodded. "Martin used to say she spent all her time in her garden and reading. And that she always listened to music at night. There's a piece I think she'll like."

"Can I see?" Jessica took the record from Clem. "Franz Liszt. Piano?" She looked at Clem. "Why? I mean, what made you think to give this?"

He hunched his shoulders, remembering. "I heard it one night in the hospital. There was a gramophone in the hall. Guys were always playing different music, American jazz, for the most part. One night, someone put on a scratchy record. Piano music. It was nice. Then they played the other side, and…"

Jessica waited for him to continue. "And what?"

Clem shrugged and squinted at a memory. "Something happened. The room grew quiet. And we – well, I felt like – it was the first time I felt – like things might be all right. That the world still had something to offer besides suffering and sorrow. I think we all felt that. I heard several of the guys sniffling – it was the strangest thing." He took a deep breath. "I think it let us hope. It let us know that there was something beautiful out there…" He shook away his words and focused his attention ahead of him.

Jessica looked closely at Clem. "You think it might help her?"

"I don't know. Maybe."

"How will she know which one?"

"She'll know."

Jessica's brow creased and she scanned the two sides. Then she read, "Consolation No. 3 – is that the one?"

He nodded.

"That's what I love about you Clem. You've always been so good-hearted. You were always nice to everyone at school, that's what I remember. You helped everyone – you helped that boy who came to town, remember him? George something. He didn't have anyone else and you helped him with his 4-H project. And he won second place and was so happy. And I remember you sticking up for Jimmy in the schoolyard. He was always getting into trouble." She twisted her mouth in indecision. "You probably don't remember it, but you picked me up once when I fell while I was roller skating."

Clem smiled. "I remember that, all right. You were always on the run – climbing trees, roller skating. When I'd come over to see Eugene, you'd be running through the corn fields or swinging as high as you could on that swing in the oak tree. You were never still for a minute."

Jessica hadn't intended to walk as far as Mrs. Fletcher's, but they found themselves outside her house. The woman opened her door and nodded to Clem.

"Afternoon, Clement. I heard you made it home. Welcome back." Her hands locked in front of her, her chin slightly raised. A defensive stance – don't come too close. Her iron-gray hair was pulled into a low bun. She cast a disapproving eye at Jessica.

"Good afternoon, Mrs. Fletcher," Jessica said in a small voice.

The woman ignored her and turned back to Clem. "I'd ask you in but I'm busy at the moment.

Perhaps you could stop by tomorrow. I'd sure love to talk to you."

Jessica felt that she had intruded and was in the way.

Clem walked up to the porch. "Sure. I just wanted to say hello and give you this. I bought it in New York City on my way back home. Had a few hours. I know how you like music."

"Why, thank you, Clement. That's very thoughtful." Her face and posture softened, and she took a deep breath. "Come by tomorrow for lunch, why don't you?"

Clem nodded. "That'd be real nice. See you tomorrow, then."

Mrs. Fletcher gave him a smile, and a curt nod to Jessica, and went inside.

Jessica twisted her hands in her coat pocket. "Sorry, Clem. I shouldn't have come. I don't think she likes me. I used to pick her flowers when I was little. I don't think she's ever forgiven me."

Clem smiled. "I don't think she approves of pretty girls in general. You know the girls were always after Martin. Or rather, he was always after them. I guess she knew that one day one of them would take him away from her. She never counted on it being the war."

Jessica hadn't heard a word. She was smiling widely, her eyes full of hope. "You think I'm pretty, Clem?"

He gave a side glance to her and shoved his hands in his pockets. "Don't be daft."

She tucked her chin at the odd word. "*Daft?*"

He gave a chuckle at the word he had used. "That's what Nigel always said – fella I was in hospital with."

Jessica waited to hear more, her eyes bright with curiosity.

"He was from Manchester. Legs blown off, his right hand mangled. The nurses would come in all cheery and ask him how he was feeling – and that would be his answer."

He pointed his head to Mrs. Fletcher's house. "Sometimes anger is what gets people through a tough time."

Jessica glanced back at the house, then over at Clem. "Did it help Nigel?"

He shook his head. "He didn't make it."

They walked in silence a few moments, then Jessica searched his face. "Why were you in the hospital, Clem? Were you hurt?"

He hunched his shoulders together and looked away. "I don't want to talk about it."

"Of course, not. I'm sorry. I shouldn't have asked."

They walked the rest of the way in silence. When they stepped inside the American Legion Hall, Jessica turned to him. "Can I get you something from the refreshment table? Something to warm you up?"

"Thanks, no. I promised Donny a matinee show. Some Western he wants to see."

Jessica waited, hoping he might invite her to go along. But he simply said goodbye and walked away from her.

She took off her coat and stood next to Ursula at the table. She picked up a cookie and bit into it.

"Are you all right?" Ursula asked, placing her hand on Jessica. "Did something happen?"

"No. Nothing happened. But you know what I think? I think there are a lot of sad people out there. More than you would ever know."

Ursula gave a soft smile. "I think you're right. We never know what's inside other people, or what sorrow they have. All the more reason to be gentle with them."

Jessica finished the cookie, deep in thought. Then she brushed the crumbs from her hands. "Let's go find Eugene. The cafe will be packed if we don't get there soon. Then we can do the grocery shopping."

Chapter 13

❧

Henry and Dusty sat at a low table near the counter at The Red String Curio Store playing a game of checkers. Near the back entrance, with the door wide open, Mr. G coached Gabriel on touching up the rocker with oak stain. Billy sat on the floor next to Gabriel, pointing out places that needed a little more color. He was on his belly now, looking underneath the rungs.

"The underside looks pretty good."

Mr. G nodded approvingly. "Remember, a deft touch is all you need." He carefully inspected the chair. "We'll let it dry. Then I'd say it's ready for a light coat of oil."

"We'll bring it to Mrs. Kuntzman's basement for that," said Gabriel. "We want it close at hand, so we can carry it over at any time. Henry's going to help us."

"Excellent plan. A little oil, a deep polishing, and it will gleam like new. Finish up here, boys, then come up front and we'll cut into the *tarte aux pommes* from Mademoiselle Amy. She's slicing it up now. We're her official tasters."

Billy jumped to his feet and dusted off his clothes.

The little bell rang at the door and voices were raised in greeting. "I believe Tommy and Mickey have arrived," said Mr. G, hurrying away to greet them.

Tommy and Mickey came into the shop and gathered around the game of checkers. "Hi, Henry. Is Amy here?" Tommy asked brightly, looking around.

"Hello, Tommy, Mickey," Henry answered. "She's in the office dishing out the apple tart for us all to taste." He smiled as he made a jump, causing Dusty to sit up and frown.

Tommy peeked into the open office. Amy's back was to him as she placed slices of tart on an assortment of small floral plates. He motioned to Mr. G that he wanted to make a payment on the locket, and they walked to the counter. Mickey seated himself next to Dusty and Henry, studying their checker moves.

Mr. G whispered to Tommy. "I must say, you've chosen the ideal gift for Amy. Perhaps you can place a small photograph of yourself in it," he added with a wink.

"If she wants." Tommy shrugged but couldn't hide his smile. "You know Mr. G, this is going to be the best Christmas ever. The war's over. Dad's on his way home. Everybody is happy."

"You're right, Tommy. Parades, homecomings, celebrations everywhere you look. This might be our most extraordinary Christmas in living memory." He closed the register draw with a clang. "We'll have our own little celebration – right now. I'll play some Christmas music on the phonograph, we'll all sample your French project, and we'll raise a glass of – " He rubbed his chin as he considered what to offer the group. His finger shot up. "Tea, of course! Let me go and boil the water."

The little bell rang again, and they looked up. "And here's Junior! Greetings! Good timing, Junior. We're about to taste Tommy and Amy's French project – *tarte aux pommes*. Have a seat. Have a seat."

Junior eased himself into a deep wing-backed chair, leaned his cane against it, and gently rubbed his hands, his knees.

Mr. G motioned to Tommy. "Why don't you gather Gabriel and Billy for our celebration. They're in the back finishing up with the staining. And a fine job they've done."

Tommy slapped Mickey on the back. "Let's go see how they're doing." He poked his head into the office. "Hey, Amy. Mr. G is going to make tea to go with our tart. I'll be right back to help." He noticed that she nodded but didn't say anything.

He and Mickey made their way through the maze, coming across shoppers poring over old books, turning over objects, and inspecting items on the various shelves.

Tommy smiled when he saw the rocking chair. "It's looking real good, Gabriel."

"A deft coat of oil is all it needs, once this dries," said Gabriel.

Tommy nodded. "Right. We'll take it to Mrs. Kuntzman's and finish working on it until Christmas."

"And when you're ready to deliver it, I'll come to stand guard," added Billy, "and help with the doors. I'm good at that kind of thing."

Gabriel stood and brushed at his pants. "And I'll stay home and make sure Mom doesn't run to the store or anything."

"Come on," said Mickey. "Let's go taste the tart-o-whatever."

Billy jumped up and closed the back door, causing a gust of wind to blow in. "Much better. It's freezing out there."

Gabriel sneezed, instinctively holding the staining cloth to his face.

Billy's eyes widened and he pointed at Gabriel, laughing. "Your nose!" he cried, barely able to get the words out. Tommy and Mickey looked back and laughed at the dark streaks on his face.

"Oops!" Gabriel said, trying to rub at it with the other end of the cloth.

"S – stop, Gabriel!" Tommy said, bent over with laughter. "You're making it worse."

Mickey found another rag and made a few wipes at Gabriel's face. "I think you're going to need soap. Maybe a little sandpaper!"

Gabriel lifted his shirt and continued to wipe at his nose as the four boys wound their way back to the front counter. They pulled up an assortment of chairs and footstools and gathered around the checker game.

While Gabriel chatted with Dusty, Tommy helped Amy and Mr. G with the tart and teacups. When they were all gathered around with a cup of tea and a plate of dessert, Mr. G raised his teacup. "To the resounding success of Amy and Tommy's *tarte aux pommes*! And to the best Christmas ever!"

"Hear, hear!" said Junior.

Billy and Gabriel bit into the dessert and widened their eyes in delight. Low hums and sounds of enjoyment came from all the tasters.

Tommy kept trying to catch Amy's eye, but she busied herself with going back and forth to the small kitchen in the office, bringing a sugar bowl and a small creamer to the counter.

Henry admired the fanned-out slices of apples on the tart. "A little work of art. I promised Martha – Mrs. Kuntzman, that is – that I'd bring her a slice."

"We already set aside a piece for her," said Tommy. "It was her idea after all. She guided us through every step of the way."

"Heavenly," Dusty pronounced, taking another bite.

"Indeed, divine!" added Henry.

Junior slowly savored another forkful. "Amy, this tastes as if it's been baked in the celestial bakeries."

Amy smiled at their comments but remained uncharacteristically quiet.

"Well done!" said Mr. G. "I foresee high marks on your project!"

Tommy beamed at Amy as he enjoyed another bite.

"Double jump!" Dusty cried out in triumph. "I finally got you, Mr. H!"

Henry leaned forward and looked at the board. "So you did, so you did," he said, more interested in taking another bite of his apple tart.

"Ah," said Dusty, leaning back in his chair. "The sweetness of triumph! How about two out of three?"

Henry finished his slice and gave a firm nod. "You're on, sir, you're on."

Mr. G jumped up to help a customer who had finally decided on a music box, Mickey went to get more hot water for his tea, and Billy and Gabriel scooted closer to the checker board.

Amy looked up from her tea and spoke almost in a whisper to Tommy. "I – I have to go home."

"Already?" Tommy realized that he hadn't heard her laugh once. She brought her cup and plate to the little sink in the office.

"Can you walk with me, Tommy?" She slipped on her coat, leaving her long hair tucked inside.

"Sure." He finished his tea on the way to the kitchen, and pulled on his coat. "Everyone sure liked our *tarte aux pommes*. Wait until our class tastes it. We'll have to slice it into tiny slivers. Or maybe we can make two tarts."

When Amy started to pull her hair from inside her coat, Tommy helped her. He gathered her tresses gently in his hands. "Your hair's so long.

And soft." He placed it down her back, and almost jumped when he saw tears in her eyes. "Amy!"

Tommy called out to Gabriel over his shoulder. "I'll meet you at home, Gabe. Don't be late!" He waved to Mickey who had raised his head from the game, and then walked out of the store with Amy.

A few minutes later, Mr. G returned and looked around. "Our group appears smaller."

"Tommy had to walk Amy home," said Gabriel, finishing his dessert. He carried a few empty plates into the kitchen.

Junior finished his tea and announced, "Game two goes to Henry Hankel!"

"Henry Hankel," said Mr. G. "Nice alliterative ring to it."

Dusty rubbed his hands together and scraped the last bit of tart from his plate. "And now. The tiebreaker." He and Henry set up their pieces.

Mr. G hooked his thumbs around his suspenders, rocked on his heels and, seeing only a few customers browsing, turned to Billy and Gabriel. "How about word, gentlemen?"

Billy's head popped up. "Can I find it?"

"Of course."

Billy stood behind the unabridged dictionary, covered his eyes with one hand, and opened the book. "I'll try the beginning this time."

Mr. G took a seat in the cane rocker and lifted his teacup. "Nothing more enjoyable than a cup of tea in the late afternoon," he said, musing aloud. "With friends. At Christmastime." He took another sip and smiled out at his friends, his shop.

"Ready?" said Billy, landing on a word.

"Go ahead, Billy," said Gabriel, sitting on a footstool. He folded his arms on his knees and listened.

Billy pronounced a word and read the definition. "*Without angels. Not having angels.*"

Gabriel raised his head and wrinkled his forehead in thought. "Huh. Not sure what that even means."

Mr. G also looked up. "Leave it to Master Billy to find such an unusual word." He rubbed his chin and cast his eyes to the ceiling. "Without angels. Without angels. Curious concept."

Henry moved a checker piece and screwed up his face. "As opposed to *with* angels?"

Dusty turned his head to the left, then the right. "Without angels..."

"What say you, Dusty?" asked Henry, following Dusty's move and then moving another piece. "You're the scholar here."

"I'm not so sure that Mr. G isn't more the scholar than I."

Billy and Gabriel exchanged the same look, puzzling out who was the real scholar.

Dusty leaned back in his chair. "To be without angels. Now, is that in opposition to having angels? A sort of attitude or position taken against the concept?"

Junior chimed in. "How would that work, anyway? I'm trying to imagine a world, any world, without angels. Not sure I like it." He massaged his knees again.

Billy looked up from the page. "What would we put at the top of our Christmas tree?" He tapped his cheek a few times. "I guess we could use a star. Or Santa."

"I like the world better *with* angels," Gabriel decided.

Dusty made another move. "I have to agree with you, Gabriel." He steepled his fingertips together. "What would the works of Raphael or Tintoretto or Michelangelo be without angels? A great loss for us all."

Junior nodded. "The great masters have painted angels for centuries – perhaps beginning with the cherubs and Cupid in Greek mythology."

"Indeed," said Dusty. "Until the Renaissance artists depicted muscular, more masculine, angels. Before that, angels were rather ethereal and feminine."

Mr. G remained silent, pondering. "I can't make much sense out of the word. Billy, read the word and definition again, this time include the etymology. Knowing the root might aid our comprehension."

Billy found the word again and began to read: "Agonic. Without – " He put his face close to the page. "Whoops!" he cried and let out a snort of laughter. "I read it wrong."

Gabriel jumped up beside him and read the definition: "Agonic. Without – " and he also began to laugh. "It says, 'without *angles*,' not angels! It's a mathematical term."

Mickey playfully swatted Billy. "You goofball. Putting us all on the wrong track."

Junior's bushy eyebrows furrowed. "We just wasted a good ten minutes on a complete and utter misconception?"

"And a double-jump wins the match!" cried Henry.

Dusty leaned forward in exasperation. "I protest! My mind was on that – that – devilish concept about angels!"

Gabriel noticed that Junior was wincing and rubbing his hands and knees. "Can I get you more tea?"

Junior shook his head. "It's going to rain, Gabriel. I can feel it in my bones. He cocked his head and examined his hands, trying to flex the twisted fingers. "No. I'd say snow is on the way. Lots of it."

"Let me get you a dram, Junior," said Mr. G, jumping to his feet. "To help dull the pain."

"I won't say no to that. Much obliged."

Mr. G came back with a small etched glass of amber liquor and handed it to Junior. A customer called out for Mr. G from the back of the shop. "Coming!" he replied. "I must tend to business," he said to the group, and disappeared into the labyrinth.

A cuckoo clock chimed, and Billy ran to see the bird emerging from the clock. "Holy mackerel! Mickey – we're late!"

"That clock's not right, remember?" said Mickey. "But we better get going."

Billy smacked his forehead. "I keep forgetting. Coming with us, Gabriel?"

"Sure." Gabriel grabbed his coat, hollered out his goodbyes, and left with Mickey and Billy.

At the apartment, Lillian had just put Charlotte down for a nap. She finished setting the table, looking out the window now and again. "I don't believe it – late again! Both of them!"

She grew increasingly angry the later it got. Had she made the wrong decision in allowing the boys to work? Perhaps they were both too young?

Gabriel suddenly rushed in through the door. "I'm home!"

"You're late again, Gabriel!"

"I am?" he asked, looking at the clock.

She took a closer look at him. "What's on your nose?" She lifted his hands. "And all over your hands?"

"Oh. That." He dashed to the bathroom and was soon soaping up his hands and rubbing at his nose. "Billy and I were working on something," he hollered, hoping she wouldn't press him.

Lillian came and stood by the door. "What exactly were you working on?"

Gabriel hesitated a moment too long.

"What are you two up to? And where's Tommy?"

"I thought he was here." Gabriel examined his face in the mirror and rubbed at his face.

She crossed her arms. "I thought we agreed – no more secrets!"

He dried his face with a towel. "This isn't a secret. It's something else. What's for dinner? I'm starved!"

Lillian was about to lose her temper when Tommy walked in, his eyes red.

"Tommy! What is it?"

He dropped onto the couch and held a pillow on his lap.

"Tommy? What's wrong?" Lillian sat next to him and cupped her hand around his cheek. "What is it, Tommy?"

His mouth quivered, and his words came out all crumbled. "Amy. She's moving back to Ohio!"

"Oh, Tommy." Lillian embraced him. "I'm so sorry, sweetheart."

Tommy tried to be strong, but his face grew more strained until he couldn't keep back the tears. "Nothing will ever be the same!" He buried his face in the pillow.

Lillian put her arms around him, wondering what to say. She looked over at Gabriel who was staring down at the floor. They had all grown to love Amy over the years.

"Tell me what you know," said Lillian. "What exactly did Amy say?"

Tommy kept the pillow on his lap and fumbled with the corners, trying to begin. "She just found out. This morning. Her dad got his old job back. They still have their house back there. So…" His shoulders dropped as if a sudden weight had been placed on them. "Her mom wants Amy to finish the school year here, but her dad says she might as well start in the new year."

Gabriel had gone to the bookshelf and now moved to the other side of the couch with the atlas opened to the United States. "Look, Tommy. Ohio isn't very far away. It's kind of close." He passed the book to Tommy.

Tommy stared at the page. "It looks far."

"Not by train," Gabriel said brightly. "We could jump a train and be there in no time. Like hobos! It'll be an adventure! Pack some food, a couple of blankets – "

"There will be no jumping trains!" Lillian looked sternly at Gabriel, knowing that he was perfectly capable of such an – adventure.

Gabriel twisted his mouth in disappointment and leaned back into the couch. After a brief silence, he nodded slowly, as if weighing different options.

"Mom's right. Why travel in a dusty old box-car when we could be comfortable inside the train? We're working men now. We can save our money and go visit her. Any time we want."

Lillian was about to stop Gabriel's wild imaginings, but she held her tongue. Tommy had turned to Gabriel, as if considering the possibility.

"Have our meals in the dining car and watch the world pass by." Gabriel linked his arms behind his head. "And at night, from a comfortable berth, we could open the curtains and look up at the stars. Be in Ohio by morning."

Tommy sat up, envisioning such a trip. "A day? That's not long."

Gabriel nodded. "A quick overnight journey."

Lillian wondered if Gabriel was serious in his suggestions, or if he was simply trying to make

Tommy feel better. She observed him closely, surprised that he had been able to lessen Tommy's despair.

"Or," said Gabriel, opening his right palm as if presenting yet another offer, "we could work as porters on the train. It might be cheaper that way."

Lillian stood. "Come. We'll discuss it over dinner. You two must be hungry."

"We got a lot of options, Tommy. Mr. G says when life presents you with a difficult situation, you have two choices. Accept it or do something about it."

Tommy scooted in his chair and dished out a piece of chicken cacciatore. "Well, I'm *not* accepting it."

The conversation branched off into several directions the future might take: wait and see what happens – maybe Amy's father would change his mind. Perhaps stopping by Ohio on their way to Kate's farm in the summer. "Maybe Amy could come with us. She would love the farm," Tommy said with a hint of hope coming back into his voice.

Just as they were finishing dinner, Charlotte's cries from the bedroom shifted their attention once more.

"Tommy," said Lillian, "can you get Charlotte?"

"Sure." He jumped up and was soon amusing his baby sister in the living room.

Gabriel raised his face to Lillian. For a brief moment, she caught a new expression in his eyes. Older, wiser, and – reassuring. As if he had been in control in shifting Tommy's mood and was checking to see if he had gotten away with it, or if she would be angry.

Lillian smiled at him, strangely comforted. She gave his shoulder a light squeeze. "Go and sit with Tommy. I'll clean up here."

While she washed the dishes, she heard enough laughter coming from the living room to ease her mind about Tommy.

Gabriel plugged in the Christmas tree lights, and they took turns holding Charlotte and showing her different ornaments.

"Here's a shiny brass trumpet," said Gabriel. "And up there is a soldier. And over here," he lifted an ornament with his free hand, "is my old Santa ornament." He handed her to Tommy. "Look at her eyes, Tommy. She has Christmas tree lights in them."

Tommy lifted her and smiled. "She loves the tree. Wait until Dad sees her." He called over his shoulder. "Mom, can we leave the tree up until Dad gets home?"

Lillian came into the living room and smiled in agreement. Tonight, she would agree to anything.

*

Later that night, after she had bathed and fed Charlotte and after the boys were asleep, Lillian sat in front of the Christmas tree. She rocked Charlotte in her arms and thought about Tommy and Gabriel.

They were so close, similar in so many ways, best friends – and yet so different. Tommy had always been popular, smart in school and good in sports, an achiever, protective of others, shy with the girls. Gabriel was more comfortable in his skin, cared less about what others thought of him, and was often driven by his curiosity. He tended to befriend unusual people and was at ease with everyone, even girls.

Tommy had an underlying tension about him, the weight of the world on his shoulders. Was it because he was the elder and had to step up at an earlier age? He was older when Tom died – perhaps he had felt the loss more. Had she unwittingly put too much pressure on him? And yet he was rock solid, dependable. She never had to worry about him.

All these years, it had been Gabriel who most concerned her. She had worried that he was too much like her – too dreamy, too much in his own world, and would always be at odds with school and routines and things he was supposed to do. Now she realized that he was full of his own kind of confidence and joy.

She realized that Tommy was the more vulnerable one. He was more unsure of himself, and worried about what others thought of him, worried if he was doing the right thing, and was caught off balance when the world threw him a curve.

Gabriel – *Gabriel*, she thought with a shake of her head, was the more resilient of the two. They were both smart and determined. They would both succeed in life, she was sure of that. But Gabriel might have more fun doing so.

She shook away her fruitless worrying. Perhaps it was simply the differences in personalities, differences that made them so delightfully their own. And so compatible as brothers. She knew they would always look out for each other.

She lifted Charlotte and held her close, cradling her head against her shoulder. "And now they have you." She kissed her cheek and carried her to her crib. She looked down at the sleeping face and imagined that Charles was there with her, his arm around her shoulder. How happy he would be.

Before going to bed, she went into the boys' room and gazed down at them. She remembered how she used to tuck them in and read stories to them. They seemed so old now – fourteen and eleven. How quickly the years flew by. She leaned over them and kissed their foreheads and smoothed their hair, her heart bursting with love. Soon, soon – their happiness would be complete. The years of longing, the years of waiting, would be behind them.

*

After his rounds, Red stopped off at a small pub for dinner, a rather quiet one where he could usually find a table away from the crowds. He shook the rain from his jacket, hung it up, and rubbed his hands together. Snow was in the forecast, the temperature was dropping. He had read that in the States, as in Europe, the winter was a cold one, unusually so. He placed his order, along with a cup of tea to warm up.

All day he had been tempted to place a call to Charles to let him know there was a flight for him – but three days ago, a similar arrangement had fallen through. He would hate to disappoint him.

And yet, he had a good feeling about this flight. Nova Scotia, then on to Toronto – Charles could take a bus or train from there. Maybe even a flight. He had read about the long delays at all the U.S. train and bus stations, as well as airports. The highways were clogged with returning servicemen – it was one enormous, country-wide traffic jam, with no end in sight.

Red counted the days until Christmas. If Charles didn't catch this flight, he'd be lucky to get home in January. If it didn't work out, they could spend the holiday together, if either of them felt up to it. Several families had already invited Red to Christmas dinner. They all had children. Maybe Charles would enjoy that. Or maybe it would be too painful.

He glanced out the window as he finished his meal – a simple stew and a heel of bread. Through the rain-drizzled windowpanes, he watched the people pass by, probably hurrying home to a loved one. Suddenly, his heart lurched as a woman with auburn hair passed by. He sat up and looked closer. No. This woman pushed a pram and a small child held her hand. And the walk was all wrong. He rubbed his eyes.

It must be all Charles's talk of going home. Red realized that he had been "seeing" Izzy again, as he used to. Mirages. Visions. Dreams. He could be staring out at traffic – and catch a glimpse of her in the way a woman wore her hat. Or at a restaurant, dining, and suddenly catch from afar, the way a woman threw her head back to laugh. Or he could be talking with a patient outside the hospital and he would see her – stopping to look in a window, walking with her hands in her coat pockets. Or, with an ache – always with a gripping heartache – her arm linked with a man's. Izzy. She had become a part of him. And there was no undoing it. Three thousand miles hadn't changed a thing. A sham marriage hadn't changed a thing. A war had come between them, but always she was there – tucked away inside his heart. He would die with her locked safely there.

She had moved on, as she should have. But he could never let her go. Would he ever be brave enough to return home – to see her again, knowing that she was not his? He didn't think he could bear it. Or to see her married to another man. She hadn't married as of yet. He often wondered if that should give him any cause for hope.

No. He had done the unpardonable. It was hard for him to believe what he had done. It was as if someone else had inhabited him briefly and went along with the idea of marriage – while he was recovering. It was all a blur. Only Izzy was real. Only their time together, their long walks, their peaceful sleeps in each other's arms. In all the spinning, dizzying world, only Izzy was real. But she had moved on.

But then why had she written this past year? Charles had told him of the incident last Christmas when he was home. How stunned Izzy had been to hear that his marriage was long over. That news had jarred him. To think that Izzy had believed him married all those years. In his heart, he had only been married to her. He should have listened to her, back before he joined the Canadian Air Force. She had wanted to get married. He had said no. He had wanted to protect her. If he had listened to her, they would still be together. He would be going home to her now.

What to do – stay in England or go home? Part of him wanted to stay and help out. A bigger part of him wanted to go home. Home to a green land full of happy people and standing cities – to full tables and happy children. He wondered how long the rationing would last in England. And the continent. Home. To a land untouched by bombs and fire and wraith-like figures wandering, searching for food, for a home, for family. So much was gone. He felt none of the euphoria others did. In the beginning he did. But then the reports started to come in – of revenge and retribution. In Czechoslovakia, France, Belgium. German civilians lined up along roads and shot in the back. Thousands of women in France humiliated for consorting with Germans – many of the charges unfounded, but people were out for blood and perhaps now was the time to settle an old score with a woman who had rebuffed a suitor. Some were killed. What was the point of defeating evil if the victor then behaved in the same way? He pressed on his eyes. And the Soviets. What they were doing to German women turned his stomach. Maybe he should go home. Try to do some good there. But live in the same city as Izzy and not be able to see her? He couldn't imagine it. It was all so awful. He couldn't bear any of it –

"Anything else, sir?"

Red gripped the cup between his hands.

"Can I bring anything else?"

Red realized that someone had been talking to him. He looked up, momentarily perplexed to find a kindly old woman smiling down at him. Flyaway white hair, kind blue eyes, a tray under her arm, a gentle hand on his shoulder. Red teared up at the simple kindness she showed him.

She patted his shoulder. "I think you could do with a warmup. I'll be right back with a fresh cup."

Red nodded his thanks.

What a kind old woman. He had a feeling that he would always remember those few seconds of maternal gentleness in a cold and dismal world. A reminder of what they had been fighting for, a reminder of what he had to live for – goodness, kindness...

He looked around and took comfort in the solidity of the oak tables and chairs, the drizzle running down the window panes, the anchoring of laughter and conversations, a clang from the kitchen, the smells of food, a flash of headlights outside. At a table by the window, a couple leaned into each other with love in their eyes. A group of men stood at the bar, arms flung around shoulders, a friendly slap on the back in greeting as someone joined them. Humanity. Simple, beautiful humanity that made him want to weep.

The elderly waitress returned with a cup of steaming tea and a shot of whiskey. "On the house, soldier." She patted his shoulder again and left to tend another table.

"Thank you." His words came out in a whisper.

Red added the shot of whiskey to his tea and drank gratefully, allowing it to warm him through and through. After a few minutes, he realized how dark the day had become, and paid his bill.

He put on his coat and hat and left the restaurant. Outside, he pulled his collar up, and walked through the sleety rain. Though it was dark, he made his way to the park, and stood near the bench. He looked out over the river and softly spoke his evening prayer: "Izzy."

The lamplight near the small arched bridge glowed in the cold rain. A few scattered lights reflected on the river. He turned around and walked to his room.

Chapter 14

❀

As usual, Ursula stood at the kitchen window in the morning, waiting to see if Friedrich would be dropped off by Mr. Creight. Though she tried to be level-headed about their situation, she sometimes indulged in happy visions of the future. Imagining the day when Friedrich would be able to return. How they would have a house of their own, or perhaps move to a city and start life afresh.

Her hand went to her earring and a soft smile transformed her face. Friedrich promised to buy her an amethyst ring to match the earrings, like the one he saw last year when he was working over at the river. Perhaps even the same one, he had said. Perhaps it would still be there. They would cross the river, picnic along the water, and visit the little shop where he saw the ring. He would buy it, slip it on her finger, and call her his wife.

Her smile slowly left her lips. Friedrich was being used more and more at the camp. Their time together was getting shorter and shorter. In truth, their future was an utter blank. Perhaps none of those things she dreamed about would ever happen. Perhaps he would be kept away for a long time. Perhaps...

She abandoned those thoughts and clung to the one thing she was sure of. That she would wait for Friedrich. Until she was old and gray, she would wait for him, or seek him out and bring him back to her...

"You're wasting your time," Eugene said to her, coming into the kitchen. "It's almost 10:00. They would have been here by now."

Kate sat at the table, reviewing her accounts notebook. She glared at Eugene over her reading glasses, then addressed Ursula. "Why don't you come into town with us, Ursula? We'll only be gone a few hours. Jessica wants to do a little shopping while I help Mildred organize the raffle for the food drive. Shirley's over in Greenfield visiting her cousin, so Jessica will be on her own."

Ursula shook her head. "I think I'll get started on the ironing. But if you don't mind, I'd like to take a walk while Frankie's asleep."

"Of course. I'll listen for him. Bundle up, though. It's cold out there. More snow's on the way."

Kate watched Ursula as she left the house and walked down the lane. Brisk, restless steps. "She's ready to burst from the tension."

Eugene ignored Kate's comment and went into the pantry, opening and closing cupboards. "Where'd you move that jar of nails you always kept? I need to fix the shelf in the cellar."

When he didn't get an answer, he stuck his head out of the pantry and saw Kate staring at him with her arms folded.

He leaned against the doorjamb to the pantry. "Go ahead. Say what's on your mind, Mom."

"I don't like the way you speak to the girls. Especially Ursula."

"I just pointed out that they're not coming today."

"It's the tone you always use with her. Abrupt, disapproving – as if she needs any more trouble in her life. Even when Friedrich is here, she can't speak freely to him."

"That's because of Creight."

"And you. And you know it."

"I stood up for her at the Legion hall."

"And called more attention to her predicament."

Eugene threw his hands up. "I can't do anything right."

"I'm not saying that. You were right to defend her, but you have to be sensitive to her situation. It hasn't been easy for her. And you talk to Jessica as if she's still ten years old."

"What are you saying, Mom?"

"That you need to see your sisters in a different light. They're not the girls they were when you left. That was almost four years ago. They did the work of my sons during the war – especially before we got the POWs."

Eugene looked down at the floor, weighing her words. He brushed his foot over the worn linoleum. "You're right. I do still think of them as kids." He shook his head. "I've missed out on four years of their lives. I forget that they've grown and changed."

"They plowed and took care of the animals. Milked the cows and sold it at the market, along with eggs. I consulted them in all decisions. I discussed the finances with Ursula and relied heavily on her judgment. They have good heads on their shoulders. Jessica's worked hard on becoming a teacher and never let it get in the way of her work on the farm. Ursula's a mother now, but that hasn't stopped her from doing any of her daily chores. She had big dreams of going to college. And now what hope does she have? Sometimes I see her paging through her schoolbooks and it breaks my heart."

"Jeez, I feel like a heel." Eugene plopped down at the kitchen table and stared out at the bleak winter sky. "Sorry, Mom. I'll try to do better."

"I know you will." Kate placed her hand on his shoulder. "I know what you're made of. And I know you've got your own worries. But you were always close with your sisters and I don't want you to lose that."

Eugene leaned his elbows on the table, regarding his mother with love. "You always did keep us all in line. I was on my own for so long. I guess I got a little isolated, and selfish."

"I'm sure you had to be that way, to survive. But you're home now. And we need you. Being the eldest, you always had a big influence on the others."

When he smiled at her, Kate caught a glimmer of her son before he left for war. Her heart swelled to know that he was still there, and that time and healing would slowly bring him back.

Jessica ran down the stairs and came into the kitchen. "I'm ready when you are." She looked around. "Where's Ursula?"

"Out walking," said Kate. She checked her handbag and closed it with a snap. "We'll go as soon as she's back."

"You don't have to wait. I'll be here," said Eugene.

"What if Frankie wakes?" Kate considered it but then shook her head. "I'll call Mildred and let her know we'll be a few minutes late."

"I know what to do. Warm up the milk, check the temperature." Eugene mimed shaking a few drops on his wrist. "I remember doing it for you, Jess."

"For me?" Jessica was incredulous. "Is that true, Mom?"

"Eugene was the eldest and was a big help to me with all you kids. Especially you and Paul. He'd watch you for hours. Pull you around the farm in the wagon. Remember that, Eugene?" Kate asked from the hallway, pulling out her coat from the closet.

"Sure do. Paul liked to ride on my shoulders. You liked the wagon."

"Did I?" asked Jessica. "I remember that old wagon. I remember trying to sit in it after you gave it a fresh coat of paint and getting red paint all over my clothes."

"And face," Eugene added with a chuckle.

Kate came back into the kitchen with her coat and hat on. "Well, since Frankie is in good hands, we can leave."

Jessica gave Eugene an impulsive hug. "Can we bring you anything from town?"

He laughed. "No. And take your time. Frankie and I will hold down the fort."

Mrs. Bloomfield and Kate chatted all the way into town. Jessica sat in the back seat, staring out at the snow-covered fields and woods. She did her best not to think about Clem. She couldn't help but wonder if there was someone he was sweet on, something he was keeping to himself. She saw how the girls looked at him in town. Everyone thought he was handsome. And kind. Her childhood affection for him had grown into something deeper. And it hurt that he didn't want her.

They pulled into town. "Look how busy the square is," said Mildred Bloomfield. "Shirley will be sorry she missed it."

"I'm sorry Ursula didn't come," added Kate, as she got out of the car. "Jessica, would you mind picking up some stamps for me? I still have a few more Christmas cards to send out." She handed Jessica an extra dollar. "In case you want to stop at the soda fountain."

"Thanks, Mom."

Jessica stopped at the five-and-dime and browsed at crayons, paint sets, and colored paper for possible art projects for her students. For now, she purchased a small box of multi-colored foiled stars for when she graded papers. One of the older teachers criticized her for being too soft on the children, but Jessica firmly believed that encouragement and praise brought about the best results.

Then she went to Arnold's and looked at fabric and a few of the ready-made dresses. She lingered over a pretty dress with pale buttercups and wispy green leaves. It would be a nice dress for teaching. She would think about it.

She walked around the town square, taking in all the decorations. Even though it was daytime, colored lights twined around the fir trees and added a sense of cheer to the overcast day. There was the Santa Claus house with its crooked little chimney. Soon there would be long lines of children waiting to see him. The square bustled with holiday shoppers and workers on their lunch break.

So many happy people. She tried to catch the holiday cheer, but her spirit remained weighted down with thoughts about Clem. Again, she tried not to think about him. She thought about the Christmas school play. She thought about her brothers coming home. And how happy they would all be, even if they didn't make it home in time for Christmas. She thought about the Christmas dance and wondered if Clem would go. Probably not. She thought about Christmas baking, and how pretty their Christmas tree looked. She thought about the fluffy teddy bear for Frankie already wrapped and tucked under the Christmas tree. She thought about all these happy things and waited for that burst of joy that usually filled her. Maybe she was tired.

She made her way to the Post Office, stopping to admire the pine boughs twisted around the railings and the wreaths tied with big red bows on the double doors. She waited in the line of people sending and receiving packages. Everyone so happy and busy.

With a start, Jessica realized that the woman next in line was Mrs. Fletcher. She was sending a package.

"Afternoon, Mrs. Fletcher," said the elderly clerk, Mr. Whiting. "I haven't seen you in a long time. Nice to see you out and about."

"I'm sending a present to my niece. It's best to keep busy. Especially at the holidays."

Jessica heard them chatting about the cold weather and the various Christmas drives and activities. She stared straight down at her shoes, hoping that Mrs. Fletcher would simply walk past her.

She turned her head and busied herself with her purse as Mrs. Fletcher passed by. Jessica exchanged a few words with Mr. Whiting and purchased her stamps. She slipped them in her purse and turned to leave.

There was Mrs. Fletcher, standing by the door as she pulled on her gloves. Jessica sensed that she was waiting for her. She pretended to see her just now. "Oh, hello Mrs. Fletcher."

The woman gave a brief nod. "You're Kate's youngest."

"Yes, ma'am. Jessica."

"You used to pick my flowers."

Jessica swallowed, bewildered. "I know. I'm sorry. They were always so pretty and – "

"How's Clem?"

Jessica stood speechless for a few moments. "I – I don't know. I haven't seen him." She opened the door to leave, annoyed to find that Mrs. Fletcher was also leaving. Jessica held the door open for her.

The older woman raised her chin and looked down at Jessica. "Clem's a good boy."

Jessica bristled at the accusatory tone. "Yes, he is."

"Kindhearted. Hard working. Loyal. You could do no better than Clem. I wouldn't have expected him to fancy someone so young and flighty."

Jessica's mouth dropped open. "He doesn't! I mean, I'm not! I mean – " Jessica took a deep breath and spoke calmly. "You're mistaken on both points, Mrs. Fletcher. Goodbye."

Mrs. Fletcher followed her down the steps. "Oh, come now. I saw how he looked at you. And his manner when he spoke about you when he came to lunch. I'm old but I'm not blind. I pretended not to notice, but when he took off his jacket, your photograph fell out of his pocket."

Jessica's cheeks turned pink. She noticed the creases of merriment at Mrs. Fletcher's eyes. Was she making fun of her? Jessica gave a silent nod goodbye and walked briskly away. Had she looked back, she would have found the older woman smiling in full approval of her.

Jessica's earlier despondency was now replaced with anger. She went into the soda fountain shop, took a seat at the counter, and ordered two scoops of vanilla ice cream with chocolate syrup. And whipped cream. She took a big bite and recalled every word of Mrs. Fletcher's. Flighty? The nerve of that woman! And speaking to me as if I was out to hurt Clem. Had he said something against her to Mrs. Fletcher? But then what did she mean – 'I saw the way he looked at you.' Jessica couldn't make sense of it.

The more she thought about it, the angrier she became. She decided there was only one thing to do. Action was always better than fretting. She paid, left the soda fountain, and made her way to Clem's house. She took a deep breath and knocked at the door.

Donny answered, smiling widely. "Hi, Miss Jessica."

"Afternoon, Donny. Is Clem home?"

Donny opened the door for her to step inside. "We were just working in the kitchen. Come on in."

"I'll wait out here, thank you."

Donny left to get Clem, who soon appeared with a wrench in his hand. "Jessica?"

"I won't keep you." Though she tried to sound stern, her heart melted. Clem wore a deep green plaid shirt that brought out the color of his eyes. Only then did she realize how foolish she was being.

Clem waited expectantly.

Jessica gulped and tried to muster up her earlier anger. "I just ran into Mrs. Fletcher. She seems to think I'm after you and that it would be disastrous for you. Did you tell her anything?"

"Course not. There's nothing to tell."

Jessica blinked in frustration. "Exactly! That's what I told her." She waited for him to say something.

They stared at each other. Jessica's feelings for Clem swelled, and her resolve to stand firm weakened. "Of course, there could be, if you weren't so – "

"So what?"

"So stubborn. And so against me trying to be friends with you."

"I told you, Jessica, that's not for us. Just leave it alone."

"But why? You could at least give me a reason. Is something wrong with me? Do you and Mrs. Fletcher think I'm chasing all the boys, passing out my photograph?"

He opened his mouth to say something, but remained quiet, looking past her.

She took a sharp intake of breath. "So that's it!"

Clem threw the wrench down and took a step towards her. "Sometimes a fella just needs to be alone. Can't you understand?"

"No! I don't see why we – "

"Leave me alone, Jessica. I'm all messed up."

She took a step forward, pained by his words. "Can't I help?"

"You don't know anything! And I don't want your pity!"

He whipped around and slammed the door behind him.

"That's not what I'm offering!" she yelled at the door. She waited a moment, and then ran down the steps and crossed the yard. "Oh, why did I come?"

"Miss Jessica!"

She turned around and saw Donny running after her.

He glanced behind him to make sure they were alone. "Clem didn't mean that."

"He despises me!" She sniffed and took a hankie from her pocket. "He thinks I'm flighty."

"Nah, that's not it. He's just – I don't know what it is. But I know he likes you."

"Hardly!" Then she softened. "Thank you, Donny. I know you're just trying to be nice."

They walked quietly to the end of the street.

Donny stopped, uncertain about proceeding. "I know it's none of my business – "

"What? What is it? I can't figure him out. One moment he's nice and the next… Has he said something?"

"No. Nothing." Donny appeared uncomfortable, as if unsure about speaking. "But all he does is look at that picture of you. That's the only time he smiles. Honestly."

Jessica's mouth opened and then closed. "I don't believe it!"

"It's true, all right. He doesn't know that I know, but he keeps your picture under his pillow. Then carries it around in his pocket. Just this morning I saw him looking at it. He put it away real quick and I pretended not to see it."

She stood with her eyebrows creased.

Donny shrugged, as if he didn't know what it all meant either. "Well, I better go."

"Thank you, Donny," Jessica called after him, as he ran back up the street.

Jessica walked slowly back to the town square, more confused than ever about Clem.

Christmastime 1945

Chapter 15

֍

When Tommy came home from school, Lillian made a quick trip to the corner grocery store to pick up a few items for her dinner with Izzy that night. She was delighted that Mrs. Mancetti had the cheese and olives in stock that Izzy so loved.

Lillian hurried home with her bag of groceries. She and the boys were looking forward to seeing Izzy. And thank goodness, Tommy was in a much better frame of mind, now that Amy would be finishing up the school year here. Mrs. Little had convinced her husband that it was to Amy's benefit to do so. Tommy and Amy were already making plans for Tommy's first visit to her over the summer.

When Lillian opened the door, she saw Tommy sitting on the couch with his schoolbooks. He jumped up to take the bag of groceries. "Getting your homework done?" Lillian asked, taking off her coat and hat.

Tommy frowned. "French. The project with Amy was fun, but this grammar is hard." He brought the groceries to the kitchen.

Lillian peeked over at Charlotte. Still sound asleep. Then she turned, surprised to see Gabriel at the kitchen table, doing his school work.

"Gabriel! I thought you were at Scouts."

"It was canceled for tonight. So, I'm getting started on my math homework."

"Oh, what a shame! There was a young man outside, asking for you. A soldier – Army Air Forces. I told him you would be home in a few hours." Lillian began to take out the groceries and set them on the counter. "I invited him to wait but he said he had a train to catch."

Gabriel searched his mind. "The only soldiers I know have already gone home for Christmas or are still stuck in the hospital."

"Maybe he had the wrong address," said Tommy.

Gabriel gave it some thought. "Did he tell you his name?"

Lillian set the vegetables near the sink to rinse. "What was it? Staff sergeant – Hmm. Devlon? No, that wasn't it." She took out two boxes of pasta. "What do you think – lasagna or spaghetti Bolognese tonight?"

"Lasagna," both boys answered.

Gabriel focused on his geometry lesson, positioning his protractor to calculate the degrees of various angles.

"A handsome young man, friendly and courteous," Lillian continued, as she put away the rest of the items. "Though awfully young-looking to be a staff sergeant. Oh, look at these olives! Mrs. Mancetti just got them in." She took out a colander and began rinsing the vegetables. "What was his name. Damion? No." Then she held up her finger. "Demain! That was it. Staff Sergeant Demain."

"Sounds like French for *tomorrow*," said Tommy.

Gabriel's head snapped up – and he exploded out of his chair. "Tiny!" He ran to the window, shoved it open, and stuck his head out looking left and right. In the distance he saw a man in uniform. "TINY!" he hollered. The figure spun around, took off his cap and waved it high. Gabriel flew out of the apartment, crying, "It's Tiny!"

Tommy's mouth dropped open. "Tiny Tomorrow?"

Lillian looked at Tommy with wide eyes. "Could it be?"

Tommy ran to the open window and leaned out. He saw Gabriel run up to the soldier. "I don't believe it!"

Lillian also leaned out, clutching the carrots. "After all these years!"

"Tiny!" Gabriel cried, running up and almost knocking him over in a hug. "Tiny! Is it really you?" He leaned back to look at his old friend. "I can't believe it!"

Tiny was now a good head taller than Gabriel and had filled out considerably. He laughed. "No one has called me Tiny since I left here."

"No wonder – look at you! Army Air Forces!"

"I became a tail gunner, just like I said I would."

"I didn't think you'd be old enough to get in."

"Well, that's the thing, Gabriel." Tiny pushed his cap back and tilted his head to one side, and for a moment, Gabriel caught a glimpse of the scrawny boy he had met in the park four years ago foraging for firewood. "The orphanage never knew the exact date of my birth." He broke out into a smile. "So, I made one up that allowed me to enlist! One of the advantages of being an orphan."

"Holy Toledo! You gotta come back and tell me everything! Jeez, I was afraid I'd never hear from you again."

"I'd love to Gabriel. And I want to visit Father Dwyer. I stopped by but he wasn't there. I left a note for him saying I'd be back. And I want to see Mrs. Mancetti." He glanced at his military watch. "But I have to catch a train. To Wisconsin," he added with a wide smile, just begging to be explained.

"Wisconsin? Who the heck lives there?"

"My wife," Tiny said with a proud grin. "Molly."

"Your wife? You're married?" Gabriel smacked his head in disbelief.

Tiny nodded. "I met Molly outside of the air-base. She was a WASP – she can fly! I'm going to meet her family in Wisconsin for Christmas. Then we're coming back to visit. I want you to meet her."

"I have to! We'll have a celebration dinner for you! And we'll go to Mancetti's and see if they recognize you. When will you be back this way?"

"End of next month. What about you, Gabriel? What's new with you?"

"I got a baby sister! Charlotte. I wish you could see her."

"A sister!" Tiny leaned his head to one side. "I never had a sister. I counted myself lucky to have a brother." A hint of sorrow filled his eyes. "You remember him, don't you Gabriel?"

"Marcel? Sure, I do. I'll never forget him. He was a good older brother to you. He'd be proud as heck to see you like this."

"I think he would." Gabriel's response had righted things for Tiny, and his grin returned. "A brother and a sister! Count yourself lucky, Gabriel. And your father? He's all right?"

"All right and on his way. He telegraphed from London. He's coming home!"

"I've often thought about him. I'll never forget how he helped me. Didn't know me from Adam, and he emptied his wallet for me, tried to get me to stay."

"He'll be so happy to see you, to know that you made it. They'll all want to see you! Sure you can't stop by?"

"I can't miss my train. The snowstorms are even worse in the Midwest. Causing all kind of havoc. I don't dare miss the chance to be with my wife for Christmas. But I'll be back next month. Then we'll catch up. I promise."

Gabriel gave him a big squeeze. "It was sure good seeing you, Tiny. What a Christmas present!"

"For me, too. Well, better run. I'll see you soon, Gabriel. Merry Christmas!"

"Merry Christmas, Tiny!" Gabriel stood in his stocking feet, smiling from ear to ear, as he waved goodbye to his old friend.

*

"Tiny Tomorrow!" Izzy mused, as Gabriel recounted his surprise meeting over dinner. "I remember hearing all about him. You thought he was an imaginary friend of Gabriel's."

"I did," said Lillian, laughing at the memory. "I was never so surprised in all my life. And now I'll finally get to meet him. And his wife!"

Tommy had listened, deep in thought. "He's the most mysterious person I ever met. Just when I was busting Gabriel's chops about making up stories, the police came – remember? Spider threw a rock through Mancetti's window? And I saw this skinny boy looking scared to death. Mr. Mancetti blamed him and tried to grab him by the collar, but he wriggled free and fled – fast as lighting. Gabriel cried – 'Run, Tiny!' And that's when I knew he was a real person." Tommy shook his head. "I'll never forget it. Not as long as I live."

Lillian leaned over and squeezed Gabriel's arm. "I'm so happy he's alive and well – and married! Oh, I can't wait to tell Charles!"

Izzy had insisted on holding Charlotte when she began to cry, but now Charlotte was fast asleep. Lillian gently took her and carried her to the bassinette.

"My goodness, but the years go by quickly," Izzy said. "It seems like yesterday that I first heard about Tiny." Izzy said yes to another serving of lasagna and looked over at Tommy and Gabriel. "And both of you with jobs now! I knew Tommy was working at Mancetti's – but now you at The Red String Curio Store?"

Gabriel smiled proudly. "At first Mom didn't want me to work, but now she says it's okay, since I'm learning so much."

"What are you learning?" Izzy asked. "How to make sales? How to count change?"

"No. Mr. G does that. I help people find things."

"I bet you're good at it. Mr. G," said Izzy. "What does the *G* stand for?"

"I asked him that question myself. He said I could take my pick. His name is Gilbert Gossett Gillingham. He said his mother was fond of alliteration."

Izzy exchanged a look of amusement with Lillian. "So, besides helping people find things, what else are you learning?"

"Poetry, for one thing. Junior is always reading poetry to us and we help him decide which frames to put them in. Then Mr. G sells them, and they split the profit."

Gabriel bit into a breadstick. "And Mr. G has a lot of maps and globes and books around the shop. He has one of those big dictionaries and sometimes he'll say: 'Master Gabriel, how about a word?' Or, 'Mr. H, would you do us the honor?'"

Everything Gabriel related caused Izzy to chuckle. "And who's Mr. H?"

"That's Henry."

"So, Henry visits the shop?" Izzy asked, taking a sip of wine.

Gabriel nodded. "He likes to talk with Mr. G. And he plays checkers with Dusty. Dusty used to be an archeology professor. He's an Egyptologist."

Izzy looked up in surprise. "Does The Red String sell artifacts?"

"No. Well, there could be some things in all those shelves. Dusty's wife and Mr. G's wife used to be friends."

Lillian raised her head. "There's a Mrs. G?"

Gabriel helped himself to more lasagna. "There was. Before she died. That was a long time ago. She was a painter. Her name was Violet, and she loved violets. All around the shop are paintings of little purple flowers, some of them by her – but most of them are not for sale. There's a little glass vase on the counter and when Mr. G can find them, he buys fresh violets for it."

Izzy placed her hand on her heart. "How touching."

Tommy was paying attention to Gabriel's descriptions and had to agree. "It is kind of interesting there. Lots of different people come in. Besides shoppers, there are collectors. And theater people, looking for stuff for stage sets."

Gabriel nodded. "Mr. G said an umbrella stand from his shop made it to Broadway recently. Front and center."

"It all sounds very intriguing," said Izzy, eyeing Gabriel with curiosity.

Lillian wore a skeptical expression, still unsure whether the curio shop was a wholesome environment for Gabriel. She was beginning to believe that it was, but still had some reservations.

"And sometimes, if it's quiet, we just talk about things."

Izzy was genuinely curious. "What do you two talk about? The shop?"

"Yes. And if there's something I don't know, I ask him about it. He usually knows the answer. Like cockles."

Izzy raised her eyebrows.

"He explained that 'warms the cockles of my heart' doesn't mean clams. It comes from Latin for heart. And yesterday I asked him why people say a quarter past the hour and a quarter to – but they only say half past, not half to. That kind of stuff."

Izzy pressed her lips together to keep from smiling.

"Dusty, Junior, Henry, Mr. G. They talk about everything," added Tommy. "The weather, the source of the Nile, who the best playwrights are, the Civil War, which countries make the best chocolate…"

"All sorts of things," Gabriel said. He spread his hand, as if offering choices. "Whether or not there are angels, death – "

"Death?" said Lillian, sitting up in her chair. She looked at Izzy with a helpless expression that said, *You see what I mean?*

Gabriel nodded and finished chewing his food. "Junior says death is a good deal."

"A good deal?" Izzy asked.

"Yeah – he said you don't have to do anything. You can forget about your doctors telling you to do this, do that. You can just lie there and sleep. No pain at all. Says his old hands and knees will finally get some peace. He's looking forward to it," Gabriel said cheerfully, and took a swig of milk.

Izzy leaned her head, slightly concerned. "But – won't he miss life?"

Gabriel shook his head. "He'll be too busy. He said his spirit will be roaming the universe. Finally getting some answers to a whole lot of questions."

"An interesting point of view," Lillian said, looking at Izzy.

Izzy resumed eating, greatly amused by everything Gabriel recounted. "I must say, it sounds like quite an interesting place. I'll have to stop by."

Gabriel's head popped up. "That'd be swell! You'll fit right in!"

Izzy looked over at Lillian, and they both burst into laughter.

Over dessert, the conversation shifted to Tommy. Izzy listened with interest as he talked about his work at Mancetti's, his time at the veterans' hospital, and his relief that Amy wouldn't be moving back to Ohio until after the school year.

Izzy regarded Tommy with tenderness. "I'm so happy to hear that she'll be here until the summer."

"Me too," said Tommy.

"So am I!" Gabriel added, bringing his plate to the sink.

"I'll clean up later, boys. You can get ready for bed."

While they said their goodnights to Izzy, Lillian checked on Charlotte. Then she poured Izzy a glass of sherry, fixed a cup of tea for herself, and set them on the coffee table.

"Tiny, Mr. G, Mr. H!" Izzy said with a laugh. "An Egyptologist, a poet? I must say, it's a colorful world that Gabriel inhabits."

Lillian turned on the radio and soft music filled the apartment. "He's always been that way. I don't know if I should be concerned or not. At first, I worried about the eccentricity of the place, the people. But he's so happy."

"There's no denying he's getting quite an education," added Izzy. "Of sorts." She leaned back and looked out at the lit Christmas tree, the Victorian holiday cards on the mantel, the bunches of holly placed around the room. "You have a lovely life, Lilly. Beautiful children, a loving husband, you're working as an artist. A life brimming with beauty and love. You must be so happy."

"I am. Sometimes I pinch myself to make sure it's all real. When Charles finally returns home, then I'll believe it."

Words from the radio announcer caught their attention. "*We now continue our tribute to Mr. Glenn Miller, marking the one-year anniversary of the disappearance of his plane over the English Channel...*"

Izzy let out a deep sigh. "What a loss!"

Lillian listened to the melodic strains and nodded. "So much has been lost with the war."

Izzy's shoulders moved to the rhythm, and she gave a wistful smile. "My God, how we loved to dance to Glenn Miller."

Lillian had been observing Izzy. All night, she could see that something was on her mind. In between her laughter and conversations, a shadow would fill her eyes. Sadness? Regret?

Izzy let out a sigh and sipped her sherry. "It's funny how you can be so sure of something, only to discover that you're mistaken. Hearing about Tiny reminds me of this time last year, right here. Do you remember?"

"I certainly do." Lillian recalled the exact moment when Charles, assuming Izzy already knew, casually mentioned that Red's marriage to his nurse had lasted only a month or so.

"I was stunned," said Izzy. "I had been living with a false idea for so long, that it really spun my head around. It took me quite some time to adjust to that new reality."

Lillian took a sip of her tea. "I was stunned, too. I can only imagine how profoundly it must have affected you."

They sat quietly, both of them staring at the lights on the Christmas tree, lost in their own thoughts. Then Izzy gently spoke. "I heard back from Red."

Lillian set her cup down. "He answered your letter?"

Izzy slowly nodded.

Lillian sat expectantly, unable to decide if it was good news or bad.

"He said he'll be working at the veterans' hospital through the holidays and would most likely stay in London for months, if not years."

"I see." She realized that Izzy had hoped Red was coming home. "Did he – answer your question?"

"Whether he loved her?" Izzy leaned back and nodded. "He said love never came into it. He said they were two drowning people grasping at each other in order not to sink into darkness. Locked in a sort of struggle – and when it was over, the marriage was also over." Izzy took a sip of sherry. "She reconnected with a childhood sweetheart and married him. Red said he was happy for her."

Izzy sat silently, then pulled out his letter from her handbag and read:

As far as love, I will say this only once
and then no more. I have loved only you.
That has never changed. I don't expect forgiveness.
I'm only telling you because you asked.
I will always want the best for you, Izzy, and
I hope that one day you will find love again.

She folded the letter and held onto it.

"Oh, Izzy. You two have never stopped loving one another. What will you do?"

"I don't know." She put the letter away and took another sip of sherry. "Wait for him to return and then see."

"But what if he doesn't return home for years?"

Izzy turned to Lillian. "The thing is, I don't feel that I'll really know what to do until I see his face. If I could see him, look him in the eye and see what's there, then I would know. I would know what to do." Izzy twisted her glass around in her hand.

Lillian smiled gently. "Then there's only one thing for you to do."

Chapter 16

～

The farmhouse kitchen grew festive as Kate and the girls worked on their Christmas baking. Jessica and Ed had gone out earlier to cut pine boughs, and now the greenery framed the kitchen doorway, emitting a fresh woodland scent. And Kate had placed the embroidered Christmas runner on the kitchen table, along with a vase of holly that Ursula had gathered on her walk.

Frankie sat in his high chair banging a spoon while Ursula fed him mashed yams. Kate opened the oven door and took out a batch of Christmas cookies. She set them on the counter to cool, and added another batch to the oven.

"We haven't made fudge since 1942 – imagine that!" said Jessica. She had set out the ingredients for fudge and was now checking them against the recipe card.

"We didn't make a lot of things with the rationing. Well, this year will be different," said Kate, chopping walnuts for the fudge. "I do hope we hear from Jimmy and Paul soon. They so enjoy Christmas and all the holiday foods."

Jessica eyed the warm, fragrant cookies. "Eugene!" she cried. "The cookies are done. Come taste them." She waited a moment, and not getting a response, hollered again. "Eugene, the cookies – "

"I heard you the first time. I'm not deaf!" He sat at the dining room table reading up on the GI Bill.

Jessica rolled her eyes and lifted down the vanilla bottle.

"There's the mail truck," said Ursula, glancing out the window.

Assuming Eugene would want to know the mail had arrived, Jessica called out into the dining room. "Eugene, the mail truck just left – "

"Why do you have to yell everything? God dang, it's enough to give anyone a headache."

Jessica opened her mouth and put her hand on her hip as she watched him go upstairs. His door closed with a bang.

"I thought I was doing him a favor by letting him know."

"Leave him be," said Kate. Eugene's spirits had been high for a few days, but he had slowly sunk back into sullenness.

Ursula looked from Jessica to Kate. "This is the first day he hasn't wanted to check the mail."

Kate leaned against the counter with a worried look in her eye. "Why don't you go and bring in the mail, Jessica."

Jessica frowned as she pulled on her boots and jacket. "He thinks he's the only one with any heartache. If he would just look around he'd see it everywhere. It's still no excuse to yell at people who are just trying to help."

She kicked at the snow as she walked down the lane. At the end, she checked the mailbox, and gathered a handful of cards and letters. Ed came down the road and pulled up next to her. "Ride?"

"Sure!" Jessica stepped up on the running board and enjoyed the lift to the house.

"Thanks, Ed." She hopped off and stood by his window. "Come on inside. Mom and Ursula just baked cookies and we're starting on the fudge."

"Thanks, but I was just heading to the Bloomfield's when I saw you. Thought you'd like a lift. But save Opal a piece of that fudge. She loves nothin' better."

"A piece? We'll put at least two rolls in your Christmas basket!"

Jessica ran up the porch stairs and went inside. After slipping off her coat and boots, she went into the kitchen and inhaled deeply. "Smells heavenly!" She reached for a cookie and began sifting through the mail – then she let out a gasp.

Kate and Ursula looked up. Jessica brought the letter in her hand closer, reading the address again.

"What?" asked Ursula.

Jessica opened her eyes wide.

Kate had been lifting the cookies off the cookie sheet with a spatula and setting them on a platter. "Don't keep us guessing! What is it?"

Jessica showed them the letter. The return address was from Iowa. It read simply *The Kinnan Farm, Route 4.*

They all looked from one to another.

"Maybe it's the letter he's been waiting for," Ursula said.

Kate's brow furrowed. "Or it could be bad news from her family."

They ran various scenarios through their minds, fearful of what the letter might contain.

"Go and give it to him," said Kate. "And don't say anything. Do you hear? Just give him the letter and come back down."

Jessica ran up the stairs and stopped abruptly outside Eugene's door. She was suddenly filled with dread. She didn't want anything to hurt her brother. She looked down at the letter, and then raised her hand and gently rapped on the door. When she knocked a second time, the door whipped open. Jessica saw that Eugene was trying to appear annoyed, but his eyes were red. She handed him the letter.

His expression changed to alertness as he read the address. He snatched the letter and shut the door.

Jessica waited outside, wringing her hands. She heard the rustle of paper, the letter being read. She quietly went downstairs, stopping once to look up at his door, then continued into the kitchen. Kate and Ursula waited expectantly. She gave a small shrug and looked back towards the stairs.

Kate began pacing the kitchen, still holding the spatula. Ursula sat down. Then stood. The longer the silence, the more worried they became. Jessica put her hand to her mouth. "He seemed so sad," she said, her voice quivering.

Only Frankie's babbling broke the utter silence that now filled the room.

Suddenly, Eugene's door flew open. "Mom!" he cried, running down the stairs and into the kitchen.

They all jumped to attention. Eugene was smiling widely, though his cheeks were shining with tears.

"Mom! It's from Edna! She's alive! Thank God, she's fine. She made it home!" He squeezed Kate and lifted her off her feet.

"I'm so happy, Eugene! What does she say?"

He held the letter out, searching for certain lines. "It took her a while to get home. There were delays...storms at sea..." He smiled up at Kate. "She hopes I haven't forgotten about her. *Not a day goes by without my thinking of you. Now I'm hoping against hope that the local girls haven't snatched you up.*" Eugene laughed at the absurdity of that remark. "*Please write – or better yet, call me, if you can get through.*" He looked up, beaming. "She wants to see me. She wants me to call her!"

Jessica gave him a shove. "Well, what are you waiting for? Call her!" They followed him to the telephone in the hallway. He picked up the receiver and placed his call, clearing his throat as he waited for an answer. After several more attempts, the call finally went through. He choked up on hearing Edna's voice.

Kate and Ursula went back into the kitchen, pulling Jessica along with them.

Eugene was overcome with pent-up emotion and he dropped onto the hall bench. "Edna." His voice cracked. "I just got your letter. I was so afraid something happened to you." He broke down, giving into the months of desperate worry. Then after static and fragmented words and talking over one another, his tone grew happier and happier.

Kate peeked around the corner at him, and paced the kitchen again, this time in joy. She lifted her apron to dab her eyes. She had never seen Eugene so happy – he was in love! Some of the things they heard him say caused them to gape at one another in astonishment.

"You could be here for Christmas! With me – with us. I can show you the farm. My brothers aren't home yet, but my sisters are here, and Mom. And Frankie – oh, you'll love him. He makes you happy just to look at him." Eugene listened and nodded. "Me too, Edna. Every single day…" He jumped to his feet. "Sure, I can! That's less than a week! I waited this long, I can wait another week. Sure. Just let me know. I can be there anytime, just say when." Then he lowered his voice. "I love you, too. With all my heart."

Eugene came into the kitchen, wiping at his face and smiling. "You're all going to meet her!" He turned quickly to Kate. "That's all right, isn't it Mom? I invited her to come for Christmas."

"Of course, it's all right! I couldn't be happier." She squeezed Eugene tight.

"Her brother's driving some fella home for Christmas to Davenport, so she can catch a ride that far. I told her I can meet her there and bring her here for a visit. She wants to meet you all. And I'll meet her family when I take her back." He sank into a chair, and for a moment appeared stunned. "I can't believe it – after so long not knowing…"

Jessica pulled out the chair next to him and sat on the edge. "I can't wait to meet her. What's she like?"

"You'll like her, Jess. You, too, Ursula. You'll all love her. You won't be able to help yourselves." Frankie was banging on his tray again. Ursula started to quiet him, but Eugene jumped up and lifted Frankie. "Especially you!" He walked around the kitchen, bouncing Frankie into laughter. "I've been waiting for so long to hear if she's all right. And now, she'll be here in a week!" He faced Jessica and Ursula. "Let's go to town! Come on, Mom. I need you to help me buy her something."

"I can't leave in the middle of baking. You kids go."

"I'll go!" Jessica jumped up. "I'll just change and be right back down."

Eugene turned to Ursula. "How about it, Ursula? Come with us."

"Thanks, Eugene. But I need to feed Frankie and put him down for a nap." She took Frankie from him and smiled. "I'm really happy for you."

Eugene draped his arm around Kate's shoulder. "Edna said on the train back from New York, all she thought about was sitting on the porch with me at night. I had told her how peaceful it was."

"That'll have to wait until spring. Oh, I'm so happy for you, son. It will be good to have her here. I wish your brothers would be able to meet her. I don't know why they haven't gotten word to me. Either of them."

"Now you're sounding like me, fretting over nothing. My letter came through, didn't it? Be patient, Mom."

"You're right. Oh, I'm so happy. A week! I'll have to get the house in order."

Jessica was soon back in the kitchen. "Let's go, Romeo," she cried, pulling on her coat and dashing out the door.

Eugene grabbed his flight jacket and started to follow Jessica outside – but then he went back into the kitchen and hugged Kate in happiness. He briefly put his arm around Ursula as he gave Frankie a quick tickle goodbye. "Edna loves kids. She won't be able to leave you alone."

The gratitude Kate saw in Ursula's eyes was almost painful to witness. She followed Eugene to the door and waved goodbye.

On the drive into town, Eugene talked about how he would show Edna the farm and the town, and how he would take her to the Christmas dance, and bring her to the Bloomfield's party. Only once did he show disappointment. "I wish Ursula would've come with us."

"Why would she do that when you've been such a bear to her?"

"I know, I know. I've been hard on her." Eugene's face darkened with guilt. "It took me a while to – to get used to the idea of her married to a – German."

"His name is Friedrich."

"Friedrich. And I still think it's wrong. Dead wrong. But I don't like to see her looking so worried. To be honest, I hoped it was all a mistake and that she would come to her senses. But it's obvious they belong together."

Jessica threw her hands up and let them fall on her lap. "Well, about time! So now that you're happy, you're all right with other people being happy."

"That's not it, Jess. I was angry. Angry at the kind of life she's going to have. Angry that Germans were on our farm! Angry – angry at everything."

"Ursula needs all the help she can get, especially from her family."

"I know. Mom and I talked about it. Figuring out how to get him back here."

Jessica's head snapped up and she was about to speak but Eugene cut her off.

"And that was *before* I got Edna's letter, so don't say anything."

After several minutes Eugene became aware of Jessica's silence. "This is the longest you've gone without talking since I got home. What's eating you?"

"You can talk."

"I had good reason for being upset. I thought the love of my life was gone."

Jessica turned and studied Eugene's expression. "She must be something special."

"She is. I never thought I'd find someone like her. That just goes to show you, Jess, you can never give up."

"You sure have a lot of wisdom now that things are going your way."

Eugene laughed out loud and began humming under his breath, tapping his fingers in rhythm on the steering wheel.

Jessica stared out the window, deep in thought. "Did you know Clem was injured?"

"I heard he was. Why?"

"I was just wondering what happened. Do you know?"

Eugene shook his head. "No. But he saw some awful fighting." He glanced over at Jessica, wondering what was on her mind. "Clem's a good guy."

"I know he is! Why does everyone have to speak to me like that about him? Like I'm going to hurt him."

"I didn't say that." He shifted gears as they came into town and looked over at Jessica. "He's a good six or seven years older than you, Jess."

Her face tightened at the remark. "Dad was twelve years older than Mom."

"Are you going to see him? Is he expecting you?"

"No. But I've got something to say to him."

"Well, go easy on him."

Jessica threw him another look of outrage, and Eugene put up his hands, laughing. "All right, all right. Clem can fight his own battles." He pulled into the town square and parked the truck. "Come on, you gotta help me. I want to get her something special."

Jessica jumped out of the truck. "Well, let's start at Arnold's. They have some real pretty dresses and cardigans in for the holidays."

Eugene stopped. "I was thinking of something else."

Jessica lead the way, calling over her shoulder, "Like what?"

"Like a ring."

Jessica spun around. "Are you serious?"

"She's the girl for me. No doubt about it."

"Hmm, I think you know her a lot better than you let on. Well let's go into the jewelry store and see what they have."

A half hour later, they walked out, Eugene all smiles. "It's perfect. I know it is. C'mon. Let's go look at Arnold's. I want her to have some presents to unwrap. This," he said, tucking the small package into his coat pocket, "will be a surprise."

Just as Eugene opened the door to Arnold's, Jessica spotted Clem across the way.

"Clem!" she called out to him.

"Jeez, you sure are one for hollering." Eugene shook his head and stepped inside the store.

Clem saw her, and began walking in the other direction.

"Clem!" Jessica called out again and crossed the street. She caught up with him and stood in front of him. "You can ignore me all you want, Clem, but I've got something to say to you!"

He looked around and let out a moan at what was coming.

"Are you listening?"

"I know what you're going to say, Jessica, and you've got every right to tell me what a heel I am. And you're right. You deserve a hell of a lot better, and you're just wasting your time on me. I tried to tell you that before, but you wouldn't listen. Maybe now you know and – "

Jessica raised her eyes to the sky. "Are you finished?"

He dropped his hands to his side and looked her in the eye.

Jessica knew that she would always remember this moment. A few tiny snowflakes drifted from the sky. The air was sharp and clean. She should have felt cold, yet she was filled with warmth as she looked at Clem. His green flannel shirt showed under his jacket, making his eyes even greener. He was trying so hard to keep a distance, to chase her away. Yet everything he did, every word he spoke, drew her closer.

"Go ahead," he said. "I'm listening."

She took a step towards him, held his face between her hands, and kissed him on the mouth. "I'm going to marry you, Clem Corrigan. And I don't care how long it takes."

Taken aback, he watched her turn around, cross the street, and go directly into Arnold's, without once looking back at him. The protective wall around his heart had been smashed with a deft touch – soft as a whisper, with all the force of a gale.

Now, only the truth would serve.

*

The lowering sun turned the snowy world outside into a golden and rosy landscape. Ursula stood at the living room window with Frankie on her hip, hoping for a glimpse of Friedrich. Mr. Creight had taken him and Gustav in the morning to the Bloomfield farm to help finish with the old shed they were tearing down. They now came back at end of day to return the tools.

Eugene saw Ursula stationed at the window and shook his head. He walked into the kitchen and stood next to Kate at the stove. Jessica was setting the table. "When the hell is Otto coming back?"

"Any day," said Kate.

Eugene huffed in exasperation and leaned in to whisper. "She waits for Friedrich all day, every day, just for a word or a glimpse of him. That damned Creight is always in the way."

Kate raised her eyebrows in disbelief.

"I know, I know. I haven't been much better."

"Well, I'm glad you've come to your senses because I've fixed my mind. The next time Friedrich and Gustav are here for the day, I'm cooking them an early Christmas dinner. And we'll all eat together at the dining room table."

Eugene went to the window and saw Ed and Mr. Creight talking outside the machine shed, while Friedrich and Gustav cleaned the tools.

Kate added a chunk of butter to the pan of corn. "I've already decided that I'm going to bake them a – "

"This is all wrong!" Eugene said, grabbing his jacket. He stormed out the door and stood on the porch.

Kate was taken by surprise at his sudden action and followed him.

"Friedrich!" Eugene called out.

His angry tone caused the men to look up.

"Over here! We need you inside." Eugene looked straight at Creight, daring him to interfere.

Creight simply nodded at Friedrich to go ahead, and continued his conversation with Ed.

Friedrich set down the tools. It was the first time Eugene had ever called him by name. As he walked up the steps, he tried to read the expression on Eugene's face.

"Go on inside," Eugene said gently, gesturing to the door that Kate held open. Then he walked out to Gustav and gave him a hand with the tools.

Ursula had seen the exchange from the window and stood rigid, unsure what Eugene had in mind. But when Kate showed Friedrich into the living room, she flooded with joy.

Kate left them alone and went back to the kitchen.

Friedrich embraced Ursula and Frankie. He held his son close and kissed Ursula, wrapping his arm around her. They sat on the couch, and with Frankie on his lap, they leaned into a tender embrace.

"It's been so long since I've held you, Friedrich." They clung to each other tightly, as if afraid to let go.

He put her hair behind her ear and touched her amethyst earrings. His eyes filled with sadness. "I promised I would give you a ring to match."

"And you will! Don't speak like that." She pulled back a little, alarmed at the tone of resignation in his voice.

"Ursula. These few minutes are a gift from your brother. We may not have another chance to say our goodbye."

"Our *goodbye*?" Ursula sat back, her eyes filled with fear. "Do you know something? Did they tell you something?"

"No. But I don't think I will be here much longer. I think – "

Ursula stopped his words with a kiss. "The camp needs you. They're using you more and more. And now it's almost Christmas. Nothing will happen anytime soon. You'll most likely be here until all the POWs have – "

"They're closing the branch camps. It's just a matter of time before – "

"But yours is still open. Surely – "

"Ursula, please listen!"

The edge of anger silenced her. She leaned back and angled her head warily, afraid of what he was going to say.

Frankie had climbed off his lap to play with one of his toys. Friedrich clasped Ursula's hands.

"Our time is short. We must be prepared."

"But the camp needs you. There's still so much work to do. We need you on the farm." Her words sounded flat, even to her ears.

"We must speak about your future. I've tried many times to discuss this with you and you never want to talk about it."

"*Our* future!" Ursula's breathing quickened. "And we've already discussed it, Friedrich. As soon as you're repatriated we'll work on getting you back here. But that's many months away."

Friedrich studied Ursula's face – her eyes darted around as if seeking escape. He couldn't add to her misery.

He lifted Frankie and spoke cheerfully as he walked around with him. "If I have to leave, you be a good boy for your mother. And when I come back, I'll teach you how to build things. And we'll go fishing and hiking." Friedrich smiled to Ursula, then lifted Frankie high above his head. "Would you like that?"

Ursula rose to her feet. "Stop it! I know what you're doing! You don't think you'll survive, and you want me to remember you like this. You will survive! Do you hear me? You will be strong, and resolute, and you will never give up. You must, Friedrich!" She embraced him, her heart pounding wildly.

He put his arm around her. "My Ursula. I will do everything you say. But we must be realistic.

Anything could happen. You mustn't wait for me if – if…"

Ursula pushed him away, her eyes afire. "I won't wait for you! I'll go and find you myself. I will! I'll bring you home – " Her voice broke, and she turned her back to him.

He saw that Mr. Creight had started his truck, ready to go. Friedrich cradled Frankie's head on his shoulder and rocked him. In his ear, he whispered that he loved him, and handed him to Ursula.

"I must go." He smiled sadly at the anger that glittered in her deep blue eyes. His hands framed her face. "My beautiful Ursula. My wife." He kissed her and quickly left.

Ursula's body shook with suppressed anger and fear. She went upstairs with Frankie and stood in her bedroom window. As the truck took Friedrich away, she wept freely, releasing her grief in low moans. She lay down with Frankie, and curled around him, sobbing.

Kate checked on her several times. When she brought up a tray of supper to her, she found her at the window again, staring out into the darkness. Frankie was asleep in his crib.

She put her arm around Ursula's shoulder. "Come eat something." She guided her to the chair next to her bed.

Ursula sat and spoke calmly. "I argued with Friedrich. For the first time. I was furious with him. He spoke as if he might not survive."

Kate stroked Ursula's hair. "He knows how afraid you are. He understands you're not angry at him."

Ursula looked up with haunted eyes. "I'm so afraid. I won't be there to protect him. I won't even know what's happening to him." Ursula pressed her hands to her face. "He wanted to talk about it and I refused. He needed to talk and I – I just couldn't."

Kate sat on the bed and took Ursula's hand. "You have to be strong. He needs to know that you'll be fine. That's the only gift that you can give him."

Ursula wiped away her tears.

"Write him a letter. Tell him how you feel. He'll take those words with him."

Ursula slowly nodded and the grief finally lessened in her face.

"We'll hope for the best," said Kate. "We'll hope that he'll still be here into the spring. I've been looking into sponsorship for him. And I've written to Charles to see if there's anything he can do when he returns home. Have hope, Ursula. And stay strong for him and Frankie."

Ursula straightened and raised her chin. "I will." She squeezed her mother's hand.

Kate rose to her feet. "That's my girl. I've never known you to be weak. Now eat your dinner. And then write your letter. And we're going to make a nice Christmas dinner for him and Gustav. I'll arrange it with Otto. We'll turn on the Christmas tree lights and give them a meal to remember. How about that?"

Ursula took a deep breath and blew out the last of her sadness. "Yes. We'll give them a real Christmas dinner. I'll show him how strong I can be."

Kate did her best to sound cheerful. "We have a lot to be thankful for this Christmas. The war is over. Eugene is home and in love! We'll be meeting Edna soon. And Jimmy and Paul should both be stateside by now. It will be our first Christmas as a family in a long time. And then we'll start preparing for Jimmy and Gladys's wedding in January!"

A tentative smile came to Ursula's lips, though her words were full of sorrow. "It will be a wonderful Christmas."

Kate's smile slowly deepened. "And you and I will be there for each other. We're strong, you and I, and we can bear a lot." Kate turned at the door and looked back, her heart melting at the sad loveliness of her daughter.

Ursula took out pen and paper to write her letter. She checked on Frankie and smiled down at him. "Your papa will come back." She leaned over and kissed their sleeping baby. "And we will be here waiting for him."

Chapter 17

∽

Lillian walked home from her meeting with Mrs. Huntington brimming with happiness. Rather, she expected to be brimming with happiness and waited for the surge to hit her. After all, the five-book adventure series, covers and illustrations, was hers. She couldn't wait to step into the world described in the books – adventure, mystery, fantasy – all from the perspective of a young boy. It would be months of living in and exploring a world of wonder.

She looked around her, trying to coax the happiness into being. Christmas was everywhere, happiness was everywhere, and Charles would be home soon. Wouldn't he? She tried to ignore the dread growing inside her.

Something was not right. She should have heard from him by now. He was in London where he could send a letter or a telegram. What had happened to him? Why wasn't he contacting her? Was he ill again and didn't want to worry her? She had sent a Christmas card to Red and hoped to hear back from him soon. Maybe he could shed some light –

So deep in thought was she, that as she rounded the corner of her block, she stumbled into a mother and her two children.

"I'm so sorry. I wasn't looking."

Lillian lifted her head, determined not to entertain any dark thoughts. She was sure to hear from Charles any day. Instead, she imagined him coming home from work and greeting him with an embrace. Dinner would be ready, she would have spent all day on her drawings, and could look forward to a relaxing evening together. Or perhaps they would go out to dinner, or all go out as a family to –

She came to a halt. There was Gabriel, with Billy, coming up from the basement stairs of the brownstone where Mrs. Kuntzman lived – and there was an unmistakable furtive manner to their behavior.

Lillian crossed the street. When the boys turned, there she was, arms crossed. Their faces filled with surprise – and guilt. She raised her eyebrows, waiting for an explanation.

"Oh, hi, Mom. We were just working on something."

"Care to tell me what?"

Gabriel looked up at the clouds, considering how to answer.

Lillian turned to Billy. He zipped his lips and threw away an imaginary key.

Her eyes widened at his audacity. "All right. What's going on?" She looked from Gabriel to Billy.

"I cannot tell a lie!" Billy announced with a smile. "So, I won't say anything!" and he ran off, clearly enjoying himself.

Infuriated, she was just about to demand an answer from Gabriel when Tommy and Mickey came out of the basement. They also had guilt all over their faces.

"Well! Are you two in on this?"

Tommy snapped his head to Gabriel. "You *told* her?"

"No!"

"Told me what?" Lillian demanded.

Mickey took a few slow steps backwards, hoping to leave unnoticed. "I better check on Billy," he said, hurrying away.

From inside her apartment, Mrs. Kuntzman had seen the exchange. She knocked on the window and waved them inside.

Lillian fixed Tommy and Gabriel with her sternest eye. "When we get home, you're both going to give me an answer!" She climbed the steps and walked into the vestibule.

Tommy whispered to Gabriel. "We can't wait. We have to tell her."

"You're right. It's not going as planned." Gabriel screwed up his mouth in thought, then he grabbed Tommy's arm. "Listen. You stall. I'll get Henry to help me take the rocker home."

Mrs. Kuntzman pulled Lillian inside and gave the boys a wink. "Come inside, come inside. Charlotte was an angel, all day."

"Inside, boys," Lillian said, trying to conceal her anger.

While Lillian gathered Charlotte in her arms, Tommy whispered something to Henry and Mrs. Kuntzman. They nodded, and Henry made a small motion with his head to Gabriel.

"Come into kitchen," said Mrs. Kuntzman. "You must try my... I make new kind of cookie. Come taste."

"I should get Charlotte home, and – "

"Come, come." Mrs. Kuntzman showed her into the kitchen. "I make butter cookies. Last week, but still fresh."

Tommy followed them into the kitchen. "They're really good, Mom. Try one."

Lillian looked at the plate of two cookies. She sat down and tasted a cookie, while Mrs. Kuntzman gave a detailed description of the apple tart she made with Amy and Tommy, and how carefully they had fanned out the apple slices.

Lillian smiled, and stood to leave.

But Mrs. Kuntzman held her arm. "Tommy said you meet with your artist boss?"

"Mrs. Huntington. Yes. I'll be working on a book series. A children's fantasy."

"That's great news, Mom!" Tommy cried. "I knew you'd get it."

Mrs. Kuntzman clasped her hands. "This calls for a toast!" She went to her cupboard. "Now, what do I have? Hmm. How about a glass of kirsch to celebrate? Brandy made with cherries. Now, where did I put it?" She moved around a few dishes in her cupboard. "It must be here somewhere…"

"Thank you, Mrs. Kuntzman, but I must be going." Lillian walked to the living room, looking for Gabriel, and felt her temper rise again. "Now where's Gabriel?"

Mrs. Kuntzman followed her, smiling sweetly. "He helps Henry with something."

Lillian gave a huff of exasperation. "Get your coat, Tommy."

Mrs. Kuntzman went to the window and glanced out. "Such a big help, both Tommy and Gabriel. Ah! Did I ever show pictures of my hometown?" She moved to the bookshelf and began pulling out a large album.

"Perhaps another time. I really must be getting home."

Tommy took a long time putting on his coat and wrestling the baby carriage out the door, causing Lillian's impatience to mount.

"Goodbye, Charlotte." Mrs. Kuntzman kissed her again and tucked the blanket around her, and then rearranged it. She stood in the doorway, looking down the street.

Just then Billy called out from half a block away, his hands cupped around his mouth. "The coast is clear!" and he ran up the stairs to his brownstone.

"What was that all about?" Lillian asked Tommy.

He shrugged. "You know how Billy is…"

"I know you boys are up to something. And you're going to tell me what it is. Gabriel is hiding something, I can tell."

In her heart she knew that Gabriel wouldn't do anything wrong, but he was maddeningly unpredictable. Just when she thought things had settled down, there was always some new mystery to untangle. Ahead of her, she saw Henry coming towards them. Alone.

"And now there's Henry!" she said, walking up to him. "I thought Gabriel was with you!"

"He was. Giving me a hand with something." He looked down at his shoes and smiled. "A fine boy. Fine boys you have." He patted Tommy's arm.

"Well – where is he?"

"Gabriel? He's at home."

Lillian pressed her lips together in exasperation. "Thank you, Henry." She picked up her pace until they reached their brownstone. She lifted Charlotte into her arms while Tommy maneuvered the carriage inside. Then he collapsed it and parked it beneath the stairs.

"Wait for me!" Tommy called, hurrying after her. He rushed past her on the second landing, opened the door to their apartment, and peeked inside.

"All set!" said Gabriel.

Lillian had had enough, and she pushed the door open. "What is going – "

There was Gabriel smiling widely. The Christmas tree lights cast the room in a merry glow, and Christmas music played from the radio.

In the middle of the living room stood a beautiful, carved wooden rocking chair with a red ribbon tied around its back.

Gabriel stood next to it, sweeping open his arm in presentation. "Happy early Christmas! Sorry about lying by omission but we wanted it to be a surprise."

Tommy moved to the other side of the rocker. "Merry Christmas, Mom! Give it a try."

Lillian stood with her mouth open, looking from the chair to Tommy and Gabriel, and back to the gleaming rocking chair. Then she surprised them both by bursting into tears. Charlotte also began to cry, whimpering softly. Lillian sat in the chair and gently rocked, holding Charlotte close.

Gabriel shot a troubled look to Tommy. "We thought it would make you happy. We weren't trying to cause trouble or make you sad."

Tommy placed his hand on the back of the rocker. "Sorry if we worried you, Mom."

Lillian put her hand on his. "I have the best sons in the whole world. I'm not angry, I'm so happy." She kissed Charlotte and pulled Gabriel to her and kissed him, and then did the same to Tommy. "I love you both so much. Charles will be so proud of you." She tried to smile but her pent-up tears poured forth. "I just don't know why I haven't heard from him. It's not like him. He would have gotten word to me if he could. I'm so afraid he's sick again or – "

"Dad's fine, Mom," said Gabriel. "We got his telegram that he arrived in London, didn't we? He's on his way home."

"He's probably half way across the Atlantic Ocean by now," added Tommy. "Everything's all jammed up with everyone coming back. He'll be home any day now. You'll see."

Lillian wiped away her tears and forced a smile. "I'm sure you're right. He'll be home very soon and we'll all be together." She stood and only now really examined the chair. "Oh, how beautiful!" She touched the red bow and ran her hand across the carved back.

"Amy tied the ribbon," said Tommy.

"Tommy and I did the sanding and staining and polishing. With some help from Mr. G and Henry. And Mickey and Billy."

"So, *this* is what you've all been up to!" Lillian said laughing. "And I like to think of myself as an observant person! I completely missed it." She sat back down in the chair, nestled Charlotte against her, and began to rock. "Oh, I can't wait to tell Charles what a surprise you gave me. My darling boys!"

Tommy and Gabriel stood, each with a hand on the back of the rocking chair, filling her in on the details of how they had thought of various gifts, how they had decided on the rocker, and how they had kept it in Mrs. Kuntzman's basement until it was ready.

"It all makes sense now," said Lillian, smiling at the sweet subterfuge of them all.

Gabriel peeked down at Charlotte and spoke in a low voice. "Look! It works. Just like you said it would, Mom. Charlotte's sound asleep."

*

When Red placed an envelope on his aide's desk to be mailed, he spotted the telegram he wrote to Lillian informing her of Charles's flight. "Barkley! This was supposed to go out days ago!"

The young man jumped up from his desk, his eyes wide, staring at the note. He smacked his head.

"So sorry, sir. I completely forgot! I don't know how that happened, sir. Shall I still send it?"

Red placed a hand on the young man's shoulder and smiled. "Please. This is one telegram that will bring happiness."

"Yes sir, sir," he said with a salute. "On the double, sir." He grabbed his jacket and cap and ran out of the room.

When word had come through confirming the flight, there had been no time for Charles to do anything but write a hasty note. Red promised he would send it via telegram, notifying Lillian of his plans.

Charles had pulled a thick envelope from his jacket. "I was just about to mail it. A letter to Lillian I've been writing for over a month." He tucked it back inside his jacket and broke into a smile. "I guess I can hand deliver it now."

Red counted the days since Charles had left – the telegram would most likely arrive late. He gave a deep sigh and finished straightening up his desk. The sounds of the office were diminishing, fewer typewriters clanked away, the coming and going of messengers had lessened, the telephones rang only occasionally now. Red rubbed his eyes and went to the window, leaning against the ledge.

He watched the world outside, people shopping, going about their business. Down the street in front of the shops, people stepped off the late afternoon bus from London. Visiting for the holidays, perhaps. Or come to visit some of the patients, or –

His heart stopped. A woman stepped down from the bus, looked around her, and continued down the sidewalk. A woman so like Izzy. Nobody – nobody in the world moved like Izzy. Brisk, with a purpose. That was her walk, the way she carried herself – even the hair color under the hat was hers. A second bus came from the other direction, blocking his view – when it passed, the woman was gone.

Red dashed out of the office and grabbed the railing as he sped down three flights of stairs taking them two at a time. He ran out of the building and down the block, looking to the left and right. He should have been able to see the woman. Had she stepped into a shop? A hotel? He walked up and down the street, looking in the windows, checking both sides of the street. There was no woman.

Was he dreaming again? It was getting worse – but this time was so real. He had felt a rush in his veins, a prickling in his skin, a physical thrill of recognition. But the mirage had vanished. He squeezed his eyes shut. Would it always be so?

Deflated, depressed, he stood indecisive. Should he put in a few more hours? Go home? Get something to eat? The vision had stirred up the pain he tried so hard to ignore.

He hoped a walk along the river would steady him.

The day was already fading. Shafts of sunlight struck the water, reflecting the ripples from the swimming ducks. He walked to his bench. The horizon was shot with gold, outlining thick clouds of purple with a shimmery rim.

He looked at the bare trees lining the small river. He smiled as two children ran ahead of their mother and crossed the arched bridge. The mother called out to them to wait for her. From the other direction, a woman crossed the footbridge. She stood in the middle and placed her hands on the stone wall.

Again, the deep ache stirred inside Red. He squinted towards the bridge. It was the same figure as before, he was sure. In a green coat and hat. With that way of moving. Tall and graceful, so sure of herself, that was it. But that was all it was.

He turned away, refusing to believe in a shade of hair, a particular gait, a burst of laughter from someone else. He took out the picture of Izzy, solid and real. Such love of life in her face. Such love for him.

His lips moved into a smile, an involuntary response, mixing memory into the vision – but he couldn't, wouldn't, give in to hallucinations that fueled his desperate longing. He narrowed his eyes against the setting sun. He realized that the woman was walking towards him. Or was he dreaming?

Red pinched the bridge of his nose and rubbed his eyes. He looked again. His heartbeat began to quicken in response to that old beloved image. As the figure came closer, his heart pounded. This was madness, he told himself. The sun was in his eyes and he turned his head aside. He saw it was a real woman, and he felt doubly foolish – was it more foolish to mistake a dream for a person, or a person for a dream?

As the figure approached, he told himself to get a grip – it must be someone with a question about one of the patients. Surely. For it couldn't be, it wasn't possible – and he no longer believed in the impossible. The setting sun cast a halo around the woman's auburn hair.

The figure was slowing her steps as she moved in front of him.

Red froze, afraid to move lest the sweet vision disappear.

Then the woman took another step forward, blocking out the sun.

There she stood. Tears burned in his eyes on seeing the beautiful face – either he had completely lost his mind, or – or –

Izzy smiled down at him, and the look in his eyes answered all her questions. She softly spoke.

"Hello, Red."

Chapter 18

❦

Another snowfall blanketed the farm, creating a soft white world. The bright morning sun caused the icicles hanging from the roof to drip slowly, and the snow glittered as if sprinkled with diamond dust. The farmhouse kitchen, always warm and welcoming, became even more inviting with the scents of bread baking in the oven and freshly made coffee. Ursula brought the coffee pot to Kate and Eugene and filled their cups.

"One more cup and then I need to get moving," said Eugene. "I'm going to give Burly a hand with a set of shelves he's making."

Ursula rested her hand on Eugene's shoulder as she topped his cup. An unspoken truce had come about for which Kate was grateful. She smiled at her two dark-haired children, her mother's heart full of love. She glanced at Jessica, wondering why she was so quiet this morning.

"More water for your tea, Jessica?" Kate asked. "The kettle's still hot."

"No thanks, Mom." Jessica reviewed the program for the school Christmas show, jotting down a few notes.

"Are you nervous?" asked Ursula, sitting down beside her.

"Not at all. I'm looking forward to it."

"You have stronger nerves than I do," said Kate, jumping up to take two loaves of bread out of the oven.

"Ahh." Eugene caught the aroma and inhaled. "Nothing like fresh baked bread."

"Especially on a snowy day like this," said Ursula, cupping her hands around her coffee.

Kate spun around and faced the table. "Let's cut into one of these loaves right now. How about it – with butter and apricot jam?" She was already reaching for the plates. "Or perhaps a little honey."

Eugene exchanged a smile with Ursula and Jessica. "You know we can't say no to that, Mom. Burly and Joe are going to wonder what's taking me so long."

They began spreading butter, jam, and honey onto slices of warm bread, enjoying the second breakfast.

"And Clem?" asked Kate. "Is he joining you as well?"

"No. He's busy or something. Been real quiet lately." Eugene gave it some thought and then cocked his head towards Jessica. "What'd you say to Clem the other day in town? Ever since then, I can't get him to go out. Neither can Burly."

Jessica gathered her notes and spoke in a matter-of-fact manner. "I told him I was going to marry him." She took a sip of tea.

The kitchen filled with silence. Kate, Ursula, and Eugene stared wide-eyed at Jessica.

"You're joking," said Eugene.

Jessica stacked the program and notes. "Nope."

Eugene set his coffee cup down. "Now why'd you have to go and scare a guy like that? Chances are he'll never come around again."

No sooner had he spoken than they heard a truck pull up outside. Kate went to the window, looked out, and turned around. "It's Clem."

Jessica placed her papers on the hutch, lifted her jacket from the coat hook, and walked outside to meet him.

Ursula and Eugene stood next to Kate at the window, baffled by Jessica's calm confidence.

Clem got out of his truck, shoved his hands in his pockets, and looked at Jessica. "I know it's cold out, but can you walk with me a bit?"

"Let's go out to the pasture. It's so pretty in the snow." Jessica led the way, with Clem walking just a step behind, eyeing her with a wistful sadness.

When they reached the fence, Jessica faced him, waiting for him to make the next move.

Clem looked out at the pasture, and the white-limbed trees along the creek, and then down at the snowy ground before him. "Jessica, there's something I have to tell you. You're too nice a girl to deserve anything but the truth."

Her eyebrows lifted slightly, but inside her heart pounded.

"I can't marry you."

"Why?" Tears stung her eyes at his decisive words.

Clem turned away from her questioning eyes. "If things were different, I'd be the happiest man on earth to be married to you."

"But?"

He opened and closed his hands and started to speak. He swallowed and took a breath – but the words wouldn't come.

"What is it, Clem?"

He looked at her, and then away. After a few moments, he slowly nodded, as if convincing himself to go through with it. "You know I was in the hospital. You know I was injured."

Worry flooded Jessica's face. "Are you still ill? Are you not well?"

"I am well. I'm fine now. But – "

"But what? Tell me, Clem."

"I don't think – the doctors say – the thing is, Jessica" – he faced her directly. "Most likely, I can't have children." He looked down, not wanting to see the disappointment in her eyes.

She scanned his face, his eyes, his mouth, making sense of his words. "You mean – it's not about me?"

He raised his face in surprise. "Of course, not! How can you think that? You're the loveliest thing I've ever known. It's because – I can't give you the life you deserve."

Jessica threw her arms around him. "Oh, Clem. I'm so relieved! I thought you didn't like me or had someone else or something."

He pulled her arms off and took a step back. "Jessica. I don't think you understand what I'm saying."

"Of course, I do. But it's *you* I care about, Clem. It's you I want."

He leaned his arms on the snowy fence and fixed his eyes on the pasture. "No, Jessica. I would never do that to you. You – you would be the perfect mother, kind and gentle, happy. I can see you with children all around you – "

"I already have that! I'll be a teacher soon and will have kids coming out of my ears! I don't need any of my own. Not as long as I have you." She put her hand on his cheek and turned his face to her.

"Jessica, you're young and so beautiful. I just couldn't take that away from you. It wouldn't be right."

Jessica again embraced him and looked into his eyes. "Listen to me, Clem. If we don't have any children, that will be all right. Maybe we will, maybe we won't – that's something that's true for all couples. Look at Ed and Opal. Look how happy they've been all these years together." She took his hands and pressed them to her heart. "But we'll have each other."

Clem tried to read her face, wanting to give in to the fullness of his heart.

She caressed his cheek. "You would still kiss me, wouldn't you? And hold me close at night?"

"Of course, I would." He looped his arms around her, indulging in her nearness, her warmth, the silkiness of her hair against his cheek.

Jessica rested her head on his chest and smiled when his embrace tightened. She raised her face to him. "So, you'll marry me?"

He had to smile at her determination. "We'll wait. If you still want to marry me in a few years –"

"No! I'm not waiting for a few years."

"We'll give it some time."

"You can give it some time if you want. For me, it's official. We're courting as of now! Within a year, we'll be married." Jessica kissed him on the mouth, and he pressed her close in a deep embrace.

Clem buried his face in her hair, kissed her neck, and almost choked on his words. "I never thought I'd ever be this happy."

Jessica squeezed him tight. "This is just the beginning, Clem. Just you wait and see how happy we're going to be!"

Kate, Ursula, and Eugene waited at the window, craning their necks towards the pasture. They had seen Clem and Jessica walk in that direction, both with their hands in their pockets, looking straight ahead. Now they were returning, arms and hands linked, eyes on each other, smiling and talking. They stopped to kiss – twice – and squeezed each other tight, as they walked towards the farmhouse.

Eugene dropped his hands to his sides. "I'll be damned."

*

Later in the day, the kitchen was once more the center of homey happiness. Kate was making fried chicken and mashed potatoes, a favorite of all her children. She hummed, her hands covered in flour, as she coated the pieces of chicken.

Ursula had peeled the potatoes and now added them to a large pan of water. She dried her hands on the dish towel and smiled at the laughter coming from Frankie upstairs. Jessica was giving him his bath, letting him splash all he wanted, no doubt.

Jessica had already taken her bath, dried her hair, applied a touch of lavender oil to her wrists, and laid out her pale pink dress. Clem was coming to dinner, and she wanted to look her best.

Eugene had just arrived from Burly's and was stomping the snow off his boots on the porch. He walked into the kitchen.

"How are the roads, son?"

"Clear, for the most part." He watched Kate place the chicken into the pan, the oil popping like a small applause. "Promise me you'll make this meal for Edna. No one makes fried chicken as good as you."

"Of course, I will. I can't wait to have her try some of my recipes."

The telephone began to ring. Kate held up her flour-dusted hands. "Can you answer it?"

Eugene went to the hallway. "Hello, Ed, I missed you earlier –" His voice was cut off as he listened. He walked with the receiver to the entrance of the kitchen, eyes fixed on Kate and Ursula, his eyebrows pinched tight.

Bad news. They stood rigid, waiting for him to speak.

"We're on our way. Thanks, Ed."

Kate placed her hand to her heart. "What? What happened?"

Eugene looked at Ursula. Her hand gripped the back of a chair.

"It's Friedrich. He's leaving – now. They're boarding buses that will take them to Chicago. Then by train out east – to ship out."

"No!" Ursula's voice came out in a whisper. "Not like this! I have to see him. I must see him!"

"Get your coat," said Eugene. "I'll bring the truck around."

Ursula ran upstairs to get the letter she had written, grabbed her coat, and dashed out the door just as Eugene pulled up.

He sped down the lane and turned onto the country road, stepping on the gas. He honked at and passed the car ahead of him, then cursed when a tractor pulled out onto the road. He lay on the horn, managing to swerve around it, skidding as he straightened the wheels.

They drove in silence. Eugene looked over now and then at Ursula. He tried to quell her fears with fragmented conversation.

"Thank God, the roads are clear. Don't worry, Ursula. We'll chase the bus down if we have to. Hopefully, Otto will be there to help us. We'll get there…"

When they pulled up to the camp, they came to a halt, and Eugene cursed. There at the gate stood Mr. Creight.

Eugene pounded his hands on the steering wheel. "Creight! Of all the rotten luck! Let me try to find Otto."

Ursula opened her door.

"Ursula! Creight's the last person – "

But Ursula had already jumped out of the truck and was running towards Mr. Creight. He took her arm and hurried her off to where the buses were being boarded.

When Eugene tried to follow, he was stopped by one of the guards and began arguing with him.

Mr. Creight went up to the last bus, spoke to the driver, and waited.

After a moment, Friedrich stepped off the bus, his face drawn with sadness. Until he saw Ursula standing before him.

"Ursula!" He embraced her and held her tight. "I feared I wouldn't be able to say goodbye." He squeezed her again, and noticed Mr. Creight, who was motioning down the line.

The camp commander was checking off the first bus, and its door closed. He moved to the next bus.

"Friedrich – " Her words broke, and she pressed the letter into his hands.

He took it gratefully and pulled a note from his pocket and gave it to her. "I didn't have time to write all I wanted to. It happened so suddenly. All it says is that I love you." He kissed her. "And that I will do everything in my power to come back to you as soon as possible." He kissed her again.

Ursula wrapped her arms around his neck and spoke into his ear. "I love you, my darling."

Eugene now ran up and put a hand on Friedrich's shoulder. "You take care of yourself and stay strong. We'll get you back here. We'll take good care of Ursula and Frankie. Don't you worry."

Friedrich's eyes glistened with gratitude. "Thank you."

The camp commander blew his whistle and motioned for Friedrich to board the bus.

Ursula stood mute, taking in every last detail of him. He stood strong and tried to appear hopeful, though his eyes filled with anguish. "I'll write. As soon as I can." Then he broke. His eyes welled with tears and he whispered in her ear, "I love you."

They clung to each other and kissed passionately one last time. Then Friedrich released Ursula's hands from him, took a step back, and boarded the bus.

Eugene put his arm around Ursula. He saw tears stream down her cheeks, and her body trembled, but she didn't make a sound.

They watched the convoy of buses pull out of the camp and turn onto the road.

Mr. Creight took a step forward and stood next to Ursula. She took his hand and squeezed it. "Thank you." She tried to give him a brave smile and saw that tears stood in his eyes.

He patted her hand. "You let me know if there's anything I can ever do for you."

Ursula reached up and kissed his cheek.

Eugene extended his hand. "Abe."

Mr. Creight shook it, and then walked away.

Eugene and Ursula slowly walked back to the truck and drove home. Once again, Eugene tried to provide comfort with whatever words came to mind. "We'll get him back. We'll find out where he is. He'll be fine, Ursula. He'll be fine."

"Thank God, you acted quickly, Eugene. Thank you for that."

"I want you to know that I'll do everything I can for you and Frankie. We all will. And we'll get Friedrich back. We will."

Eugene kept looking over at Ursula sitting straight-backed and stoic. "Mom told me that you and Jessica had changed. Had grown up and were strong and capable. I don't think I realized it until today."

Ursula stared out at the snowy fields all around and the long black road ahead of her. The sun sank into the horizon without any fanfare. Instead, the day grew dimmer, darker, almost imperceptibly. Nightfall blanketed the earth, hiding its sorrow.

*

The chicken was warming in the oven and the potatoes had been mashed. But there was none of the happiness that usually accompanied the comforting meal. Kate was setting the table, muttering to herself. "Finding out in a call like that! Not even giving us a chance to say goodbye."

Jessica stood at the window. "Poor Ursula. I hope they were able to get there in time. I hope she had a chance to say goodbye." She saw the truck turn into the lane. "Here they are, Mom."

Eugene hurried over to Ursula as she stepped out of the truck. He had his arm ready for support in case she should need it. But she walked straight and tall and strong.

Kate and Jessica went out to greet her on the porch and walked with her into the kitchen. They closely watched her face.

"Did you reach him in time?"

"Were you able to see him?" asked Kate, enfolding Ursula.

Only then, safe in her mother's arms, did Ursula break down sobbing.

Eugene placed a hand on Ursula's back. "We did. She had a few minutes before he had to board the bus. Abe Creight was there. Helped her to see him in time." Eugene shook his head. "Surprising the hell out of me."

"That's how we knew," said Kate. "I called Ed back and he explained that Abe was at the camp and saw what was happening. Tried to call us but couldn't get through, so he called Ed."

Ursula raised her face. "If it hadn't been for him – and Eugene – I would have missed him."

Kate pulled out a chair for Ursula to sit. "Let me fix you a cup of tea."

Ursula wiped her eyes. "I'll be all right, Mom. I've known this day was coming for a long time."

The telephone rang, and Eugene answered it. "Ed. Yes. We're back. We caught him just in time. Abe helped us…"

Jessica sat next to Ursula and hugged her. "I'm so sorry, Ursula. I feel so bad that Mom and I couldn't say goodbye to him. But at least you did."

Kate stood next to Ursula and stroked her hair. Ursula raise her tear-stained face. "I gave him my letter. And he gave me one." She lifted it out of her pocket, and pressed it to her heart. The tears started to her eyes again.

"Oh, Ursula," said Jessica. "He'll be back. Hopefully, soon."

Ursula knew it would not be soon. But she nodded and gave a hint of a smile, to ease their hearts.

"Ursula, Clem's coming to dinner. Is that all right? I was going to call and tell him not to but Mom said it might help for him to be here."

"Of course. It will be good to have him here with us."

Kate lit the burner on the stove and filled the tea kettle. Eugene had just gotten off the telephone with Ed when it rang again. He answered it and handed the receiver to Jessica. She spoke briefly and then sat next to Ursula.

"That was Sue Ellen. She just heard about Friedrich. Opal called Mrs. Bloomfield earlier to see if she knew anything more. I told her we'd call back later when we have more information."

Ursula sat drained, staring out at the table.

The phone rang a third time, and Jessica jumped up to answer it, speaking in low tones. She came back into the kitchen. "That was Shirley. I guess Sue Ellen just told her."

Kate huffed at the intrusion and steeped the tea. "Jessica, get some honey from the pantry. A little sweetness always helps." She looked over at Eugene. "Do we know where they're going?"

"The guard said they're taking the bus to Chicago. Then straight to Camp Shanks in New York for processing. Then a ship to – well, we don't know where."

"But we'll find out," said Kate. "We'll write to him as soon as we can." She placed the tea in front of Ursula and sat next to her. "Have a few sips. I made it strong and sweet."

When the telephone rang again, Kate exploded out of her chair. "If that damn phone rings one more time!" She picked it up, and stood in the kitchen doorway, her fist on her hip, scowling at the phone. "Hello! What? I can't understand a word you're saying. Who – " She shook her head in disgust and waved Eugene over. "This must be for you. Sounds like a couple of drunken sailors!"

Eugene took the receiver, covering his other ear to hear better. "Speak up – I can't hear you – I can't hear – Well, if you'd both stop talking and singing at the same time then maybe I could hear you." Eugene's eye opened wide and he threw his head back in a long roll of laughter. "Mom! Mom, get over here!"

Kate looked at him like he'd lost his mind.

"Mom!" he said, doubling over in howls, and wiping his eyes. "It's your sons!"

Kate jumped up and ran to the receiver. "Jimmy? Paul? Is that you? My God, you're *together*?

Where are you? Why didn't you tell me – " She started to laugh, then cry, listening to them share a phone. "Ursula, Jessica! Come quick!"

They all crowded around the telephone receiver, trying to make sense of the noisy fragments. "*Kansas City?* They're in Kansas City!" She handed the phone to Eugene and lifted her apron to dry her eyes.

Eugene took the phone, smiling in joy as he listened to them. "Only you two could pull that off. Yes, we're all here waiting for you. Hey, you'll get to meet my girl, Edna! I'm picking her up – What? a double wedding? Give me a chance to ask her first!" His expression changed to one of urgency. "Well, get going – don't you dare miss it. We'll be at the station tomorr – !" He stared at the receiver.

Kate, Jessica, and Ursula looked from the phone to his face.

"Their train is being called," he said, still laughing and wiping at his cheeks. "Damn, I miss those two."

Jessica took the receiver, listened, and placed it back on the phone. "What'd they say? I could barely hear them. Are they really in Kansas City? That's means they'll be here *tomorrow!*"

They all gathered round the table while Eugene spoke. "Apparently, they bumped into each other by chance in San Diego and finagled their tickets to be on the same train. They've been trying to call us from stations along the way, but the lines for the telephones were always too long. Snow storms are causing major delays, and several trains have been canceled. But their train is leaving soon. They'll be here tomorrow!"

"I just can't believe it," cried Kate. "Tomorrow! After all this time of worrying. And in time for Christmas!" She embraced Ursula. "You see? Things will work out. All will be well. Before you know it, Friedrich will be here again." She turned to Eugene. "Call Ed and let him know. Then call the Bloomfields. Jessica, we'll have to make sure we have everything for a feast! We'll make a big batch of eggnog."

"And a plum pudding with rum sauce!" Jessica heard a truck pull up outside and ran to the window. "That's Clem! Wait 'til he hears!" she cried, dashing out the door.

Frankie's cries could be heard from Kate's bedroom. Ursula rose to her feet. "I'll get him. I'll wash up a bit before coming down."

Kate walked with her down the hall. Her joy changed to heartache as Ursula picked up Frankie and held him close, quietly weeping.

"Don't despair. We'll find a way to bring Friedrich back."

Ursula nodded and went upstairs with Frankie.

*

Late that night, Ursula stood at her bedroom window gazing down into the farmyard. No more would she search for Friedrich's handsome face out there. No more would there be a chance of his arriving to the farm. Now when she looked out the windows, she would see only the farmyard, the fields. They would no longer hold the possibility that her beloved might suddenly appear and raise his eyes to her window.

She lifted the corner of her shawl to wipe her eyes. She looked out at the emptiness and sought out the points of lights in the darkness. The light over the barn door casting a yellow patch in the farmyard. A few lights from the neighboring farms across the fields. Headlights from a lone car or truck traveling the country roads. In the distance, she saw the tiny lights of a train threading its way through the countryside, and heard the long, plaintive pull of the whistle.

Now the waiting begins, she told herself. Now she must be strong and believe that all will be well. Three of her brothers had survived the war. They would go on to live full, happy lives. For much of two years, she had been fortunate enough to have Friedrich close to her, while so many people had their loved ones torn from them.

Now it was her turn. There would be sleepless nights, and she would collapse from time to time, and cry herself to sleep. Then she would touch her earrings that he had kissed, read his letters, and gaze upon their child, and gather up her strength again.

She had decided long ago that, when the time came, she would be strong and brave and not cast a gloom on the others. She would accept the love from her family, grateful for all they had done. She would join them as they all sat in front of the beautiful Christmas tree, and she would see the love in the eyes of Eugene for Edna, and in Jessica's for Clem. And in her mother's eyes for her children. Soon the house would be full of life again, and the sad years would be behind them. And she would wait. And check the mail and write long letters. She would store up memories to tell Friedrich for the day he returned.

Ursula raised her eyes to the near-full moon, so like the night two years ago when Friedrich had brought her beauty – the tree below her window glowing with candles. A soft smile came to her lips as she realized how much of Friedrich was still there with her – imbued in the landscape, in the seasons, in Christmas. In the sweet baby who looked so much like him.

Ursula walked to where Frankie lay fast asleep and leaned over to kiss his cheek. "Goodnight, my love," she softly said. "We will be here, waiting for you."

Chapter 19

❦

In the late afternoon, Tommy sat deep in thought with his math book opened before him, and Gabriel was stretched out on the couch reading. Lillian rocked Charlotte on her lap while she spoke to her sister on the telephone. Big, soft snowflakes drifted past the windows.

"Annette? Hello?" She hung up the receiver. "That's twice we lost our connection. I suppose I should get started on dinner, anyway." She rocked back and forth a few times.

Tommy bit the pencil eraser. "Mom?"

"Yes, Tommy?"

"I've been thinking – I think I'd like to be called *Tom* now, instead of *Tommy*. What do you think?"

She rested her eyes on him – his voice deepening, the faintest shadow on his upper lip, his long limbs – and felt a pang of sorrow that her children were growing up so fast. "I think it's a good idea."

"I asked Amy and she thought it was a good idea too." He sat up straighter and smiled as he continued his homework.

Lillian let out a deep sigh. "I'm reluctant to leave my rocking chair. I don't know how I ever managed without one."

Tommy looked up. "Charlotte sure likes it."

"I bet Dad will like to rock her in it too," said Gabriel.

"I'm sure he will," said Lillian, rising to her feet. She held Charlotte in one arm and hummed and sang as she moved about the kitchen. "*Haven't felt like this, my dear, since you went away, it's been a long, long time.*"

Lillian saw that Gabriel had gotten up and was standing in front of the calendar in the kitchen.

"Are you finished with your book, Gabriel?"

"No. I was just thinking – *if* Dad is on a ship in the Atlantic, then there's a chance that he could still get here in time for Christmas."

"Not unless he's a or two day out," said Tommy.

Lillian suppressed her worry about Charles. It was Christmastime, and she wouldn't let the boys see her fear. She stood next to Gabriel and glanced at the calendar. "I'd say there's a chance that he could still get here in December. But even if it's January, we'll have a belated Christmas. This year we'll have two Christmases. One starting tomorrow with Christmas Eve, and one when your father arrives."

Gabriel smiled, but kept his eyes on the calendar, estimating possible arrival dates.

When the telephone rang, Tommy answered it. "Hello?"

"That'll be Annette calling back," said Lillian, going back to the living room.

Tommy shrugged and handed the receiver to Lillian. "It's for Dad."

Lillian lifted it to her ear, puzzled. "Hello? This is Mrs. Drooms. Yes. Who?"

She shifted Charlotte to her other hip and blinked as she tried to make sense of the words coming from the receiver. "I'm sorry?" She angled the telephone receiver out so that Tommy and Gabriel could also hear. A young man's voice came through.

"Sergeant Stokes. Little Wheel, they call me. I promised I'd telephone to let you know. I was in line for over an hour, then just when it's my turn, this private runs up and begs for the phone booth to call his mother, and well, I didn't have the heart to say no."

Lillian smiled. "That was very kind of you, Sergeant Stokes. You said you're calling for Charles? Charles Drooms?"

"Yes, ma'am. I mean, No. That is, I'm calling *for* him. My buddies and I wanted to thank him again. We were on the same train from – "

Lillian held the receiver away from her ear as the young man began hollering.

"Hold your horses! I waited an hour for this spot – all right, all right. Just a minute. Let me finish!"

Tommy and Gabriel covered their mouths, laughing.

Lillian looked up at the ceiling. "I'm sorry, but – " She raised her voice. "I can barely hear you. Charles isn't here, I'm afraid – he's in London. London! Would you like for me to take a message for you?"

"That's what I'm trying to tell you, ma'am. He asked me to call to let you know that he's on his way – back off, bud – it's my turn!"

Lillian's brow creased in frustration. "On his way – from where?"

"Penn Station. I thought by now he'd be home and – "

Lillian stared at the receiver, dropped it, and ran to the window. She handed Charlotte to Tommy, pushed up the window, and leaned out. Then, looking in the other direction, she saw a tall figure carrying a duffle bag. She sucked in her breath, peered closer, and screamed – "CHARLES!" The figure stopped, looked up, and met her gaze. "CHARLES!" she yelled again and dashed out of the apartment.

Tommy ran to the window and looked out. "DAD!"

Gabriel was now trying to get to the window. Tommy shoved Charlotte into his arms and bolted out the door.

Gabriel leaned out and spotted Charles. "DAD!" He looked around and, realizing there was no one to hand Charlotte to, he grabbed her blanket and ran out of the apartment with her.

When Charles saw Lillian running towards him, he dropped his duffle bag and ran to her. They met in an embrace, both of them crying and laughing and kissing and talking over one another.

"How is it possible? I thought you were still in London!"

"Didn't you get my telegram?"

"Dad!" cried Tommy, running up and hugging him.

"Tommy!" Charles squeezed him, while Lillian looked on through smiles and tears.

"Dad!" Gabriel came running, holding a baby. "Dad! You're home." Gabriel ran into his open arms. "Dad, this is Charlotte!"

Charles's smile dropped, and his mouth opened in awe at the sweet baby.

Lillian laughed and pulled the blanket away from Charlotte's face so that Charles could see her. "Your daughter." She lifted her up for Charles to hold.

Charles cradled her tenderly, and gazed at her in wonder. He broke into a smile. "My daughter!" He kissed her forehead, and then kissed Lillian again, and turned to Tommy and Gabriel. "And my sons. Look at you – you're both a good head taller!"

"You're back, Dad!" cried Tommy.

Gabriel squeezed Charles. "You're really here! You made it for Christmas!"

Charles smiled down at Charlotte, and wrapped his other arm around Lillian, kissing her again and again. Then, smiling down at his family, his heart bursting with love, he gave a wide smile. "Let's go home!"

"Yes," cried Lillian, her eyes shining in happiness. "Let's go home!"

Epilogue

◦❦◦

July 1948

A beautiful summer day spread across Kate's farm. A light breeze carried the fragrance of freshly mowed hay, honeysuckle, and roses – a medley of green and floral scents released by the sun's warmth. White butterflies flitted and landed among the flowers, along with a few dragonflies that briefly hovered and then disappeared.

A perfect day, thought Lillian. She stood in the shade of the old oak tree, using her watercolors to capture the profusion of hollyhocks that grew alongside the barn. She swished the paintbrush in the jar of water, deciding on which pigments to capture the deep rose-colored blooms – there was a hint of warmth to them. She would need to add a touch of ochre…

The sound of laughter drew her attention to the porch. Kate, Charles, and Edna sat with glasses of lemonade, watching Eugene pull Frankie and Charlotte in the red wagon. The two children shrieked in delight as Eugene sped up and then slowed down, over and over. Edna rocked a baby in her arms, and Kate bounced Eugene's older daughter on her lap.

Lillian was almost tempted to start another painting of the farmhouse, so struck was she by its charm. The white of the house, the green of the shutters and shade trees. Kate's yellow, blue, and orange flowers lining the sidewalk and fence.

She was glad they were staying a full two weeks – there were so many things she wanted to paint. She caught Charles's eye and smiled. They had arrived two days earlier and were already enjoying the slower pace of the farm. Tom and Gabriel were out in the back watching their uncles Paul and Clem put on the final touches to a much-needed addition to the farmhouse for Eugene and Edna and their two children.

The house had grown smaller. Besides Kate, Ursula and Frankie, and Eugene and his family, Paul still lived at home, though he was going to be married in the fall. He and his fiancée had purchased a two-story house in town, just a few blocks from where Jessica and Clem lived with Clem's father, Donny, and Nathaniel.

There was Clem now, with his small son on his shoulders. Nathaniel, with his wide green eyes and wavy brown hair, was a miniature version of Clem. They walked to where Jessica and Donny leaned over the garden, picking cucumbers and tomatoes. When Jessica stood and reached up to kiss Clem, it was clear that they were expecting another child. There was no hiding the love between them.

Lillian mixed the colors and dabbed at the painting. This was their third visit to the farm since the war. Each visit was an indulgence in wide skies, long walks along the country road, and a trove of sketches and paintings that she finished working on back in New York City. And each visit included the introduction of a new grandchild or two of Kate's.

Lillian was looking forward to seeing Jimmy and his family again, later in the day at the town's summer festival. Jimmy had twin boys, a baby girl, and another on the way. He and Gladys had purchased a farm a few miles away and were frequently at Kate's. Kate had told Lillian that she loved being a grandmother and couldn't be any happier, though Lillian had detected a hint of sorrow that briefly darkened Kate's eyes. Perhaps thinking about Francis. Or Ursula.

There was still no word about Friedrich. There had been only a handful of letters from him in '46 and even fewer in '47. He had been moved to various POW mining camps in France, but there had been no word from him for almost a year. Apparently, there had been a terrible explosion at the last mine where he worked and several prisoners went missing afterwards. Escaped or killed, no one knew.

Charles had been in contact with the Red Cross and several offices at the War Department trying to track him down, and recently had cause for hope. A man who fit the description of Friedrich had been recuperating at a hospital soon after France released the last of their prisoners in the spring. But that trail, like so many others, had gone cold.

There was no confirmed information about Friedrich. Had he survived the explosion? Had he been wounded, or had he escaped? Was he still lying in hospital? Had he been moved to Germany? When the letters stopped coming, Ursula had wanted to go and search for him, but Eugene had pointed out the futility of her wandering around countries where she didn't speak the language. Where would she look – in France, Germany? Somewhere else?

Lillian sighed at the situation, well understanding the agony of waiting. She added a few more leaves to the hollyhocks, and then rinsed her brush. She saw Ursula strolling up the country road, returning from one of her solitary walks. Even from afar, there was an air of wistfulness about her. Lillian watched her pause to inhale the honeysuckle covering the fence – she picked one of the small yellow flowers, pinched off the bottom, and tasted the drop of nectar at its base. In her hand she held a bunch of wildflowers.

Before turning onto the farm lane, Ursula stopped to check the mail. She sifted through the letters, and hung her head for a moment. Then she glanced up at the puffy white clouds before walking towards the house.

"Mommy!" cried Frankie, running down the lane to her. She scooped him up in her arms and kissed his cheek. Then he wriggled free and ran back to Charlotte and the wagon.

Ursula walked over to the oak tree. "Hello, Aunt Lillian." She tilted her head to study the painting. "How lovely."

As always, Lillian was struck by Ursula's beauty that only seemed to deepen with the years. She wore a dark blue and purple floral dress that caught the color of her eyes and flowed around her slim figure. Her long hair blew in the summer breeze, revealing her amethyst earrings.

"I've tried to capture their charm," said Lillian, standing back to view the canvas.

"Simple hollyhocks," said Ursula. She offered to hold the painting while Lillian gathered her supplies and collapsed the easel. "You've captured them exactly – and yet added something. They appear even more beautiful. A piece of summer to be treasured."

Lillian smiled at the comment. "I've always loved hollyhocks. An old-fashioned flower. Always leaning towards the sun and blooming in such happiness." She looked again at the tall stalks abloom with color, tapering off to small round buds. Lush green leaves nestled flowers of pale pink with dark centers, soft yellow, purple, white, bright pink. "Quaint and lovely. Especially growing against the barn like this."

They walked together to the farmhouse, reminiscing about Lillian's first visit when they had gathered lavender to make bath oil, and discussed how they would make another batch on this trip.

"We can get started on it tomorrow, if you like," said Ursula. "I have several dried bunches from last summer we can use."

They saw that Kate and the others had gone inside.

"I suppose we should start getting the hampers ready," said Ursula.

"I'm looking forward to the town's festival. We've never been here in July, so this will be a new experience for us."

"You'll like it. There's a small band and a few rides for the kids. Booths selling homemade jams and honey, pies and cakes. Mom sent Jimmy ahead to spread out our blankets. She has a favorite spot in the shade of the maple trees."

When Lillian and Ursula entered the kitchen, they found that Kate and Jessica were making a few peanut butter sandwiches for the children and placing them in picnic baskets, along with cookies, peaches and plums, and jars of lemonade.

Charles and Eugene sat at the table talking with Clem, who held Nathaniel on his lap.

Kate turned on seeing Lillian and Ursula. "Ah, there you are. Have a seat. How about a glass of lemonade? Is that the mail?"

Ursula nodded and set the mail on the table. She placed the wildflowers in a jar of water and then lifted down two glasses from the cupboard.

Eugene leaned forward and glanced at the magazines and letters. "Here's one for you, Mom. From Butte, Montana."

"Butte, Montana?" Kate finished pouring out the lemonade and set the pitcher down. "I don't know anyone there."

"It's addressed to you." He handed the letter to Kate.

Ursula, warm from her walk, sat next to Lillian and took a long sip of the refreshing lemonade.

"There must be some mistake." Kate reached for her reading glasses and squinted at the postmark. "I can't make out the name." She took a kitchen knife and opened the letter. Her brow wrinkled at the unfamiliar handwriting and she flipped the letter over to look at the signature. "Gustav!" She cried out in joy. "Oh my God, it's from Gustav!"

Kate turned to Charles and Lillian. "One of our POWs. He's alive! And living in Butte, Montana, of all places." She sat down and started to read the letter from the top.

"Gustav?" cried Jessica, holding a knife and jelly jar. "What does he say?" She cast a glance at Ursula.

Lillian also looked at Ursula and saw the tension in her face as she waited to hear.

While Kate read the letter, Jessica related what they knew of Gustav. "He wrote soon after his return to Germany to say that his family – his wife and children – didn't survive. That he didn't know what he was going to do. He seemed utterly lost. We wrote and wrote but we didn't hear back from him." In a quieter voice, she added. "And you know about Karl – our other POW."

Lillian and Charles nodded. Two years ago, Karl's death had been confirmed by the Red Cross. When Karl had first shipped out to Europe, Kate and her family had been relieved to know that he would not be sent to a Soviet POW camp. But then the news came that he had been assigned to clear mine fields in France, a job he was wholly unqualified for, as were the other young men who worked alongside him. Apparently, his last words to his fellow POWs was to tell them to stand back. Kate and her daughters had grieved over his death.

Kate kept scanning the letter, jumping down a few paragraphs, then back up, to find the key points. "He says for the past year he's been working in a copper mine in Butte. He was sponsored by an uncle who had moved to Montana before the war…" She gave a small gasp. "He says he's met a German widow there and that they'll be getting married in the fall. That America had always been a place of happiness for him – and he mentions the farm. And that they're planning a trip back here next year, to see us all again." Kate looked up and smiled at her children. "I can't wait to tell Ed. He grew quite close to them all."

Ursula couldn't contain herself. "Does he say anything – else?"

Kate shook her head and flipped the letter over again. "He asks if we've had any news of Friedrich. I'll write and let him know that we're still following leads. And are hopeful," she added with a bright smile.

She leaned over and squeezed Ursula's hand. "Gustav made it, and I'm sure Friedrich did, too." She glanced up at the clock. "Look at the time! We need to get a move on. Let me see if Edna needs any help with the babies."

Within an hour, the picnic baskets were loaded into cars and trucks, and everyone piled in wherever there was room. Eugene and Edna and their two children were the first to leave. They had a folding table and a few chairs they wanted to set up before everyone else arrived.

Tom, Gabriel, and Donny rode in the back of Clem's pickup. Kate, Ursula, and Lillian loaded up the old Studebaker sedan with two picnic baskets.

"Go ahead and climb in," said Kate to Lillian. "I'm just going to grab my hat."

Charlotte and Frankie, each holding a stuffed animal, sat next to Ursula in the back seat. Just as Charles and Paul were about to drive off in Paul's truck, Kate ran down the steps and hollered out to Charles that he had a telephone call.

He ran back in to take the call. "We'll be right behind you," he said as Kate started the car.

"It must be his office again," said Lillian, turning around to Ursula. "As soon as he leaves, they remember a hundred things they meant to ask him." She laughed lightly.

She had noticed the change in Ursula after the letter from Gustav. Though Ursula tried to appear happy, she was clearly upset. In an unspoken agreement, Kate and Lillian chatted cheerfully all the way to town, asking Ursula questions, saying how they were sure to see Ed and Opal at the picnic, and the Bloomfield family, and how Mildred Bloomfield now had four grandchildren, all boys, with another one on the way, which was sure to be a girl…

When they arrived, the town bustled with activity. Various tents and stands with refreshments lined the grassy park, and smoke poured from the barbeque area. Children played games and ran among the blankets spread out in colorful array.

Lillian and Kate each carried a picnic basket while Ursula held the hands of Frankie and Charlotte. They found the shady area where Jimmy had spread the blankets, and arranged the plates, cookies, a basket of fruit, and the jars of lemonade on the table Eugene had set up. They laughed to find Gladys chiding Jimmy for giving the kids sweets before lunch. He gave a loud kiss on her cheek and ran after the twins who were toddling off.

Charlotte and several other children gathered around Frankie who was handing out cookies before Kate could stop him. Frankie ran off, clutching several cookies in his hand, and the other kids scattered, giggling at their daring.

"Frankie!" called Ursula, but he was already out of earshot. She turned to Jessica, who leaned comfortably against Clem.

"He'll be back," laughed Jessica. "In half an hour, they'll all be hungry again."

"Would you mind keeping an eye on him? I'd like to walk for a bit."

"Of course," Jessica said, reaching up to squeeze Ursula's hand.

Ursula walked away from the festivities, wanting a few quiets moments to herself. The letter from Gustav had stirred up all her doubts and fears. She had always hoped that Gustav might have information about Friedrich through the network of prisoners – that someone might have seen him or worked with him. It came as a blow to discover that Gustav knew nothing.

She strolled to the town square where she first saw Friedrich, the fall of '43. The chance moment that had forever changed her life. She closed her eyes, remembering that autumn day. How the leaves had fluttered in the breeze, how the bus of young men had pulled up alongside her. How she had looked up and seen Friedrich, struck by the beauty of his face. How their eyes had spoken to each other's heart. She smiled at the memory and refused to give in to sadness.

She still felt him with her – when she walked around the farm, when she held Frankie in her arms, at night when she dreamed of him. There had been so many times she had started from sleep, awoken by a dream so real that she felt sure he was next to her. In her heart, she knew he was alive.

But then, why was there no word? Had his time in the camp beaten him down? Was he trying to protect her? She would not give up. She would send more letters, make more inquiries, and hope that her uncle Charles might find out what had happened, where he was. And she would send a letter to Gustav – perhaps he would know of some-one else she could write to.

Her steps took her to the church where she and Friedrich had been married. She hesitated and considered going inside – but the last time she had done so had left her red-eyed and filled with despair. She turned away and continued down the street.

After a few more minutes, she walked back towards the park and saw Jessica gathering the children for lunch. Clem helped her and steered three of the kids back to the blankets.

"Just in time," Jessica said to Ursula. "We're all ready for lunch." She turned around in frustra-tion. "Now where did Frankie get off to?"

Ursula laughed. "Here he comes, running as usual."

Frankie ran to Ursula and held up a cookie.

She bent down to kiss him. "Where were you?"

"Talking to that man." He bit into his cookie. "His cheeks were wet."

Jessica gave a sigh to Ursula. "One of the poor veterans, no doubt." She saw Clem and laughed as he tried to keep the children all together. "I better go help."

"We'll be right there."

Frankie raised his face. "He said to give this to you."

"The cookie?" Ursula laughed as Frankie took another bite. She put her hand on her hip and said playfully, "I thought that was for me."

"No, this is mine, Mommy." He finished the cookie and wiped his hands on his shirt. Then he reached into his pocket and handed her a tiny box. "*This* is for you."

Ursula stared at a small velvet box. "Frankie! Where did you – "

But he had spotted Charlotte and dashed off to play with her.

Ursula held the box in her palm and looked around her, hoping to return it to its owner. It was not something that Frankie should have.

She stared at the small velvet box, and felt a tingling in her skin. She slowly opened it – and her knees gave way. Inside, an amethyst ring glittered in the sunlight. The world swirled, and her heart beat wildly. "Friedrich," she whispered, scanning the crowd, searching, hoping, hoping – her breath caught.

There he stood, smiling at her. There stood her husband, her beloved, his arms slowly opening, his eyes locked on hers.

Lillian leaned in to Charles as they watched Tom and Gabriel helping Charlotte with her food. "I meant to ask you, Charles, was that your office calling again?"

His brow furrowed. "No," he said. "It was my contact from the War Department, with a puzzling bit of news."

Kate gathered Frankie onto her lap and looked around. "Now where's Ursula?"

Jessica had just sat down and pointed to where she had left Ursula. "She's right behind me –" She grabbed Kate's arm. "Mom!"

Kate saw Ursula standing as if frozen, and followed her gaze. "Oh, my God, it's Friedrich." Her voice broke in happiness. "It's Friedrich!"

Lillian turned, just in time to see Ursula run to a tall, handsome man. His arms enfolded her, and Ursula's arms wrapped tightly around his neck. They kissed again and again, weeping and smiling in joy.

"Thank God," Charles said softly.

Tears filled Lillian's eyes. "Charles! That telephone call – did you know?"

He kissed her and linked his hand with hers. "I hoped."

If possible, the day, at that moment, grew more beautiful. The breeze ruffled the sunlit leaves, the grass shone greener and the air smelled sweeter, and several couples and families felt a surge of gratitude at being alive and part of such happiness.

Made in the USA
Middletown, DE
26 May 2024